I0680726

WHIP IT UP ANTHOLOGY

HONEY AND DECADENCE
WENDI ZWADUK

MORE THAN VANILLA
ELIZABETH COLDWELL

SATISFYING DESIRES
VICTORIA BLISSE

FIVE COURSES
AYLA RUSE

SUBTERFUDGE
NORMANDIE ALLEMAN

THE INTERVIEW
CAITLIN RICCI

Whip It Up Anthology
ISBN # 978-1-78184-668-1
Honey and Decadence ©Copyright Wendi Zwaduk 2013
More Than Vanilla ©Copyright Elizabeth Coldwell 2013
Satisfying Desires ©Copyright Victoria Blisse 2013
Five Courses ©Copyright Ayla Ruse 2013
Subterfudge ©Copyright Normandie Alleman 2013
The Interview ©Copyright Caitlin Ricci 2013
Cover Art by Posh Gosh ©Copyright September 2013
Interior text design by Claire Siemaszkiewicz
Totally Bound Publishing

HONEY AND DECADENCE

Wendi Zwaduk

Dedication

I had to do it. Had to write this. You didn't let me give
up. You know who you are.
JPZ — Honey and Decadence makes me think of you.

Chapter One

"A hot fuck with whipped cream." Roxy cocked her hip, then stared at her co-worker, Gina. "You asked."

Gina fumbled with her tray, then placed it on the bar top. "I didn't think you'd answer me quite so honestly, or so loudly."

Roxy grinned and picked up her margarita order. "You asked, I answered." Served Gina right. Gina lived to drive her crazy. Tonight, she wasn't going to win. Roxy wound her way across the restaurant and delivered the drink orders. She checked her tables, then headed back to the registers to print up the bills.

"Hey, Roxy, do you have a moment?" Her boss, Elias McDowell, touched her arm. "I need to talk to you."

Roxy grabbed the string of receipts then followed Elias to the kitchen. "I have to deliver these." She shoved each piece of paper into the proper bill folder. "Elias?"

Of the two men who ran Delight Tonight, she liked Elias a lot. He always smiled, treated her with dignity and jumped in to help during the supper rush. She liked him, but not like Sean. Sean Malkin, Elias' partner in the restaurant, made her skin tingle. He rarely spoke and hardly visited the restaurant. When he did show up, he spent all of his time in the office. Most of the servers avoided him. Maybe it was his height or his piercing green eyes. He walked with a swagger and demanded respect wherever he went. Her pussy quivered. Thinking about the cover-model-sexy man ratcheted her heat level up so many notches.

Elias opened the door to the office, then waved his hand. "Have a seat." He took the bill folders from her hands. "Monique? Take these to her tables."

The newer server nodded to Elias. "I'll bring them back to you." She disappeared into the main banquet room, leaving Roxy alone with Elias.

"With the tips," he called after Monique, then groaned. "New servers. Got to tell them everything. Okay." Elias ushered her to the leather chairs opposite the desk. "I need you."

"Excuse me?" Roxy refused to sit. Elias could come on to the other girls, not her. She wasn't there to find a date. Hell no. She'd earned her BA in accounting and wanted to do the books for the restaurant instead of being a part of the wait staff. Unfortunately, Elias claimed to have misplaced her application for a promotion.

"I need you for a party. Sean's turning thirty-six and I want to do something nice for him." He opened a bill folder. "This is what I want to do and you're the perfect server for the job."

Roxy stared at the folded piece of paper. Nyotaimori, not accounting, like she'd hoped. Elias wanted food displayed on a human body for the consumers to eat the food directly off the presenter's skin. So he knew about her part-time job in college.

She sighed. He would know about that and not her degree. But if she played along, she'd get a chance to talk to Sean. Seeing Sean made the decision easy. "Okay, but I haven't done this in a while. Do you want me to be totally still like a mannequin or is this going to be more interactive? And since when did we start serving sushi?"

"I'm using you as the table, but I'm not using sushi. Sean's not fond of raw fish. So I thought we could modify it a little and use what he likes." Elias pocketed the paper. "If I don't hide this, he'll know and I want it to be a surprise."

"I see. You're not serving anything hot then, right?" She folded her arms. "What did you have planned?"

"Wine, fruit, cheeses and a couple other items. Mostly I want you there." Elias sat on the edge of the desk. "You're never going to believe this, but he likes you."

Roxy collapsed on the closest chair. "He what?" Elias had to be lying. Sean never talked to her other than to hand her a pay cheque. He never smiled or even looked like he wanted to be at the restaurant. And yet, she fantasised about him every time she used her vibrator.

"Sean's very"—he bowed his head—"how do I say this…particular. He's not one of those bizarre, reclusive millionaires. Trust me, neither one of us is rolling in cash, but meeting women isn't his strong point. He mentioned seeing you outside of work at the Push Club."

"He did?" She'd only been to Push twice and neither time had got her off. The guys wanted more than she preferred to give in her BDSM play. Comfort zones weren't enforced well—at least not on the two nights she'd attended. Had she seen Sean? Only one guy had even acted human and decent. She remembered she'd met him during the masquerade night. He'd worn a mask partially covering his face, leather pants and no shirt. When they'd danced, he'd held her close and murmured things about wanting to cover her in honey and lick every inch of her body. Sean barely spoke to her at work, but maybe he loosened up when he went to the club. She shivered. She remembered seeing him play with one of the subs. He'd embodied raw power and control.

"I wasn't there, so don't ask me." Elias' voice ripped her from her thoughts. "Roxy, I want you to do this. I'll prep the food, you just lie there. I'm kicking in a grand in tips, so you won't get stiffed."

"A grand?"

"Well, it does require nudity and the whole night devoted to Sean. We're normally closed on Sundays, so it's only fair."

What could she say? A night alone with Sean and a thousand dollars… One of her wildest dreams come true. A vision of Sean came to mind from the last time she'd seen him at the restaurant. His jeans hugged his muscular legs and accented the bulge between his thighs. The cotton dress shirt highlighted the green in his eyes and oozed power. His scent curled around her and she closed her eyes. The guy smelt like sex and heaven mixed with aftershave. Would he shave or leave a little scruff on his cheeks? She pressed her knees together. Thinking about Sean licking honey, or whatever it was Elias planned, off her body sent a frisson of heat through her veins. Her pussy clenched and she gripped the armrests of the chair. God, she hoped she didn't make a fool of herself. Playing the role of presentation girl had never turned her on, but having Sean involved changed everything.

Roxy met Elias' gaze. "What time do you need me to be here?"

* * * *

Sean sat at his desk in his home office and stared at the invitation. Damn Elias. He hadn't wanted to celebrate his birthday. People turned thirty-six all the time and no one made a big deal. Then again, Elias knew how much he wanted to keep his birthday quiet.

"A private party," Sean read out loud. "Probably a stripper or something equally stupid." A headache grew behind his eyes. He'd been dicked over by enough women in his lifetime to know a one-nighter with a stripper wasn't going to cut it, but he wasn't sure he wanted a full-time lover either. Hell, the nights he played at Push didn't get his rocks off. Except the one night he'd danced with the vixen in the red feathered mask.

He grinned and closed his eyes. Roxy had thought she could hide behind the red velvet. Not a chance. He'd know that body anywhere. The red satin bustier she'd worn had highlighted two of her best assets — her breasts. His mouth watered. The fishnet stockings had accentuated her statuesque legs. He longed to feel her clenched around him as he drove his cock into her pussy.

Even as a memory, he knew the feel of her slender body under his hands. That night she'd ground her ass into his groin enough times for him to memorise her curves. He longed to lash her to his St Andrew's cross and drizzle chocolate on her chest. Would she squeal? Moan? Call him a freak because he liked food play mixed with sex? She'd clutched him tighter when he'd mentioned the honey play. He could only hope and fantasise.

Then again, he'd actually have to act on his desire for her. He'd instituted the rules against staff dating. Still, he visualised her astride his lap with whipped cream decorating her body. The dark chocolate would complement her pale skin. His cock stiffened behind his zipper. He could almost feel her riding him, her moist heat enveloping him. Sean palmed his cock and groaned. He wanted the real woman, wanted to touch her and taste her.

In his mind, she smiled and clutched her sticky chest. She bit her bottom lip and her hair slid over her shoulders in tangles. Her deep brown eyes glittered as she slipped into subspace.

Sean gasped for breath, unzipped, then shoved his pants to the floor. He then wrapped his fingers around his cock and stroked. He could see her bouncing on his lap and taste the cream on her skin. She leant forward, taking his mouth in a kiss. The tastes of chocolate, cream and raw desire exploded on his tongue. Her nipples rubbed his chest and kicked his desire up another notch. Fuck, he wished he had her in person, not a daydream. His balls ached and he stroked harder. The flutters low in his belly switched to full electric shocks along his limbs. Jesus.

"I'm coming," she panted. "Sean."

Fuck yeah. Sean gripped his dick with one hand and massaged his sac with the other. He tilted his head back, opened his eyes and embraced the orgasm. Hot ribbons of cum splattered on his thighs. Good thing he'd been sitting down. He panted and glanced around the room. At least no one was around to hear him this time. He shouldn't fantasise about a woman he hardly knew, but damn, she got him off every time.

The shrill ring of his phone ended the post hand job euphoria. "Shit." Sean pulled the T-shirt up over his shoulders, then mopped up the cum on his hands and legs. He tossed the soiled clothing onto the floor then stood. He knew the ringtone.

Elias.

He could wait. Sean hiked his boxers and pants up over his hips, then answered the call. "Malkin."

"Hi to you, too," Elias replied from his end. "I take it you got the invitation."

"I did." Sean sank back onto his chair. He picked up the cream-coloured piece of paper and tapped it on the desk top. "Care to give me a few more details? Like where to go and what time?"

"That's why I called. I'd like you to come by the Delight tomorrow night. Eight p.m. sharp. If you're late, then I'm starting without you."

"You do that anyway," Sean snapped.

"But I won't be alone." Elias didn't say anything for a heartbeat, as if he wanted his words to sink in with Sean. "It's a private dinner with all the fixin's you like and I'll let you in on a secret. Your server for the night is Roxy."

Sean sat tall in his chair. Roxy? His server? Hot damn. "I'll be there."

"Thought you might. Dress casual. It's not some stuffy dinner like we normally have at Delight. I'm aiming to clog your arteries with all the good stuff. When you get here, go to the private rooms on the second floor." Before Sean could say anything else, Elias hung up.

Sean stared at his cellphone. A night with Roxy. He wasn't keen on breaking the rules, but for Roxy he would. Maybe turning thirty-six wouldn't be a shitter after all.

Chapter Two

Roxy stared at her reflection in the mirror and secured her hair in a bun on the top of her head. The look accentuated her already lanky body. She crinkled her nose. Three hours before when she'd gone through the cleaning regimen for the dinner, she'd felt more confident. This was just another job, nothing else.

Except Sean was involved.

She squared her shoulders then headed out of the bathroom on the second floor of Delight Tonight. Elias and Sean barely used the second floor unless they were catering a wedding or private party. Even then, they never used the room marked 'Office' as the office. Elias kept the books and computer downstairs off the kitchen.

"Elias?" She knocked on the door to the quaint room. "Are you ready for me?"

"Come on in," came his reply from behind the door.

She twisted the handle and a shiver of excitement raced through her veins. Only an hour longer and she'd see Sean. Elias shook out a plastic tablecloth, then covered the cushioned table.

"Hey." He grinned and patted the table. "Climb up. I'll be right back."

She shrugged out of the robe, then stretched out on the plastic. He'd specified she wear black stilettos and red lipstick. Not exactly the attire she normally wore when playing the part of the dinner table, but whatever he wanted she'd do. She stared at the ceiling and measured her breaths. "Get into the zone," she murmured. "Zone."

Every nerve ending sizzled. Her nipples beaded and no matter how much she tried, she couldn't hold still. Damn it. She wished Sean were the one decorating her and wondered what it would feel like to be under his command. A moan escaped her lips and she gritted her teeth together. She remembered the way he carried the whip at Push. Would he use that on her? Her ass tingled. She hadn't earned a good spanking in a long time. Would he talk dirty to her? Her pussy quivered and she pressed her knees tight together.

No matter how much she wanted Sean, she had a job to do.

Behind her head, the door clicked. She continued staring at the ceiling tiles and focused on anything mundane, like puppies, her work schedule for the next week and where she wanted to go shopping for a new pair of boots.

"Perfect." Elias snapped his latex gloves, grabbing her attention. "Not much longer now."

She glanced to watch him place thin circles of chilly filo dough over her breasts and her pussy. Sliced strawberries and bananas decorated around her navel in a neat pyramid. Sliced peaches ringed the pile. He arranged dollops of whipped cream on her covered nipples, then added a cherry. A tiny round cake ended up on the dough covering her groin. All in all, the set-up wasn't nearly as exotic or intricate as she'd expected.

"And it's time for me to head out." Elias wiped his hands and checked his watch. "Thanks for coming through for me. The money's in my desk downstairs. Ask Sean to open the locked drawer for you." He winked then walked out of her line of sight.

She blew out a long breath then closed her eyes. From the other side of the door, she heard Elias again. Singing?

"Happy birthday, dear Seany boy, happy birthday to you. Now go enjoy your dinner, old man."

The doorknob clicked and creaked. Roxy held as still as possible, but her hands trembled. She flattened them on the table and prayed no one would notice.

"Old man my ass." A shadow moved to her right, then something else creaked. "Roxy?"

She knew that voice. Sean. When she'd trained to do Nyotaimori, she'd learnt the art of lying still. Being around Sean made that task damned near impossible. She breathed in through her nose and out through her mouth to keep from shaking.

Sean stood beside her and picked up a strawberry, then popped it into his mouth. "Happy birthday to me," he said between bites.

Talk about a great surprise. Sean picked up a second berry, then dragged it through the whipped cream. He licked the cream off the crimson strawberry but barely tasted the fruit. He focused his attention on the sight of Roxy, his fantasy girl, covered in food. Elias knew what Sean liked and how to come through in the clinch. Sean trailed his fingers down her leg. She shivered and stuffed her hands under her bottom. He couldn't have imagined a better display for his birthday supper.

"So pretty." He sat on the chair, then leaned over her and sucked one of the cherries into his mouth. She closed her eyes and her lips parted farther. The Nyotaimori girls weren't supposed to react to the patrons—not in a traditional setting. But this, this was not traditional by a long shot. Sean dipped his finger in the whipped cream then drew a heart on her sternum.

Her cheeks flooded with colour and she whimpered.

"Talk to me, Roxy." He dragged the other cherry in the fluffy white cream, then dangled it over her mouth. "First, take a bite."

She curled her tongue around the cherry before pulling the fruit from the stem. Her brown eyes glittered and she moaned.

"So sexy." He hooked his finger in the cake, then smeared frosting on her belly. The contrast of the perky blue frosting and her pale skin turned him on. He swiped his tongue through the sugary concoction, cleaning her up. His cock thickened and the blood rushed through his body. If they were in his bedroom, he'd do so much more with her. So much more.

"Don't stop," Roxy panted. She arched her back, offering herself to him. "Please?"

Oh hell yes, he'd take things further. He scooted to the head of the table and cupped her jaw in his hand. The sugary confection on his fingers smudged on her cheek. Time to tell her about their shared past and how much he wanted to give their future a try.

"You're not wearing your red velvet mask." He pressed a kiss to her lips, then licked her bottom lip. "It's sexy as hell, but I like you better without it."

"You remembered," she whispered.

"I couldn't forget." He kissed her again, this time taking total control of the connection. He tangled their tongues and learnt her taste. When she moaned, he slid one arm behind her neck. "I want to play with you. More than anything we could do at Push and so much hotter."

Her chest heaved. "Play?" The corner of her mouth curled. "I'd love to be yours for the night."

For the night. She'd given him an opening. Sean stood, then moved the chair out of the way. Time to show her his dirtiest fantasies. "What is your safe word, beautiful?" He flicked the catch on his watch. This night needed to be special. The thick band of leather slid off his wrist and he tucked the timepiece in his pocket. He never showed off his tat on his inner wrist. For her, he would.

"Corsica." Her cheeks flushed anew. "And I call you Sir?"

"Yes, pet." He unbuckled his belt and slid it free of the loops. "Hands, pet." When she raised her arms over her head, he leaned over her again. "Do you wish to use your safe word?"

"No, Sir." She smiled and clasped her hands together.

"Good." He wrapped the belt around her wrists then plucked a strawberry from her navel. "Bite."

She opened her mouth and accepted the berry.

"If you want to use your safe word, use it. I respect you and want you to enjoy what we do."

Roxy nodded and her eyes sparkled.

"Now, what can I do with you?" He dragged his fingers through the whipped cream, coating her upper body in the sticky liquid. The strips of dough peeled from her breasts, revealing her dusky nipples. His mouth watered and he took one rosy bead in his teeth.

She arched into his touch and moaned around the berry between her teeth.

Oh yeah. The taste of strawberry and whipped cream mixed with the salt on her skin turned his senses inside out. He groaned and drew in the white cream on her belly.

Roxy writhed and whimpered. The cake wobbled over her pussy, then toppled and stuck to her inner thigh. Sean licked his lips, then kissed and nipped the frosting from her skin. She moaned and opened her legs. Nice. Sean nibbled the sugared confection and made his way to her pussy. The aroma of her excitement wafted around him and he grinned. *Damn.* He loved a turned-on woman. Loved a woman who understood his needs.

Sean dragged his tongue over her clit then backed away from her cunt. Her eyes widened again and the leaves on the top of the berry slipped from her lips. She swallowed the berry, then opened her mouth.

Hmm. What could he do with her? He moved the extra cake from her lap, then scooped the last few slices of fruit in his hand. "Come here." He sat down in the chair he'd abandoned. "Come to me."

Roxy moved her arms, then eased off the table and crawled on her knees to him.

"Undress me." He spread his knees and bit into a piece of peach. He liked seeing her struggle a bit with the belt still around her wrists. One by one, Roxy worked the buttons on his shirt, then pushed the sides of the shirt away from his chest. Sean dabbed the strawberry on his nipples. "Taste me, pet."

She eased between his legs, brushing her breasts over his abdomen. Leftover frosting spread between them. She flicked her tongue on his chest and hummed. Each tiny moan and whimper spurred him on. He threaded his fingers into her hair and freed the tresses from the pins. Her hair spilled down her shoulders and framed her face like a halo.

"Yes, pet." He guided her down his chest to the button on his jeans. "I want to feel that hot mouth on me."

Roxy glanced up at him and smiled, then unzipped him and fondled his cock. She eased him out of the boxer shorts and denim. The cool air mixed with her hot breath and made him need her more. Sean then shrugged out of his shirt, giving her ultimate access. He gripped her hair and urged his dick past her lips. He groaned. Damn, he wanted to do so many more things with her. She knew what to do and how to churn his lust.

"Enough." He swatted her bottom. "You're too good." And he hadn't experienced enough. He scooped her into his arms, then placed her on his chair. "Want to taste you." Sean buried his face between her thighs and draped her legs over his shoulders. Juice from the berries mingled with the sweet taste of her excitement. He speared one finger into her wet heat.

Roxy writhed on his hand. She raked her nails through his hair.

"Good, pet?" He palmed her breast with his free hand and pinched her nipple. "Tell me." He blew across her clit, then nipped the tiny bead of skin hard.

"Sir." She jerked forward and clamped her legs tight around his head. "Sir."

He scraped her clit again, thrilled when she keened for him. "Do you wish to use your safe word?" He knew better, but he also asked to be sure.

"No, Sir. More." She panted and draped her arms around his neck. "More."

"Absolutely." He spread her pussy lips and plunged back into her heat. Sean added a second finger and pumped, fucking her with his hand. Roxy met him thrust for thrust and groaned. Her legs quaked and she was breathing hard. Time to pull back. He stood.

"On the table, pet, on your hands and knees." He patted the cushioned surface. "Up."

Roxy stared up at him from under her lashes and licked her lips. She wobbled as she scampered into place on the table top. With the belt still around her wrists, she spread her legs. Her pussy glistened with the combination of her juices and the remnants of the fruit.

Sean fished his wallet from his back pocket, then withdrew the condom he always kept there. Part of him wanted to feel her bare skin on his. The rest of him knew better. He sheathed himself and rubbed her cream on his dick. A shiver ran through his body. He wouldn't last long, but yeah, he wanted in her. He stroked her with his fingers, then lined his dick up with her slit. Inch by delicious inch, he slid into her.

"Oh, Sir." Roxy pushed backwards, sending him deeper into her cunt. "Fuck."

"We are." Sean brought his hand down hard on her ass, the crack resounding through the room.

"Sir. More." Roxy rolled her hips, grinding on him. His balls slapped her clit with each thrust and he punctuated his movements with spanks on her bottom. She cried out and gripped the edge of the table. She squeezed him from within and held him tight.

Sean stroked her reddened skin then wrapped his arms around her. A bead of sweat slipped between his shoulder blades. He shook his head then gripped her hips.

"Come for me, pet." He thrust hard into her and tipped his head back. "Fuck." His balls tingled and he gritted his teeth. "Come, babe."

Beneath him, Roxy shivered then tensed. Her inner walls rippled and grabbed at him while he emptied his seed into the rubber. From his head to his toes, his body buzzed. *Holy shit.* Sean slumped forward and hugged her to his chest.

"Happy birthday, Sean." Roxy dropped to her elbows, sagging onto the table.

Sean sighed and pulled out of her. She'd made his birthday one to remember. Hell, he wanted to continue their tryst for the rest of the night. He tossed the used rubber into the trash can then discarded the mangled filo dough. They'd made a mess, but he didn't care. He rather liked using the spare office for his personal play area.

Sean patted her hip. "Turn over, babe." When she did, he unbuckled the belt and released her from her bonds.

Roxy rubbed her wrists. "Thank you, Sir."

"You're very welcome." He zipped his jeans then picked his shirt up off the floor. "This is for you." He draped the shirt across her shoulders. "Come here." He settled in the chair, then tugged her onto his lap. "That was the best birthday present ever. Thank you."

Roxy tucked a loose lock of her hair behind her ear and smiled. "Any time."

Chapter Three

Roxy rested her head on his shoulder. Holy fuck in a basket, she'd screwed around with Sean. Not only screwed around, but indulged in her favourite fetish — food play. Not many men liked food mixed with sex. Sean sure did. She sagged against his chest and fought to catch her breath. The night wasn't over, but for all she knew, their time together ended the moment she walked out of the room.

Did she want their night to end?

Not really.

"What happens now?" she asked. "I was only hired to be the table." She braced herself for his answer. Sean was known for playing hard and what they'd done was only a shred of what he could do. She'd seen him at work.

"My birthday isn't over." Sean squeezed her. "I'd like you to come home with me and continue what we've started."

"Sean?" She had to have heard him wrong. Sean Malkin could have any play partner he wanted. She'd witnessed the lines of women who came to the restaurant to see him.

"I never imagined I'd end up having so much fun tonight. I'm not sure I want this to end." He patted her bottom. "I want to take you home and pamper you."

Her mind spun. "I— Elias paid me to come." Her stomach soured and she scooted off his lap. Damn it to hell. She sounded like a freaking hooker. Her heart dropped to her toes and she turned away from him. She refused to look into his eyes. "I can drive myself home." Where'd she leave her clothes? In the upstairs restroom. She blinked back tears and headed across the room to the door.

"Hey."

She froze, but didn't turn around.

Sean wrapped his arms about her midsection and rested his chin on her shoulder. "Roxy, he told me he brought you in tonight. Us having sex wasn't part of the deal."

"True." She glanced down at his entwined hands. He'd taken off the watch. Three calligraphic letters were tattooed onto his inner wrist. Huh. She'd never figured him for a tattoo kind of guy, but then he never removed the watch either.

"I remember the chemistry we had at Push. No matter how I tried, I couldn't forget you." He kissed her neck below her ear, then dragged his teeth over her earlobe. "I'm very picky about who I play with. We have a connection I can't ignore. I want you and I'm pretty sure you want me, too. Let's see where this can go."

"I do want you." She clutched his folded hands, stroking her thumb over the letters on his skin. "I want more." But fear crept into her brain. She'd been honest with him. She knew how much more he could give her. Would he want her in the morning? And what about her job? They'd broken Sean's cardinal rule not to screw around with staff.

"Live for right now and put yourself in my hands again. Please, babe?" Sean kissed the side of her head. "Can't get enough of you."

Roxy threw caution to the wind. She'd worry about the repercussions of her actions later. "Then let's go."

Sean grinned. "Why don't you drive?"

She snorted. "Are you too good to drive? Or is this so you can kick me out in the morning?"

Sean followed hot on her heels as she strolled to the restroom for her clothes. "I didn't drive. Elias told me to take a cab. He's got a wicked sixth sense about stuff — like me and you."

"Wait here." She ducked into the bathroom and weighed her options. End things or give him a chance. Ending things meant she'd still have her job. Continuing meant an inevitable change in her life. Who needed status quo? Might as well give him the chance. She dressed and checked her look in the mirror, then opened the door. Sean stood in the hallway waiting for her.

"Hi, beautiful." He trailed his fingers down her arm, then held her hand. "Ready?"

Second thoughts crept in. She rubbed her temple. She wanted to be alone with him, but something felt off. "Why don't we go to Push?"

Sean nodded once then escorted her to the first floor. She hated putting a wall between them, but things had moved too fast.

"Nah, I'm not in the mood for a club." He walked her to her car then threaded his fingers into her hair and massaged her scalp. "Let's give us some time." He rested his forehead on hers. "We can go out... Tomorrow night?"

"I've got to work," she replied and her voice cracked. "I should be in bed right now so I'm not a wreck tomorrow for the lunch rush."

"Makes sense." He rubbed her nose with his and kissed her. "I'll meet you wherever you want, however you want."

"I'd like that." She placed her hand over his heart. The touch seared her to her core. Did love happen in a few hours? Could they turn white-hot lust and a shared fetish for food play into something more? She wasn't sure.

"See you tomorrow." Sean stood in the next parking spot and watched her leave.

Roxy slid onto the car seat then shut the door. The drive across town to her apartment went by in a blur. A mix of regret and relief washed over her — relief for putting the brakes on the burgeoning relationship, but regret for walking away from Sean. She knew damn well she wasn't a freak for enjoying their play, but she wondered how she'd let things happen so fast. The whole night seemed like a strange and sexy dream. The more she thought about Sean, the more she knew why she'd stopped short of going home with him. The last time she'd moved at warp speed, she'd been burned. Was Sean going to end up being another dead end or a sexy new beginning? She pulled into her driveway and stopped, then held her head in her hands and closed her eyes.

"Why do I want what I shouldn't have?" she murmured. "Why?"

Sean stuffed his hands into his pockets and watched her leave. Sex with Roxy had blown his mind. He wanted her again and again. But he understood her hesitation. Too much, too fast and she needed to control something. He dragged a long breath into his lungs then headed back into the restaurant. He needed her in his bed. Like now. If waiting meant he'd have another chance to spend time with her, then he'd do it.

Glasses clinked at the bar and light spilled from the main room. Sean crept to the banquet room and peered around the corner. Elias leaned on the bar top, glass in hand, and shook the ice. A basketball game played on the television.

"Elias." Sean rolled his shoulders then sat down on the first stool. He placed his watch on the bar top, then smoothed the wrinkles in his T-shirt. "What are you doing here? We're closed on Sunday nights."

Elias turned around and grinned. "Keeping an eye on you." He frowned. "Is Roxy in the bathroom? You're heading out?"

"She went home."

"Home? You're going after her, right?" Elias dumped the ice from his glass in the sink, then wiped the condensation ring off the wooden surface of the bar. "You two are good together. I see you showed her your tat. You never show people that tattoo."

Sean pulled his watch from his pocket then affixed the timepiece around his wrist to cover the tattoo of his initials. Damn it. He hated when Elias was right. "Just because we're good in bed doesn't mean we'll have a future together. It was one night." He leaned over the bar and grabbed a bottle of beer from the open ice chest. "It's nuts. After Rebekah, I didn't think I'd find someone. Going to Push was an outlet. No commitments, just fun. Then I saw Roxy there. We danced and flirted. She made me think about trying again, but then I didn't see her there after the first time."

"Which is why I put you two together." Elias grinned. "So what's the hold-up? She's not into your kink?"

"That's not it at all." Sean scrubbed his hand over his mouth. "I think I'm in love with her. That's nuts."

"It's not. It's called moving on." Elias tossed the towel onto the bar. "You're going to give her time, because you're a good guy, and see where things go." He tipped his head. "I know you. Then things will turn out. Why? Because you're secretive except around her and she's crazy about you."

"And you know this how?"

"Any of my girls would've jumped at the chance to make a grand serving a birthday party. Half of them would've played the role of nude serving platter, if I'd asked. Only one of them isn't afraid of the big, bad, scary Sean who never smiles and never comes into the restaurant. Roxy. Either she's really into you or she's got balls of steel." He leaned on his elbows. "Besides, she left the money in my desk. I guess she didn't feel right taking it and wanted to see you instead."

"No shit," Sean replied, not realising he'd spoken out loud. So the feelings were there. He could work with that information. "Thanks."

"For what?"

"Showing me what I already knew but didn't see." Sean slid the open but untouched bottle of beer across the bar top to Elias. "Drink that so it doesn't go to waste, then get yourself a girl."

Sean climbed the stairs to the second storey and the office he and Elias shared. He collapsed on the couch and closed his eyes. He'd pamper Roxy and show her just how much he cared about her — after some sleep.

* * * *

Sean stretched out on his couch and stared at the ceiling. Sleeping on the couch in the office hadn't worked, not when he'd still been able to smell the sweet scent of Roxy in the room. He drove himself home and collapsed on the couch in the living room. Slumber came and went, but he didn't bother to move until mid-afternoon.

Twenty-four hours earlier, he'd found the love of his life. Granted she'd been right under his nose the whole time, but at least he knew. He glanced at the clock. The restaurant closed in an hour. He'd picked up flowers for her and arranged the living room for a midnight picnic. Not the greatest idea for a date, but whatever worked. His heart raced and he palmed his cock. In less than an hour he'd see her and get to hold her again. He couldn't wait.

He imagined her on his lap again and relived the night before. The next time they played, he wanted to go all out. Chocolate, honey, whipped cream…and handcuffs. He'd been out of practice for too long, despite his jaunts to Push. He craved her submission and the smile she wore when she slipped into subspace.

Yeah, he loved her.

Sean sat up and raked his fingers through his hair. Time to tell her how he felt. He drove across town then parked at the back door of the restaurant. Flowers in hand, he strolled into the kitchen. One of the other servers, Alice, a skinny brunette with a full chest and a bright smile, wandered past him. Her shoulders bobbed and she didn't bother to look at him, but kept singing a song he didn't know.

He shrugged and made his way through the kitchen to the downstairs office. The door swung open and yet another server bounded out of the room. "That's it, Elias. I'm done." She whipped her apron at him. "Done."

Sean stepped back out of the line of fire, then poked his head into the office. "Rough day?"

Elias pinched the bridge of his nose. "Two servers quit and one threw up an hour ago. Yeah, it's great. Can you help bus tables?" He stood and grabbed a smock from the coat hook. "I can use all the help I can get."

"Sure." Sean placed the flowers on the desk. When he left the kitchen, he snagged a bus tub. "Who quit?"

"Couple of the newer girls." Elias stopped at the first table and hefted filthy dishes into the tub. "Roxy's had a rough night, too. Been a champ and hasn't complained."

Sean passed her in the main banquet room and grinned. Her hair had escaped the clip and stuck out at odd angles. Her makeup was smeared under her eyes and her smile dimmed when she saw him.

"Hey." He followed her back to the kitchen. "Rox."

She stopped and sighed. "You picked a great night to ask me out, didn't you?" She smoothed a flyaway lock of hair behind her ear. "Not the sexiest hook-up, is it?"

Hell, she looked sexy in every way. He twined their fingers, then led her to the office.

"It's a bit early for a quickie. Won't Elias get upset if we screw around on his paperwork?" She giggled, then rested her head on his shoulder. "Or is it yours?"

"My paperwork, babe." He handed her the flowers. "For you. I thought I'd be able to whisk you out of here early. Guess I was wrong." He wrapped an arm around her. "I had a hot night planned, but I've got a better idea."

"Yeah?" She sniffed the roses. "These are beautiful."

"Anything for you." He kissed her temple. "Even a nap later."

"I might take you up on that." She stood on her tiptoes then kissed him on the lips. "Then I'll have you smack my ass and drench me in chocolate." She wriggled her brows before leaving him alone in the office.

Sean watched her leave and gawked at her ass. Well, hot damn.

Chapter Four

Two hours after he'd arrived at Delight Tonight, Sean led Roxy back to his house. She dropped her bag inside the door and sagged in his arms. "This is your house?"

He shrugged and kissed the back of her head. "It's where I live."

"This is a mansion." She pulled away from him and waved her hand. "Well, a mini one, but wow." She wandered through his living room and trailed her fingers over the leather sofa and stained glass lamp, then stopped in front of the painting of dogs. "The only art I have is a concert poster from a band I saw in college. This is so cool."

He liked seeing her in his home. She offered the feminine touch he longed for, and a hot one to boot.

"Are they your dogs?" Her shoulders sagged and she sighed. She could hide her fatigue at the restaurant, but he knew better. He stood beside her and touched the painting.

"They were. Pug, my pug, had cancer. Toot, the mutt named because she had a bad case of gas, died of

old age, and Cap, my greyhound, ran out in traffic."
He cleared his throat. Other than Elias, no one knew
about his dogs and he missed them. "Sorry."

"Why?" She threaded her arms around his. "I keep
discovering sweet things about you. It's sexy."

"Yeah?" Sean swept her off her feet then carried her
to his bedroom. Roxy whimpered and clutched him
tight. "Afraid I'll drop you?" He placed her on his
bed. "You're tired. Our date can wait until the
morning."

"I'm sorry." She sighed and closed her eyes. "The
night wore me out. It's crazy. I shouldn't be this
tired."

"Sleep, babe. We had a full house and three servers
doing the work of six. You deserve a nap." Sean
stretched out beside Roxy. She completed him in
every way. She responded to his touch like no other
and she accepted his kink. He couldn't imagine being
without her, even after just a few hours together. But
things couldn't go so easily. They never did for him.
In one way or another, she'd realise she wanted more
than him. She'd leave, just like the others.

He stroked her hair and listened to the cadence of
her sleeping breaths. He wanted to leave her. To walk
away and never look back. They'd played just once
and he'd got what he wanted. But something about
her pulled him back. He wanted her for more than a
play thing. He wanted forever.

"Love you, Roxy."

Sean pulled the blanket over her body then strode
across the room. No more thinking about the past.
Time to embrace the future. In the morning, they'd
talk — then they'd play.

He dug through the bag of toys he'd purchased earlier in the day and arranged them on the dresser. He'd show her the time of her life.

* * * *

Roxy flopped onto her back and snuggled against the warm object at her side. *Warm?* She slapped at the thing beside her before opening her eyes.

"Good morning to you, too." Sean reclined on his side, one arm tucked under his head. "Feel better?"

"Yeah." She glanced down at her outfit. Still dressed. "How long have I been out?"

"All night." He smiled. "You fell asleep on me."

Great job, Roxy. She gritted her teeth. "I'm sorry."

"Why? You were tired." He shrugged. "Having you beside me wasn't a hardship. I like spending time with you, sweetheart."

Realisation washed over her. She had spent the night with him. He'd been what she wanted. A gentleman. Her feelings for him grew. So did her desire. "I believe last night you mentioned something about playing." She spotted the St Andrew's cross in the corner and lust pooled low in her belly. "Something about honey and chocolate? And maybe the cross? We can create our own little Push, right here."

"Yes, babe."

She scooted across the bed and met him for a kiss. Sean took over the connection and rolled her onto her back. His tongue tangled with hers and he rubbed his burgeoning erection against her upper thigh.

"I want to tie you up and spank your ass." He palmed her breast. "Then cover you in honey and chocolate to soothe the pain." Sean tweaked her nipple. "Honey, dribbling from here." Another tweak. "Ready and waiting for me to lick you clean."

Roxy panted and nodded. "Yes."

"Tell me your safe word. We don't play until you tell me." The possession in his eyes resonated in his voice.

"Corsica, Sir." She loved this kind of interplay and craved his dominance.

"Very good, pet. Disrobe for me. Slow." He rested on his elbow and crossed his ankles. "Show me all your secrets."

Roxy stood, then eased her shirt up over her head. Her hair slipped free from the clip and tickled her shoulders. She focused on Sean, then folded the shirt and placed it at her feet. Her work jeans ended up in a pile on the floor. She turned around, showing him her ass, and folded the denim. When she glanced over her shoulder, he grinned.

"More." He waved his finger. "Everything."

She licked her lips, then hooked her thumbs under the straps of her bra. The clasp popped free, allowing the cups to slide away from her breasts. A rush of cooler air spread over her chest and her nipples responded in kind. She gasped, letting the lingerie land in a heap. Most Doms expected their playmate to abide by certain directions, like tidiness. What would he do if she ignored the mandates?

"You didn't fold it. Or don't you want to play by the unspoken rules?" He glanced down at the bra. "Should I punish you?"

A frisson of excitement rang through her. "Do what you see fit, Sir." She slid one hand down her belly to the elastic of her panties, then tugged. The cotton eased down her hips and landed on the floor, giving him a view of her body. She bowed her head and clasped her hands behind her back.

Sean stood, then crossed the room and circled her. He touched her ass, swatting her skin, then tweaked her nipple. "Tell me your limits."

"Sir?" She kept her gaze on the floor. "No wax, blood, needles, bruises, choking. I trust you to know when to push and when to hold back."

"Good, pet." He tipped her jaw to look her in the eye. "I want you to be happy and enjoy our play. Use your safe word and we'll stop, then return to that play later. Do you understand?"

"Yes, Sir." She spread her feet. "Thank you, Sir."

"Sexy." Sean disappeared from her line of sight, but she heard his footsteps on the floor. Something clinked. She wanted to look at what he held, but didn't dare.

"This," he said, holding a thick leather collar before her, "is just for play right now. I like my subs in the bedroom, but I don't expect you to be one everywhere. Do you accept?" He'd ditched his sleep pants and his cock pointed to her. The veins stuck out and the blunt head jabbed into her belly.

"Yes, Sir." When he clicked the buckle in place at her throat, her nerves calmed. She closed her eyes a moment and breathed. Heat flowed through her veins and her skin prickled. "Thank you, Sir."

"Now about that punishment." Sean clipped a leash onto the D-ring of the collar. "Come." He tugged the leash then led her across the room to the cross. "Turn."

When she faced away from him, he secured her wrists in the cuffs. "Feels good?" He left her feet free. "Talk to me."

"Wonderful, Sir." She measured her breaths and braced herself for whatever he planned to do with her.

"I believe I owe you punishment." More footsteps behind her. Something cracked, then something cool touched her ass. "This," he said, "will sting. How many spanks?"

"Five, Sir." She'd guessed high, but didn't care.

"Good choice." He brought the item down on her bottom, hard. She gulped and her mind raced. *A studded paddle?* Nice. She wanted to look at the instrument of pain, but didn't dare. Another swat kissed her ass. Her skin burned and the pain morphed into pleasure in an instant. Her pussy creamed and she wriggled to stick her butt out more for his touch.

"Greedy, aren't you?" He smacked her twice more, then walked behind the cross. "Hold." He placed the handle of the paddle between her teeth, then disappeared from her vision. She listened for his every move. Something clicked. Anticipation filled her brain. What would he do next?

"I owe you one more spanking, don't I?" He kissed her shoulder and took the paddle from her teeth. "Answer me."

"Yes, Sir. May I have another? Plus another for being bad and not counting the spankings?"

"My pet." He twisted her hair around his hand, then added two more spankings.

Her bottom ached in the delicious pain. She suppressed a moan. "Thank you, Sir."

"Now to cool you down."

Chill swept over her fevered skin. She jumped at the switch in temperature. The cuffs clinked again and held her fast.

"Taste." Sean smeared the white cream over her lips. "Whipped cream for my pet."

She sucked on his fingers before letting him go.

"Damn, pet." He ground his crotch into her ass. "Tease." He swatted her with his bare hand, then rubbed more whipped cream on her skin. Sean knelt behind her and spread her ass cheeks wide. "Wet for me, too." He buried his face in her cunt lips, swirling his tongue through the cream and her liquid excitement. "So good."

Roxy gripped the arms of the cross and whimpered. He knew the right amount of licking to add to the spankings to make her mind blur. Flutters started in her belly. Too fucking early, but hell. She writhed on his tongue.

"No, pet." He kissed the inside of her thigh. "Not until I give you permission."

Sean unfastened the cuffs at her wrists, then turned her around. He reattached her to the cross, this time using the ankle cuffs as well.

Roxy panted and licked the last remnants of the cream from her lips. Sean stood across from her. Seeing him totally in control knocked her lust for a loop. He dropped the crop on the floor at her feet then picked up a bottle of lube and a vibrator.

"I want to see you come apart for me." He tapped her lips with the toy. "Get it nice and wet."

Roxy curled her tongue around the toy, coating it with her saliva. She would've preferred to suck his cock, but since he hadn't offered yet, she kept quiet.

Sean dribbled lube on his fingers, then caressed her labia. She bit down on the toy to keep from crying out. The lube warmed her delicate skin and gave him easier passage into her vagina. He pumped two fingers in her, then left her bereft.

"You please me, pet." He took the toy from her mouth and switched it on. He touched her breasts, then dragged the vibe down her belly to her cunt. "Can you hold this in for me? Show me."

Sean eased the dildo into her pussy, then stepped back. She gripped the knobby surface with her inner muscles and focused on him again. A grin lit up his face. He picked up a bottle of chocolate syrup. She shivered. Between the need in her body and the vibrator, she'd never be able to keep from coming.

"You need some decoration." He picked up the paddle and tucked it under his arm then popped the top on the bottle. Hunger and desire burned in his eyes. He stalked towards her and the muscles in his jaw clenched.

Her belly tightened. "Cover me, Sir. Drench me." Her voice dropped an octave and she whimpered. "Please?"

The vibrator slipped, rubbing her G-spot. Holy fuck in heaven. When Sean dribbled chocolate over her breasts, she moaned. Her grip on the leather cuff tightened. The chocolate slid down her chest, tickling her skin.

Sean drew a heart in the sticky brown substance, then offered her his finger. "Taste yourself."

She licked his hand, sucking on him as if she were going down on him.

"Damn, pet." He smeared his fingers over her lips. "So good."

The vibrator slipped more, then plopped on the floor with a whirring thud. He tipped his head. "Bad girl." He picked up the dildo, switched it off, then turned the paddle over in his hand. "Very bad."

"Punish me, Sir." She rolled her hips. "I need punished."

"Yes, you do," he said and punctuated each word with a swat on her pussy. The tingles in her clit exploded through her body and centred in her core.

She needed the pain, craved the rush of pleasure afterwards and longed for him. Nothing mattered but Sean and the way he manipulated her body. He spread more chocolate on her skin, then dipped his hand into the whipped cream. White dollops of cream decorated her breasts, chilling her nipples. He knelt before her and feasted on her chest.

Roxy shuddered and groaned. "Thank you, Sir." Her legs trembled and her pussy quivered. "Sir." She couldn't breathe, couldn't process all the pleasure bombarding her senses.

"I need more." Sean stood and pressed his body to hers. "God, I want inside you." He unclipped the hooks holding her cuffs in place for her wrists and ankles, then picked up the leash. "Come here." He led her to the padded bench. A board at the head of the bench featured a row of hooks and two gigantic rings on either end. "Up."

Roxy sat in the middle of the padded surface, then lifted her arms above her head.

"Good girl." Sean locked her wrist cuffs on the rings, then scooted her down on the bench. He spread her legs wide, then affixed one cuff to the large ring.

When he locked her other ankle in place, she moaned. Being on display and only for his use turned her on five times over. Her cream slid over the tender skin. Sean waved the bottle of honey, then crooked one of his eyebrows.

"I've imagined you covered in honey so many times." He drizzled a generous amount of the golden liquid down her inner thigh, then decorated her other thigh in the same way. Just as soon as he'd drenched her, he licked the sweetness from her skin. Each pass came close to her pussy without touching it. He leaned between her legs and kissed her, sharing the honey with her. The sweetness exploded on her tongue. She moaned into his mouth.

"My pet." He dragged his tongue down her labia, then turned his attention to her clit. He eased her pussy lips open and dribbled a tiny amount of honey on the tight bundle of nerves. His teeth scraped on the sensitive area, making her cry out. She pulled against the cuffs and curled her toes.

Sean stood and backed away from her. He wrapped his fingers around his cock and stroked.

Roxy flicked her tongue, licking her lips. "I'm ready, Sir."

"Can't." He grabbed a condom from the dresser. When he walked away, he gave her a great view of his muscle-corded back.

"Need you too much." He tore the corner of the packet, then sheathed himself. A groan escaped his lips and he coated his cock in lube. "You are so fucking sexy all tied up. I want to keep you there, just for my pleasure." He breached her hole and pushed. From root to tip, he filled her.

She gasped.

"Fuck." Sean gripped her hips and rolled his torso. Each plunge into her body brought her closer to orgasm.

She gritted her teeth and rode the wave of pleasure.

"Look at me." Sean rested his forehead on hers. "Can't get enough of you."

"Thank you, Sir."

He swatted her ass in time with his thrusts. The combination move kicked her passion up and put her right on the edge.

"Come for me, pet. Let go." He shook his head and his brow creased. Sean watched her from under heavily lidded eyes. "Come."

She gave in to the good feelings and let the climax wash her away. Her vision blurred and she gasped for breath. Her pussy clenched and she shivered. Above her, Sean pulled out and ripped off the condom. His seed spurted on her chest and belly. He groaned and yanked on his cock. Another ribbon of cum streaked onto her skin.

Despite the cuffs, Roxy sagged on the bench and panted. Holy shit, Sean wore her out in all the right ways. From her head to her toes, she stuck to the vinyl covering, but she didn't care. For once in her life, she was happy. A tiny voice in the back of her head screamed love—for him. Her gut response mirrored the voice. She stared at the ceiling. Thoughts raced through her brain. Listen to the voice and stay put, or erect the wall between them once again?

Sean tossed the used condom in the garbage, then unbuckled the cuffs. The collar came away from her neck and the leash ended up with it on the floor. "I love you."

When she winced and pulled away from him, he helped unfold her body, then cradled her in his arms. "What are you thinking about, Rox? Let me into your secret world."

"I'm wondering what your middle name is." The words *I love you* teetered on her tongue. Instead she blurted the first thing to come to mind. "I'm thinking about what my life would be like without you."

Chapter Five

"Come with me." Sean kissed her shoulder. "I want to spend time with you." He carried her into the bathroom, then placed her on her feet. "My middle name is Landon. Family name." He twisted the knob. She'd not only let him cover her in food, but he'd come all over her. Few women got into such play and damn it, he craved her. He wanted to tell her so many things and welcome her into his life for good. But shit. Some of his past could make her run. Then there was her reaction to his proclamation of love. She'd winced. Not the exuberant cheer he had expected.

"This is your shower? I mean, it must be, it's in your house, but wow. It's huge." Roxy slid the door open and steam billowed from the shower stall. "I love it." She stepped into the vast space and rolled her shoulders under the hot spray. The water sluiced over her body, giving her the look of a soaked goddess. His cock throbbed. He palmed his burgeoning erection.

Sean eased into the stall behind her and grabbed a washcloth. "Let me pamper you." He added soap to the cloth, then squished it to build up a hearty lather.

"I've become rather attached to you." He massaged the soapy cloth down her shoulder. "More than I ever believed."

"Me, too." Roxy brushed her hair off her shoulders. "But why me? You could have any woman you want. I'm sure all kinds of glamorous women would love to decorate your arm."

"There's a difference. Most women want the fame and perceived trappings of money. I don't have a lot of money. I've got a thriving restaurant I own with my best friend and a nice house because I inherited it from my folks." He squatted down behind her and washed her ass and legs, taking the extra time to clean the honey and chocolate off her. "Turn."

When Roxy did as he asked, he smoothed the cloth up between her legs and rubbed her pussy. "I don't trust many people. You're one of them." Roxy wobbled on her feet and clutched his shoulders. "I'm glad I chose you."

He stood and ran water through the cloth.

"What is it about you?" She draped her arms around his neck. "You're right. Most of the girls at Delight are scared of you because you always look so angry and commanding. You walked into Push like you owned the place. You don't own Push, too, do you?"

"No." He eased her backwards under the spray to dampen her hair. "I go there, but don't own it. It's a place to play. No emotions involved."

"Are your emotions involved when we play?"

His heart hammered. Time to talk about his past. "I don't love easily." Sean scrubbed the back of his hand across his mouth. "I've always been shy. Girls paid attention to me when they found out my dad had money. He owned part of a record company and sold his shares before it went belly up."

"Bet that was fun. Did you get insight into new bands?"

"He got out of that business before my time. Mom didn't have me until she was thirty-nine and Dad was forty-one." He worked the shampoo into her hair. "I never made a point to act like we had money. Girls knew and tried to date me to latch on to the status. They didn't really care about me. Then came Rebekah. We met in college. She didn't just see the dollar signs. She saw me." He bowed his head. "She turned me on to the world of BDSM and showed me things I never would've seen. I followed her headlong into the lifestyle and trained as a Dom. I did pretty well, but I wasn't one to go along with the rules. I like my subs to talk to me and I like to use food. Crazy, huh?"

"Not to me."

"She pretended to like what I got into. I fell head over heels for her and begged her to marry me. Guess that was the big flashing sign our relationship wouldn't last. She said no. I begged more, she refused even more."

"What happened?"

"She dumped me. I was too much of a freak and not hot enough in bed because I wouldn't go to some of the extremes she needed." Sean grimaced, then blinked to blot out the memories. "My heart broke and I gave up on love." He stepped under the spray to rinse off, then shook his head. "I go to Push to be around the lifestyle. You've seen it. Any fantasy you can dream up is probably being played out somewhere in that club. It's kinky and hot, but not what I want all the time."

"What do you want?"

"I want a woman who is willing to stand beside me and submit to me. Someone who doesn't want to fix me, but can handle all my quirks and kinks." He'd been blunt. Probably more than she expected. "I want you." He cupped her face in both hands. "You know how to put me in my place, then turn around and submit like a pro. I'm not broken or screwed up, but when I'm with you I feel like I'm a new man. You're hot as hell covered in satin or honey and you crave that release when you're spanked."

"I do."

"And I happen to know you earned your BA in accounting. Are you interested in helping me with the books? You can do payroll or whatever you want instead of waitressing."

"Why would you do that? We're having sex. An affair. You act like this is something that will last forever."

"This isn't just sex or an affair. My heart is in what we do one hundred per cent. I love you, Roxy. To hell with the no staff dating rule. When I'm with you, no one else exists. My stress goes away and I'm happy. I want to keep that feeling. I want you in my life. I mean it. I'm in love with you."

He held his breath and gauged her reaction. She didn't throw her arms around his neck. Didn't scream or cry. Just stared at him. She opened and closed her mouth a couple of times before she finally spoke.

"I need time." Her eyes widened and she inched away from him. "You don't know me. What if I were really some scheming bitch trying to steal all your money?" She slid the stall door open. With her back to him, she retreated out of the shower.

"Rox." He turned the water off before racing after her.

Roxy shook her head and hurried into her rumpled clothes. "I'm no good for you." She tripped getting into her jeans and tumbled backwards.

Sean caught her then carried her to the bed. "Hey." He stilled her hands with one of his and smoothed the soggy locks of her hair off her face. "We've worked together for two years now. I might not look like I pay attention, but I've watched you at the restaurant. You're kind and sweet. You go out of your way to help others and want everyone to get along. You're submissive to your core and you love with your entire heart." He rubbed his cheek on her shoulder. "Time doesn't matter to me. My heart belongs to you and has since we played the first time two nights ago, maybe even since you started working for me."

This time she wrapped her arms around his neck. "Then give me time to sort this all out. I love what we've done and I want to do more, but I'm in over my head." Tears slipped down her cheeks. "Please?"

"You know where I am." He placed her hand over his heart. "You own me. Always."

* * * *

Sean hiked his boxer shorts up over his hips, then folded his arms. She'd gone. Just like he'd figured. But this time, he wasn't worried. The spark between them hadn't died when she'd left. Nope. His feelings for her grew stronger. The past didn't own him—he owned the past and had moved on.

He picked up a picture of Rebekah he kept tucked between two tattered books on his bookshelf. The one last reminder of what he'd shared with her.

"Bekah, I thought I'd never get past what we shared." He grabbed the corners of the photograph and tore. The wounded pieces of his heart mended with each rip of the image. "You showed me the world I belong in and gave me the strength to grab what I truly want." He tossed the pieces into the fireplace. "Thanks and good riddance."

Sean flipped the switch to ignite the gas logs. The paper crinkled, sizzled, then turned to ash. He dowsed the gas, then stared out of the window to where Roxy had parked before she drove away.

"Love you, Roxy. Just don't forget about me."

* * * *

Roxy sat at the bar and stabbed her salad. She'd worked four straight split shifts in five days and the late hours had caught up with her. Each time she went into the kitchen for an order, she looked for Sean, but he didn't turn up. No gifts or little notes. Nothing. And why should he leave her anything? She'd walked out on him after he'd said he loved her.

She covered her mouth with her hand. Guys didn't confess their feelings. They bottled and compartmentalised. Not Sean. He'd been honest with her. The sex sizzled, yes, but he craved her touch, her kiss and her love, too. She balled her fist and closed her eyes. What was she hiding from?

"Hey, Rox? Is your salad okay?"

She opened her eyes and blinked back the tears. "Hi, Elias." She placed the fork on the plate then folded her hands. "It's good. I'm not as hungry as I thought."

"Huh." He stretched the soda gun and refilled her drink. "Sean said the same thing to me last night. Not hungry and lost in thought. Don't know anything about that, do you?"

"He did?" Her voice cracked and dropped an octave. "How's he doing?"

"Good, surprisingly." Elias wiped up the spilt soda, then rested his forearms on the bar top. "He told me how he feels about you."

"How he hates me." She scooted down in her seat. "I left in a hurry and didn't say things I should've said. Everything got so screwed up."

"That broke his heart, yeah, but he's more resilient than you think. We went to Push last night. I wanted a drink and a wing man. He volunteered. It's funny. I've never seen him turn down an offer to play, especially not at Push. But he did. Every time someone gave him the come-on look, he raised his glass, then refused."

"Oh."

"What are you worried about? He'll hurt you?"

"No."

"Then what? Sean's not made of money, but he'll treat you like a princess."

"What if he changes his mind and realises he wants someone else? Someone better?"

"What if you do? He's pretty well invested in you. Have you ever seen him take off that huge watch? No, except when he's with you, and why? Because he doesn't want anyone to see that tattoo of his initials. He's very protective, but when you walk in the room he opens up." Elias picked at the edge of his rag. "That's the beauty of love. You never know if or when the floor will collapse beneath you, but you have faith it won't. Sean is my best friend and I trust him with my life. He's a man of his word and his faith is in you. If he says you're the one he wants, then he means it all the way."

She stared at Elias for a long time. He was right. Sean didn't back down from her because of her looks or intelligence. Hell, he'd encouraged her to use her degree. She wiped her face. "Elias, do you need me tonight?"

"You're not quitting, are you?"

"I need to see Sean."

"Take the time you need." He grinned. "Rock his world."

She untied her apron and sprinted through the back of the restaurant to the back parking lot. Sean had said he'd wait for her. Now she had to hope he meant what he'd said.

"Don't give up on me now," she murmured and stepped on the gas. "Please, Sean." She raced across town in record time and screeched to a halt in his driveway. Roxy bolted up to the front door and pressed the bell. "Come on, Sean. It's only five in the afternoon. You've got to be home."

The storm door jiggled, then the steel door opened. Sean blinked and yawned, then rested one hand on the door frame. The sleep pants rested low on his hips and his bare feet poked out from under the worn cuffs. His hair stuck up in all directions, like he'd just rolled out of bed. "What time is it? Noon?"

"Sean, I'm sorry," she blurted. "Very sorry."

He frowned, then opened the storm door. "For what, Rox?" He stepped onto the porch. "Slow down and talk to me."

"Thinking I could do this."

Sean scratched his head, then smoothed his hair down. He glanced at his watch. "Shit. It's already five." He shook his head. "I know I just woke up, but what are you talking about?"

"I thought I could protect my heart from you. You've been right all along. When we play, my heart is involved, too. I lied to myself because I thought if I didn't fall for you, then when you dumped me it wouldn't hurt. I was wrong." The worlds rolled off her tongue at breakneck speed. She clutched her chest and fought back tears.

"I didn't dump you." Sean trailed his fingertips over her cheek, smoothing a tear off her face.

"And I fell hard for you." She couldn't breathe. "I love you, Sean. Tell me I'm not too late. Elias said you went to Push last night. I know you can find lots of others who are better for you than me." The tears fell and her resolve collapsed. "If you've got someone else, tell me."

"What are you saying, Roxy?" Sean wrapped an arm around her and rested his forehead on hers. "There's no one else but you."

"Sean, I realised I can live without you, but I don't want to. I'm sorry it took me so long to figure out that I love you." She clutched his arms. "So much."

"You've never had a thing to worry about, Rox. You're the only one I want. The only one I love."

Despite her tears, a giggle bubbled in her throat. Her fears faded and her heart soared. He loved her. Above all else, the bond they shared had survived. Roxy gazed up at her man. "Take me inside and teach my ass a lesson." She offered her hands. "Please, Sir?"

"I will." Sean scooped her into his arms. "I might lash you down so you don't run away again. Or I might leave you drenched in honey."

"I'd like that." She kissed him hard on the lips. "Will you? Drench me in honey?"

"I'm going to do more than that, but not yet." He opened the storm door, then carried her to his bedroom. "I'm never letting you go." He deposited her on the bed. "Hold still."

Sean untucked the hem of her work shirt, then eased the garment up over her head, kissing her shoulder. Her skin tingled from the touch. The spicy scent of his cologne wafted around her. He spread her out on the mattress, then unzipped her jeans.

"These have got to go," he murmured. Under his gentle touch, the pants and her panties slid down her legs. She shivered under his appraising stare.

Sean untied his sleep pants. The soft fabric slipped to the ground, revealing him to her. His abs rippled and his cock stood at attention. She balled her hands. What would he want her to do? Anticipation rippled in her mind.

"Right now I want to love you." He crawled onto the bed and settled between her legs, rubbing his cock over her pussy. "Soft and tender with no barriers." He rolled onto his back, taking her with him. Sean gathered her in his arms and kissed her. "So you never forget how much I love you."

Roxy ground her pelvis into his groin, stroking his cock over her clit. From her back to her ass, he touched and caressed. Her skin tingled and her love for him soared. She dug her nails into his shoulders, grappling to get closer to him. From little bites on her neck, to long strokes with his tongue, he touched her everywhere.

"Fuck me, Sean." She spread her legs.

"Not yet." He peered up at her, then situated his cock between her folds. Her cream slickened his path. "We're making love and I can't wait to be inside you." Sean entered her with one thrust. His balls slapped her ass and his groan filled the room.

Roxy grabbed his shoulders and tilted her head back. Each ripple and nuance of his cock stroked her from within. Fever swept over her body and her skin prickled.

Sean propped her legs on his shoulders, then grabbed her hips. His thrusts started slow and easy, but soon increased in intensity. Heat enveloped her and she rocked her torso. Her legs trembled. Little whimpers and sighs escaped her lips.

"This won't take long," Sean grunted. His brow shimmered with a veil of perspiration and his eyelids drooped shut. He gritted his teeth and the veins in his neck stood out. "Fuck."

From her head to her toes, her body quaked and she couldn't breathe. "Sean."

"Come for me," he replied. "Come." He pushed hard, filling her to the hilt. "Come."

Stars exploded behind her eyes in time with his seed spurting in her pussy. She shivered and moaned. Sean released his grasp on her hips and arranged her legs back on the bed, then collapsed on top of her. Neither of them spoke for a long moment.

Roxy willed her heart rate to slow to normal and held him close. One of the few things she'd wanted to come true had, and in the best way possible. Sean loved her.

Sean rose up on his elbows and grinned. "That was pretty wow." He tucked a lock of her hair behind her ear. "I want you in my life and business. Elias and I want a third partner—you. What do you say?"

"I'm shocked." Nervous laughter bubbled in her throat. She trailed her fingers over his chest. "I just wanted to help with the books. I never expected to fall for you. Are you sure?"

"Absolutely. You're the one we trust and I can't live without you. Plus, you've got the degree to back things up." He touched his forehead to hers. "I mean it. You're it for me."

"Then I'm all yours. Love you, Sean." No hesitation, no worries. She kissed him lightly on the lips. "Forever. And I want a tattoo to match yours."

"You want your last name tattooed across your shoulder blades?" He bobbed his brows. "Or this one?" He turned his wrist over.

"That one." She rubbed her thumb over the script letters. "Might put mine on the other side."

"I'll do that, too." He kissed her again. "Now I'm going to drizzle honey all over you and spank your ass red." He palmed her ass. "Or shall I use whipped cream?"

MORE THAN VANILLA

Elizabeth Coldwell

Dedication

For Gwenn, who toured the chocolate shops of Bruges with me. All that hard work was worth it…

Chapter One

She'd been waiting for him since she'd closed up the shop, just as he'd instructed. Naked apart from the delicate silver collar that passed for jewellery to the uninitiated but marked Oliver's ownership of her, Nina knelt in the hallway with her legs spread a little way apart and her palms resting on her thighs. A classic display position, it was one of the first things Oliver had taught her when they'd moved their relationship from being simply lovers to dominant and submissive.

It wasn't cold in the hall, not with the thick carpet beneath her legs and the radiator providing a constant, welcome warmth, yet still Nina's skin prickled and her nipples were crinkled and hard. Anticipation of her master's imminent return fuelled her body's reaction, but it was mixed with worry. The phone call he'd received the day before, asking him to meet with Mike, his accountant, at the earliest opportunity, had set alarm bells ringing. Usually Oliver only needed to discuss his financial arrangements with the man when the time came to file his yearly tax return, or when the shop's business rates were adjusted. This had sounded urgent, anything but a routine appointment.

With no clock in the hall, Nina couldn't keep accurate track of time, but by her reckoning she'd been here a good half an hour already, having stripped as soon as she'd climbed the stairs to their flat above the shop and shut the front door behind her. Oliver had left for his appointment at four o' clock, an hour before Honeyman's had closed for the evening. Even accounting for the rush-hour traffic that clogged his route through the centre of York, he should have been back by now.

He often requested her to wait for him in this position, which laid her most intimate places bare for his scrutiny the moment he stepped through the door. She usually passed the time dreaming about any faults he might have found with her recent behaviour, and how she might be punished for her misdemeanours. Today, though, she was too anxious to think about anything but what news the accountant might give him. Whatever it might be, she was sure it couldn't be good.

Honeyman's was one of the best known sweet shops in the city, in premises just off the historic Shambles, and had been in Oliver's family for over two hundred years. But in recent months the business had been struggling. Sales had been much lower than either Oliver or Nina would have liked, even over the usually busy Christmas period. Customers had shunned their ranges of traditional boxed chocolates, lollipops and bags of misshapes in favour of shops selling retro ranges of boiled sweets, or chain chocolatiers who attempted to turn buying a simple bar of fruit and nut into a luxury experience.

Honeyman's, it seemed, just wasn't fashionable anymore.

Doing her best to let her mind drift, trying to forget about their immediate troubles, Nina was startled by the sound of the door opening. Tempted as she was to glance up, Oliver had ordered her to keep her eyes downcast until he gave her permission to look at him. He didn't say a word for a good minute, the time passing in an agony of silence for Nina. She imagined him taking a lingering look at her bare curves, eyes drawn to the soft folds of her pussy, revealed between her parted thighs, and the silver ring threaded through the hood of her clit. The piercing had been carried out to mark their fifth anniversary together, and to celebrate Nina's first year as Oliver's slave. She wore it as proudly as she intended, one day soon, to wear his wedding ring. Though their marriage plans might have to be put on hold, if the business was in as much trouble as she feared. Better not to think about that now.

"Look at me, Nina," Oliver commanded.

When she gazed up, their eyes met. As always, his dark blue ones reflected his approval of her submissive posture and her strict adherence to his instructions. She would do whatever it took to please him, and he knew that. In turn, he would reward her obedience, her unashamed display of love and pride in him as her master, whether that was with gentle words or the slap of his hand on her backside. Nina had to admit it wasn't an orthodox arrangement, but it suited them both.

"You may get up now, girl," he said. "Come through to the kitchen and we'll have a cup of tea. I need to talk to you about what Mike said."

With those words, their relationship shifted back into couple mode, though Oliver didn't tell Nina to cover her nakedness with the silky robe that hung on the back of the kitchen door. Whatever news he might have to share, it obviously wasn't enough to distract him entirely from his lustful appreciation of her body.

"So," Nina asked as she bustled about spooning loose Darjeeling into the teapot and pouring boiling water onto the fragrant leaves, "is everything okay?"

Oliver paused before answering, and his hesitation told her everything she needed to know. "You know Mike's always been honest with me—with both of us. It's why I've employed him for so long, and why I consider him a friend. But he's gone through the figures in detail, and it's really not good."

Nina said nothing, just handed him a mug of tea, strong and with just a dash of milk, the way he liked it. She waited for him to continue as she sipped from her own mug.

"The truth is we're haemorrhaging money. Our takings are down twenty per cent on this time last year, and there's no sign of business picking up any time soon. I'm sure none of this is coming as a surprise to you. But Mike's told me in no uncertain terms that it can't go on."

"What does he suggest?"

"Well, he thinks we should sell up. Apparently, Café Chocolat are looking to open a branch in the city, and our premises would be ideal for their needs. They're prepared to make us a very reasonable offer, according to him."

The look on Oliver's face told her exactly how appealing he found the prospect of letting go of the family business.

"You're not seriously thinking about it, are you?"

"Nina, you know how much the shop means to me, but I can't see any other option. No one wants what Honeyman's has to offer anymore."

"Then we offer them something different." The forcefulness in Nina's tone surprised even herself. "Ollie, Honeyman's has always stood for quality, for constancy, but maybe it's time it stood for change. If we could bring the business into the twenty-first century, show people it's still the place they should be coming to for their chocolate, we could turn things around, I know we could."

"And how do you propose we do that?" There was no scepticism in his words, only a genuine interest. He might have expected her to defer to him in the bedroom, but in business he'd always treated her as his equal.

"I'm not sure. All I know is that we should forget about selling boxes of chocolates with the Minster on the lid, and those cutesy foil-wrapped kittens. People have more sophisticated tastes than that, and we should acknowledge the fact. Give them something adult, something that's not so — oh, I don't know — not so vanilla."

Despite the gravity of the situation, Oliver broke into laughter. "Well, if anyone knows about taking things beyond vanilla, it's us."

Again he fixed Nina with a look that left her in no doubt as to the strength of his desire for her, and she felt the dynamic between them change subtly. Business could wait, she told herself. There'd be time enough to talk about repelling the threat of a buy-out from Café Chocolat, and start forming plans to take Honeyman's in whatever direction was necessary to save the shop from failing. For now, soothing her master after such a fraught day had become her immediate priority.

She set her mug down on the table. "You look tired, and I'm sure your feet are aching. You've been on them most of the day, after all."

"And what did you have in mind to remedy that?" he asked.

Nina adopted her most humble expression, her pussy already growing wet at the thought of serving him. "Perhaps master would like them massaged?"

"Now, that sounds like an idea..."

Dropping to her knees, Nina unlaced each of Oliver's sensible brown brogues in turn then pulled them off, followed by his thin woollen socks. He hadn't bothered changing out of the T-shirt and jeans he'd worn in the shop for his meeting with Mike, merely pulling on an old tweed jacket over the top, a jacket he'd discarded as soon as they'd entered the kitchen. The fact that he remained almost fully dressed while she wore nothing served to emphasise the difference in their status, the happily naked slave serving her covered-up superior.

When she took Oliver's left foot in both her hands, he let out a soft sigh of pleasure, and when she used the pads of both thumbs to press the fleshiest part of his sole, he almost groaned aloud. She'd never known a man who took so much delight in having his feet played with, most of her exes preferring her to concentrate the touch of her fingers and tongue on their penis alone, but Oliver really appreciated that his body was a mass of erogenous zones. Nipples, navel, the secret place between the root of his cock and his arsehole — she could turn him into a writhing mess of sensation by licking and stroking all those sensitive spots.

However, massaging his feet gave her almost more pleasure than anything, simply because being on the floor between his legs, looking up at him as she stretched and tugged at each toe in turn, gave her a delicious feeling of servitude. This was how a good slave should please her master, by soothing him after a long, hard day and putting his desires before her own. Not that she wouldn't have her own needs well attended to by the end of the night. But for now, her world revolved around Oliver, and the way he squirmed against the seat of his chair as she took his big toe into her mouth and began to suck.

"God, Nina, that's so good. Where in the world did you learn to suck like that, you little minx?" His words spurred her on to swirl her tongue over and around that toe as lovingly as if she was orally pleasuring his dick. They both knew this was just a teasing, drawn-out prelude to the moment when she would take his fleshy crown between her lips and suck till his cum spurted down her throat. But he was content to let her take this at her own pace, trusting her to do all the things he liked best.

She let his toe slip from her mouth, turning her attention to his other foot. Though he'd been fighting to hold on until now, his restraint finally broke. "I need to be buried in your throat," he told her, and she knew exactly what he meant. Nina broke off from tonguing his instep, and reached instead for the button at the waistband of his jeans. She popped it open and slid down the zip. Already his cock was a solid bulk behind his fly, encased in tight-fitting black shorts. He shifted in his seat, giving her access to undress him further. When she pulled down his underwear, his erection bobbed free, its tip shining with juice.

Confronted by this evidence of how much her foot play had turned him on, she couldn't do anything but swallow him down with one smooth gulp. His blunt head butted at her cheek as she started to suck, while she cradled his balls in her palm. With one hand, he pushed her long, red curls aside, and she knew he wanted the best possible view of his shaft easing in and out of her lips. Even with his jeans and shorts down round his ankles, something that should only have given him a vulnerable air, Oliver didn't lose any of his innate dominance in her eyes. He'd regained his self-control, and now he would hold on with every scrap of his willpower while she did her best to bring him to the brink with her wickedly skilled mouth. It was a battle they never tired of fighting, and one that Nina knew she would win. Try as he might, her master couldn't resist the siren call of her plush lips.

"Play with yourself." Oliver sounded as if he were finding it hard to shape the words. "I want to watch you come."

Nina didn't miss a beat. While she continued to suck his cock, running her tongue over the head in languid circles, she dropped her right hand down between her thighs. At once, she encountered the slippery wetness that had pooled there, and felt the heat radiating from her core. The lightest brush of her fingers over her clit had her shuddering, and she realised that Oliver wasn't the only one who'd be fighting not to surrender too soon. The difference was that he didn't expect her to fight. He wanted to watch her lose control, to come with a couple of fingers buried in her pussy and his shaft lodged deep in her throat. Even if she'd wanted to hold out, to put on a show that would have him coming in her mouth, she simply wasn't able to do it. All the uncertainty surrounding their business was temporarily forgotten, submerged in the rush of sensation as she strummed her clit, aware of Oliver's gaze on the busy movements of her fingers.

We'll find a way, she thought, as her head swam and her pussy clutched and clutched again. *Between us, we'll do whatever it takes to save Honeyman's*. Then her orgasm poured over her, rich and sweet as chocolate, and she was lost in her own pleasure and that of her watching master.

Chapter Two

"We're going to play a game," Oliver said. Nina's ears always pricked up when he used those words, knowing that whatever he had in mind, it wouldn't be snakes and ladders—unless he could supply it with some kind of dominant twist. "I had a long, hard think about your suggestion to bring Honeyman's products into the twenty-first century, and I have some ideas for new lines I'd like your opinion on."

"I do hope that means I get to eat chocolate," Nina said, looking forward to the game already, even though she suspected it wasn't going to be as simple as she'd thought. His next words proved the truth of her suspicions.

"Now, I have a number of flavours for you to try, and I have to warn you that some of them are a radical departure from the mint creams and chocolate honeycomb we've sold for so long. And if you fail to spot what they are, then I'm afraid you'll be forced to pay a forfeit. Though there'll be a reward at the end of the game for the ones you get right, of course."

Nina grinned. "Sounds like fun."

"And as you're a true chocolate connoisseur, which is one of the many things I love about you, you should find most of them pretty easy, especially if you can see what I'm holding. That's why you're going to need to wear a blindfold."

She expected him to produce a flimsy nylon eye mask, of the type that is handed out on long-haul flights. Instead, he brought out from behind his back something he must have purchased in a sex shop. Made of thick black rubber and designed to mould closely to the contours of the wearer's face, once it was buckled into place, it blocked out all light. And Nina knew it wouldn't be coming off till Oliver decided. The thought sent an excited little thrill of pleasure skittering to her pussy. Her master might have been working all hours of the day and night forming plans to save the business over the past few weeks, but somehow he'd found time to go hunting for this beautifully kinky item—and to find the perfect way of using it on her.

For a moment she waited in darkness, only the odd rustling noise breaking the silence. She caught the faint snick of the living room door being pushed to— not that they were in any danger of being disturbed on this quiet Sunday afternoon. *Trust Oliver to be thorough about everything*, she thought. Then he came close to her. He wasn't wearing cologne, presumably so as not to distract her from any aromas the chocolate might hold, and she breathed in the warm, male scent of his skin.

"Open wide," he ordered her, and obediently she let her mouth fall open. "Now taste this, and tell me what it is."

Prepared to rise to his unusual challenge, Nina let the square of chocolate Oliver had popped into her mouth dissolve on her tongue. With the blindfold securely fastened over her eyes, it seemed her other senses had sharpened to compensate. The hit of cocoa was instant, intense and almost bitter. This blend had to be at least sixty per cent pure, she reckoned, far higher than anything they'd used till now. Following swiftly behind came a taste she recognised at once, subtle but still hot enough to leave her lips swollen and tingling, as though she'd been thoroughly kissed.

"Chilli," she pronounced, confident in her answer, "and very good dark chocolate."

"Well done," Oliver said, the words of praise bringing a warm glow in their wake. "Perhaps a slightly stiffer test is called for."

This time, she tasted white chocolate, soft and creamy. With it came a hint of something clean and herbal, naggingly familiar, but, struggle as she might, she couldn't bring its name to the front of her mind.

"Sorry, no," she said at last.

She couldn't see his face, but she knew from the tone of his voice he must be smiling in satisfaction. "I thought that might fox you. It's lemongrass."

With his love for Thai food, it shouldn't have surprised her that Oliver had chosen to blend chocolate with one of the staple spices of that particular cuisine. She wasn't entirely sure she liked the effect, but she had to admit it was a bold experiment on his part, and one that might appeal to palates other than her own.

"And as you failed that test," Oliver continued, "I'm afraid you're going to have to pay the appropriate forfeit. Remove your blouse, please."

She should have known it. Oliver liked nothing better than to engage her in games where she was forced to strip systematically—and the gradual exposure never failed to turn her on, too. Fumbling for the blouse buttons, she undid them one by one. She'd undressed in the dark so many times before, but never when that darkness had been enforced with the use of a heavy-duty blindfold. The thought of Oliver looking on, admiring the curves of her plump breasts in their scarlet lace bra as they were revealed to him, caused a trickle of juice to dampen her panties.

Once the blouse was off and Nina had dropped it to the floor, Oliver pressed the next of his chocolate creations into her mouth. This one had a gooey fondant filling, and as she bit down on it, its floral, cloying taste catapulted her right back to her childhood.

"Oh, yuck! That's just like the Parma Violets my Aunt Rosemary used to buy for me, never mind how many times I tried to tell her I didn't like them. I thought we were trying to get away from appealing to the old lady market, Ollie."

"Some old ladies are very sophisticated in their tastes," Oliver pointed out, "and, though you got the flavour partially right—it's actually violet and acacia honey—for insulting those women I'm afraid you've earned another penalty. Your shoes, please."

At his request, Nina kicked off her leopard print ballet pumps, wiggling her pink-painted toes against the carpet. The faint hint of violets still assaulted her taste buds, and when Oliver put a glass of water to her lips, encouraging her to drink it and cleanse her palate before the next offering, she did so gratefully.

"Ready for more?" he asked her.

"Of course. Just make sure the next one's something I'll like." There was a hint of brattishness about her reply, designed to push his buttons and invite him to raise the stakes.

Another fondant followed, wrapped in milk chocolate, but this one was much more to her taste. Her favourite fruit, but combined with an ingredient she couldn't quite identify, adding a moreish hint of syrup to its flavour.

"Strawberry, definitely," she told Oliver, "but you've added something to it. Whatever it is, I like it."

"Would you believe it's *balsamico*?" He pronounced the word with a mock-Italian flourish.

It didn't entirely surprise her. Eating at an upmarket restaurant in York's Micklegate Quarter a few weeks back, they'd finished the meal with a plate of luscious, ripe strawberries that had been marinated in balsamic vinegar to heighten their sweetness. Trust Oliver to have filed that combination away in his brain for future reference, having seen how much she'd enjoyed the taste.

"So, you got that one half right," Oliver continued, "but in this game, half isn't good enough. Remove your jeans, girl."

She wanted to complain that he'd bent the rules in his favour, but what else could she expect? This was going to be tricky without sight. She was relying completely on her other senses as she reached for the button and zip on her jeans, undoing them with fingers that trembled. Then she pushed them all the way down, trying not to trip over the tangle of denim as she stepped out of them.

"Ready for the next one?" her master asked, and she nodded. Standing before him in her underwear, obediently waiting for him to tease her with another sweet titbit, aroused her in a way she could never have imagined.

Nina tasted white chocolate once more, with a filling that combined a vanilla cream with—with what?

Fruit, certainly, but the flavour was almost too subtle to identify.

"Apple?" she considered aloud. "Pear?"

"Wrong, and wrong." Oliver gloated in satisfaction. "It's a good old Yorkshire combination, rhubarb and custard."

"Well, I certainly tasted the custard, but I think the rhubarb needs to be more pronounced. It's getting a little overwhelmed at the moment. This one's got potential, but you might want to tinker with it."

"We can discuss that later. For now, you'll have to pay the price of those two incorrect guesses…"

He didn't need to elaborate. Reaching behind herself, Nina unfastened the catch of her bra. She took her time about slipping the straps off her shoulders, delaying the moment when she would expose her breasts to him. When she finally pulled the cups away from her soft mounds, she heard a low groan of appreciation. It almost didn't sound like Oliver's voice, and for a moment she wondered whether they might not actually be alone in the room. *What a stupid idea*, she told herself, *you've just got him really turned on*. Still, she found herself entertaining the fantasy of a stranger, unseen by her, watching as she was made to strip bare. She grew so wet at the thought that the thin strip of cotton and lace between her legs became soaked through.

"And the rest," Oliver said, for the first time sounding impatient to see her naked. "Pear, indeed…"

The only thing preserving Nina's modesty was her flimsy panties, and now she would have to remove them. Would that be the end of the game, or did Oliver have further delicious humiliation in store for her? She hooked her fingers into the waistband, and slowly shimmied out of her underwear.

"Very good. Now hand them over."

Nina could only reach out the hand containing the crumpled, wet fabric in the vague direction of Oliver's voice. Her knuckles grazed against warm flesh, and she felt the panties being plucked from her fingers. Straining her ears, she thought she heard a long, appreciative sniff being taken, and a burning heat rose to her cheeks at the thought of her master enjoying the obvious evidence of her excitement.

"You actually did very well there," he continued, "and you've given me plenty to think about. There are more flavours I'd like you to taste, but I didn't want your palate to get jaded. And anyway, I think it's time this came off..."

He moved to stand behind her, and unbuckled the blindfold. When he whisked it away, Nina blinked a couple of times, slightly disorientated as her eyes adjusted to the sudden flood of light. And blinked again, realising her mind's wild imaginings had been exactly right.

A second man stood in the room, his face stretched in a broad grin. Dark where Oliver was fair, with messy black hair and a day's growth of stubble on his chin, he looked somehow dirty and dangerous, but in a good way, if such a thing was possible. The reason for his smile was not only because he was so obviously revelling in the sight of Nina's naked body, but because he held her panties in his fist. She hadn't given them to her master, after all, and the thought that she'd so obediently handed her worn underwear to a stranger made her feelings of shame intensify.

"I'm sorry I tricked you, Nina," Oliver said, "but it's all been for a reason."

Glancing from his crotch to that of the stranger, and noting the bulges that strained the fabric covering each one, Nina thought she knew exactly what that reason might be. His next words caused her to revise her opinion, if only a little.

"Let me introduce my companion. This is Daniel Martens, and all the chocolates you've just tasted are his creations. Daniel, this is Nina Lee, my girlfriend, business partner and, as you can't fail to have noticed, my obedient submissive."

"*Prettig kennis te maken*, Nina. Pleased to meet you," Daniel said, the guttural quality of his accent leaving Nina in no doubt that he'd been the one who'd groaned when she'd taken off her bra.

"I found Daniel when I was doing research into our new direction for the business," Oliver went on, then paused. "But why don't you tell Nina a little about yourself?" He ceded the floor to the other man.

"Well, I'm from Bruges, in Belgium, and until recently I worked for one of the leading chocolatiers in the city. However, much like Oliver, I've reached a stage where I want to try something new. I have a vision of what chocolate could be, and it isn't the boring boxes of pralines that are the staple of our business. I've always thought it could be fun, daring — outrageous, even."

Outrageous. That certainly summed up some of the flavours that had danced on Nina's tongue as she'd tried to pass her master's kinky taste test. Despite the fact that she still stood naked and vulnerable before him, it somehow felt natural, just as it did with Oliver. *Is he a dominant too?* she wondered. *Is that how Oliver found him? In some secret chat room for tops who like chocolate?* The idea brought a giggle to her lips, which she quickly suppressed.

"So Daniel and I have been talking." Oliver took up the story. "And everything that he says makes me think he is the perfect fit for us. His chocolates are of a quality that could only enhance the Honeyman brand, and his ideas would definitely make us stand out from the crowd. But I really need your opinion, Nina, before we progress any further with our discussions."

"Well, I'd be very happy to have Daniel on board if what I've just tasted is any indication of what we'll be selling in the shop," Nina said. "I'm still not sure about that violet and honey combination, though."

"Ah, taste," Daniel commented, his dark eyes twinkling. "It's such a subjective thing. And as you said yourself, so much of it is tied up with memory. But I believe that good chocolate can create good memories. Don't you agree, Oliver?"

Oliver nodded. "We can discuss all this in more detail later. Maybe the three of us can go for dinner to seal the deal. But first, there's the matter of disciplining Nina."

"Disciplining me? Whatever for?" Nina felt a pulse beating urgently between her legs, as it always did whenever her master brought up the subject of chastising her.

"Well, I said you did well in the taste test, but thinking about it, you got far more of the flavours wrong than you did right. And that deserves a spanking, don't you think?"

Nina shivered. Not only at the thought that, as always, he'd found some delightfully gratuitous excuse to spank her bottom, but that he was so openly discussing all this in front of Daniel. From here, she knew, it would only be a short step to inviting their new friend to witness her punishment—something they'd often discussed as a fantasy, but had never thought to make real. Until now.

"If you say so, Sir."

"I do, and I won't have you questioning my judgement." He went to sit on their oversized leather sofa, spreading his thighs and making a broad platform of them for her to drape herself over. "Come here, Nina."

She did as he ordered, aware of Daniel's gaze on her as she climbed onto her master's lap. He liked to have her lie so that her rump was at his left-hand side. That was his dominant hand, the one he had used so many times to warm her backside.

Once she had assumed the required position, he ran his left palm over her bare skin, taking time to explore the familiar curve of her arse cheeks. Daniel stood, the silent observer, but Nina swore she could feel the heat of his gaze as it followed the slow, sweeping movement of Oliver's hand.

"So, let's work out what you got wrong," Oliver commented, bringing Nina back to awareness of the reason why she was over his knee. "Lemongrass, that's one." As he spoke, he brought his hand sharply down against her bottom. No gentle warm-up taps today, just a stinging slap that made her bite back a whimper as heat flooded her skin.

"Sorry, Sir. I should have known." It seemed the appropriate thing to say.

"You didn't realise it was balsamic vinegar with the strawberries. That's two."

Another slap, even harder than the first. The first had fallen on her left cheek, and this one was applied to her right. She couldn't see her own bottom, but she could imagine how it would look to Daniel, with the splotchy red marks of Oliver's handprint staining each globe. The thought caused her to writhe with dark, secret pleasure as well as pain.

"And rhubarb is not apple, neither is it pear." Twin spanks, fast and with an upward motion, skelping each cheek in turn. Nina couldn't help yelling out at the force of the swats. Normally, Oliver would take time over her punishment, creating a rosy glow in her arse that would gradually deepen and build. Today, he was taking her to the limit with only a handful of slaps, and she wasn't sure whether this performance was for Daniel's benefit or his own. His cock was a rigid bar, poking into her belly, and if they'd been alone he would have wasted no time in sliding it into her slippery depths. Perhaps he would do it anyway, heedless of their audience.

He had come to a halt, and she hoped that was the end of her spanking. Her master, though, had other ideas.

"All that remains is the matter of the violet and honey. For your insolence in dismissing them as — what did you call them? — oh, yes, 'old lady sweets', I think you've earned another four slaps."

He dispensed her punishment in swift and efficient fashion, aiming two swats at flesh already crimsoned by his earlier blows, and reserving the remainder for the oh so sensitive crease where her cheeks met the tops of her thighs. That was almost more than she could stand, and she would have leapt up from his lap if he hadn't slipped his finger into the folds of her pussy and brushed her clit.

"Oh, Nina, love. You're absolutely soaking wet..." he crooned. His words, coupled with the soft, insistent touch of his fingertip on her straining bud, took her over the edge. Never had she come so soon and so hard after a spanking, but everything that had happened from the moment Oliver had first slipped the blindfold over her eyes had conspired to bring her to this place. It didn't matter that a man she barely knew was watching her as she spasmed in pleasure. If anything, it only added to the intensity of the sensation.

"Oh, master. Thank you," she managed to gasp, then she came again across his thighs, overwhelmed by the strength of her body's reaction.

Oliver smoothed her hair away from her face, murmuring soft words of love, too low for Daniel to hear. This moment following her orgasm was strictly between the two of them, but as her master encouraged her to stand on weak, trembling legs, Nina couldn't help wondering how long that might continue to be the case.

Chapter Three

They discussed the finer points of their collaboration over dinner, just as Oliver had suggested. In the lively surroundings of a tapas bar just round the corner from their home and shop, Oliver ordered a bottle of Rioja to toast their business deal—and whatever might come along with it. Nina didn't make much of a contribution to the conversation at first, too busy studying Daniel as they waited for their order to arrive. A man's attitude to food was a reflection of his attitude to sex, she'd always thought. Oliver had a hearty appetite in and out of the bedroom, and Daniel certainly seemed to savour everything that was set before them, from a dense slab of tortilla, thickly layered with onion and potato, to delicate slices of air-dried Iberian ham. He ate with relish, licking his fingers clean of garlicky oil as he polished off the last of a plate of plump tiger prawns.

From time to time, his gaze met hers, and the obvious desire in them sent a thrill through her. The only man who'd ever looked at her with such lust in his eyes was Oliver—indeed, he still did—and she found herself contemplating the prospect of what it might be like to find herself over Daniel's knee, bottom bared for a spanking.

When the waitress arrived with coffee, laced with a generous slug of Spanish brandy, Nina found her voice. Having decided that they would make Daniel's unusual—and very grown-up—flavoured chocolates the focus of their new range, talk had turned to renovating the premises.

"We're going to need to totally revamp the shop," she said. "I know it'll involve a lot of work, but it will be worth it."

"What did you have in mind?" Oliver asked, letting her have her head in a way he never did in the bedroom. When it came to matters of business, Nina was definitely not his silent partner, and it seemed he wanted Daniel to know that too.

"Well, I'd like to see the place redecorated in more dramatic shades. Purple, gold, deep brown—just like a sumptuous boudoir." Nina took a sip of her coffee, relishing the warming note of brandy as it slipped down. "And I'd like customers to be able to look through into the back of the shop and see Daniel, or whoever, at work actually making the chocolates, so they can see all the love and care that go into each one."

"You sound like you've been thinking about this for a while," Oliver commented.

She shook her head. "Not really. I mean, I knew we'd need to give the shop a facelift, particularly if we want to compete with the likes of Café Chocolat, but bringing Daniel on board gives us the opportunity to try something more radical than we otherwise might have done. What do you think?"

"I think you're crazy," Oliver said, "but I also think it could work. Daniel?"

"Well, I'll admit I've never made chocolate for an audience before, but there are many places in Belgium that have their workshop on display as you describe, and I don't foresee a problem with it."

Oliver drained the last of his coffee. "So it's decided, then. Tomorrow, I'll get the process of drawing up a contract underway, so we all know what we're bringing to this partnership, and we'll start looking at the renovation costs. It'll mean closing the shop for a few weeks, but the way business has been recently, I don't think we'll be taking too much of a financial hit."

"One last thing," Nina added. "The name's going to have to change, too."

"What do you mean?" Oliver looked startled. "The shop's been called Honeyman's forever."

"And that was fine for a long time. But this is a fresh start for us, and I think we need a name that breaks with tradition, and reflects the fact that this will be a chocolate shop for adult palates."

"Do you have anything in mind?" Despite himself, Oliver seemed intrigued.

She recalled her conversation with Oliver when they'd first talked about making changes to the business, and her conviction that they needed to project a more grown-up image. "Well, I was thinking... How about More Than Vanilla?"

Oliver considered her suggestion for a moment, his face breaking into a grin. "You little minx, you couldn't have chosen anything more perfect. It describes just what we are."

Daniel nodded his agreement, even if Nina wasn't entirely sure he grasped that her choice of name encompassed the kinky nature of her relationship with Oliver. "It's a name that people will remember, I'm sure of it."

"Well then, More Than Vanilla it is. And I think it's going to be a very successful venture," Oliver said, and motioned to the waitress to bring them their bill.

* * * *

Five weeks later, his optimism remained high, despite all the work they'd had to put in to bring the shop up to date. With the help of a local contractor, they'd opened up the premises, installing a floor-to-ceiling glass partition that led on to the workshop and would enable customers to see them as they piped and filled the chocolates. The walls had been painted in a luxurious shade of purple, and slim new display cases had been fitted, making the most of the limited space in the small shop. Nina hardly recognised the place, but she knew the changes—even letting go of Oliver's family name over the door, which had come as more of a wrench than either of them had expected—were for the better.

With all the fixtures and fittings in place, the only thing that remained was to stock the shop with Daniel's new range of flavoured chocolates, along with bars in milk, dark and white, from beans sourced in Mexico, Peru and the Dominican Republic. Honeyman's had always bought from ethical suppliers, paying a fair price for their goods, and neither Oliver nor Nina saw any reason to change that policy now.

Oliver had gone to the bank that particular afternoon, leaving Nina and Daniel hard at work. In one of the big steel vats, white chocolate was being tempered—the process repeatedly heating and cooling the chocolate so that the finished product would have a glossy texture and melt smoothly in the mouth. Daniel was all about the 'mouth feel', Nina had discovered. He wanted the eating of chocolate to be a sensual act, one to be savoured and enjoyed.

The tempered chocolate was almost ready, at which point it would be poured into small, heart-shaped moulds. These shells would then be filled with a mixture of raspberry purée, framboise liqueur and whipped cream—or, as Daniel called it, *slagroom*. Nina had picked up a few Flemish words from him while they'd been working together, including a couple she didn't think she could repeat in polite company.

"You know," he said, as Nina went to put the bowl of raspberry-flavoured cream in the fridge, "there's one thing we've never really discussed. And that's how you and Oliver come to be master and servant as well as lovers."

"You're not really interested in that, are you?" Nina paused with her hand on the fridge door handle, aware she was blushing. Just the word 'master' on Daniel's lips set her pussy fluttering. His interest in her had to be obvious to Oliver from the way he'd reacted to seeing her in the throes of submission, and to her surprise, he didn't seem to mind in the slightest. In fact, he'd been dropping heavy hints that, given the opportunity, he'd like to see her submit to the Belgian.

"But of course. Your relationship is obviously a very special one, and I think that Oliver is so lucky to have a partner like you, so submissive and obedient."

Nina's heart raced. She shouldn't be so aroused by Daniel's words, by the want in his gaze, by the knowledge that he'd seen her naked and writhing helplessly on Oliver's knee as she was brought to orgasm. Yet she knew that if he ordered her to begin stripping, just as Oliver had done when they'd played their kinky game of 'guess the flavour', she would peel off every last stitch for him.

"I knew for a long time that something was missing in the relationships I'd had with other boyfriends," she told him. "It was only when I met Oliver that I realised what that something was. Obeying his orders, letting him take control—it gives me the freedom to explore my desires to their limits. And now there's no place I'd rather be than over his knee."

"And very beautiful you look there, too." Daniel might have continued if Nina, her hands sticky with sweat, hadn't lost her grip on the stainless steel bowl and almost dropped it. Between them, they prevented it from crashing to the floor and spilling its contents, but in the process their faces and clothes were flecked with specks of the blush-tinted cream.

Despite the gravity of the situation, Nina couldn't help giggling. A blob of cream had landed on the end of Daniel's nose, and he seemed oblivious to the fact as he made sure the bowl was safely stowed in the fridge. Only when he turned back to face her did he seem to realise what had happened.

"You think this is funny, do you?" he snapped, the sudden bark in his tone sending a fresh jolt of lust down to her pussy. Certain that he wasn't as angry as he appeared to be, and that the sudden tension in the workshop stemmed from the conversation they'd been having before their near-disaster with the framboise cream, Nina bit back her giggles.

"No, Sir. I'm sorry, Sir."

It had been the right thing to say. Glancing downwards, she was certain she saw the shadow of a bulge at the crotch of his dark trousers.

"You know how much it would cost to make another bowl of that *slagroom*? The time it would take to whip it up, the time we'd waste when we could be working on the filling for the champagne and peach truffles?"

"It was an accident, Sir. I didn't mean to—" Still the cream adorned the end of Daniel's long, straight nose. Nina yearned to reach out and wipe it away. With Oliver, that would surely have earned her a punishment. Would Daniel react in the same way, and why was it so important to her to discover whether he would?

At last, he seemed to have realised where her gaze was focused. He brushed his finger over his nose, removing the cream, then brought that digit to her lips. Without needing to be told, she licked it from his finger, relishing the faint, salty taste of his skin combined with the tartness of the raspberry. Growing bolder, she sucked his finger deeper into her mouth, giving him an indication of how it might feel if she were to tongue his cock instead.

"Stop that, you wicked girl," Daniel husked as he pulled his finger free of her oral grasp.

Sure her eyes must be shining with the naughtiness of the situation, Nina stood, arms by her sides, wondering what might happen next. Oliver could return from the bank at any moment, and she could only imagine how he'd react if he walked into the workshop and saw the two of them, Nina teetering on the brink of allowing Daniel to discipline her for her unintended clumsiness. Either of them could stop this now, but she didn't want to and she was damn sure Daniel didn't, either.

"I have rules in my workshop, Nina," Daniel continued. "Rules I expect you to obey. Making an unnecessary mess is one. Laughing at the boss is another."

So he was the boss now? Nina had been aware as she'd assisted him that she was watching a superb craftsman at work, but suddenly the expression 'master of his domain' seemed much more fitting.

"So what happens if I break those rules?" Nina asked.

"Why, you have to be punished, of course. But first, you have to make sure that any cream on my body is removed—and I expect you to use your mouth to do it."

All Nina could see was a creamy spatter on Daniel's cheek, and another on the back of his hand, but she sensed he had something more in mind. As if to confirm her thoughts, he opened the fridge, took out the bowl of cream then set it down on the wide metal counter.

With efficient movements, he unbuttoned his short, white uniform tunic and removed it, then peeled off the plain white T-shirt he wore beneath. His chest was appealingly broad, his pecs covered with curly dark hair. Nina's heart raced as Daniel used a teaspoon to dig a small amount of the creamy confection from the bowl, then dolloped it onto each of his small pink nipples. The coldness of the cream didn't appear to make him shudder, and Nina marvelled at his control in suppressing any reaction. Handsome, controlled, effortlessly dominant—he shared the qualities she loved so much in Oliver, and she couldn't help but react in the same way as she did to her long-term master. Her wet panties clung to her pussy and her nipples were tight knots, pressing against her bra. Breathless, she waited for his next order.

"Clean me."

Nina stepped forward on his instruction to lick away the delicious mixture of cream, raspberries and liqueur where an errant blob still adorned his stubbled cheek. Then she turned her attention to his chest. She latched her lips onto each nipple in turn, sucking hard. She flicked her tongue over the little buds, partly to make sure she'd cleaned him thoroughly, and partly because she loved the noises he made as she did, soft gasps that betrayed his excitement.

"Very good," he said, when she finally pulled away. "But you haven't finished yet."

Even though she'd already guessed what might be coming next, she still gave a gasp of surprise when he undid his trousers and pushed them to his knees. Beneath them, he wore pale blue briefs that strained to contain his cock. Oliver had always been long and thick enough to satisfy Nina, but even constrained by cotton as it was, she could tell Daniel left him in the shade. She itched to discover what that big, beautiful thing might look like, but he didn't move to pull down his underwear.

"Bring me another spoonful of cream," he ordered, but as she turned to obey, he changed his mind. "Wait. Take your tunic off first." When she'd done as he asked, revealing that all she wore beneath it in the heat of the workshop was a white, lacy bra, he said curtly, "That, too. Let's see those lovely *borsten*."

Again he lapsed into his native Flemish, but the meaning would have been clear in any language. He wanted her breasts bare so he could feast his gaze on them. Nina flicked open the front fastening of her bra and took it off, placing it next to Daniel's tunic and T-shirt on the counter.

"*Mooi*," he murmured, reaching out to brush a finger over the barbell in her nipple. "Beautiful."

She blushed at the compliment, feeling her buds harden even further as Daniel played with them, and craving the feel of his mouth there. But this was all about pleasing him, as his reiteration of his request to fetch more cream reminded her.

When she'd done as he asked, he told her to get down on her knees in front of him. In this position, his cotton-sheathed bulge was directly in her eye line. Nina could sense its heat, its coiled potential. She glanced from it to Daniel's impassive face, revelling in the feeling of being half naked and under his command.

"Take them down," he said.

She reached for the waistband of his briefs and tugged. As she did, she caught a hint of musk and sweat, a mixture that set her mouth watering just as much as the cream and raspberries had done. His cock, freed from its prison, unfurled to its full extent. He seemed to be taking a moment to let her admire it, and she fought the urge to swallow it down before he'd had time to issue his next order.

At last, he said, "The *slagroom…*"

She needed no more in the way of instruction. Just as he'd done with his chest, she smeared cream along the length of his shaft, letting the teaspoon drop to the floor with a clatter. Holding him by the root, fingers splayed wide around the thickness of him, she began to clean him off. Her first thought as she slipped his crest between her lips was that she really couldn't remember how long it had been since she'd sucked anyone but Oliver. Her mind registered the differences between them as she continued to lick and lap. Daniel didn't just stretch her jaws more widely, he tasted sharper, brinier. She would have liked to have had Oliver here, proudly naked too, so she could alternate between them, sucking first one, then the other.

The ache in her pussy made her all too aware of her own need for satisfaction, and she dropped a hand down briefly to rub at herself through her clothing, the thick seam of her jeans creating a wonderful friction against her clit. She might have carried on stroking herself, but Daniel had begun to moan and butt his cockhead against the back of her throat. Faced with the overwhelming fact of his need to come, she let her own needs take a back seat. Hollowing her cheeks to increase the suction, she redoubled her efforts. It only took a moment or two before Daniel rewarded her with strong spurts of his semen, filling her mouth and trickling down her chin.

Which was the moment that Oliver pushed open the workshop door.

"Nina," his voice asked from somewhere behind her. "Did I give you permission to do that?"

Nina broke off from licking the last drops of creamy cum from Daniel's cock tip. Her stomach lurched. There was no way to disguise what had just happened. Was he angry with her? Had she crossed a line that might irreparably damage their relationship? Would he ever forgive her if she had? "No, Sir."

The smile he lavished on her let her know that all her fears were unfounded. "Well, make sure you ask me before you do this again. And you won't be surprised to learn this misbehaviour in my absence has earned you a spanking, will you?"

Even as she wondered if Oliver and Daniel could have cooked up this scenario between them, giving her the chance to finally submit to the Belgian, she replied, "No, Sir."

"Well, I'd love to dish it out now, but that pleasure will have to wait till later, my dear," Oliver said. "After all, we have work to do. Don't forget, we have a shop to open in two days' time…"

Chapter Four

None of them could have predicted how much interest the grand opening of More Than Vanilla would generate. They'd contacted various members of the press to invite them along, as well as food bloggers and anyone else they thought might be prepared to give the launch a mention. Nina had handed out flyers in the street, offering a ten per cent discount on the shop's first day of trading.

"If even half the people who've said they'll come along turn up, we'll do okay," Oliver predicted. Nina wondered if he was trying to reassure her, or himself. Daniel would only say that the quality of his chocolates would speak for itself, though Nina knew he was every bit as nervous as she was. After all, this was the first time he'd stepped out on his own, in a country where no one knew him. Would the public be seduced by his unique flavour combinations, and the boudoir-like aura of the shop itself?

So when the doors opened and Nina was almost rushed off her feet by the number of customers pouring through them, she rejoiced inside. She spoke to an eager young journalist from the local newspaper, who was particularly intrigued by Daniel's use of herbs and spices in his chocolates, and found herself giving a live interview to the presenter of a morning radio show, who wanted to know whether chocolate could be used to spice up a couple's love life.

"Of course," Nina assured the woman. "After all, the Aztecs believed that it has aphrodisiac qualities, and there's nothing more sensual than feeding your lover really good chocolate..."

Oliver, passing by, caught her eye and winked. Like Daniel, he was dressed in the shop uniform of black shirt with the More Than Vanilla logo on the breast pocket, and tight black slacks that hugged his arse. God, she wanted him so much at that moment! But she had to concentrate on the radio presenter's inane questions, and in getting through to the end of what was increasingly looking like it would be a more profitable day than any of them could ever have hoped.

"They really love the chocolates," Daniel told her when she managed to snatch a few moments for coffee and a sandwich. They'd put out a few samples for the press and customers to try, and the reaction of most people was to sigh in bliss as they bit into whichever treat they'd picked up, then immediately attract the attention of whoever was behind the counter and start placing an order. Boxes came in sizes that offered room for four, eight, twelve or twenty chocolates, and Daniel said he'd been amazed by the number of people opting to buy the biggest selection.

"We've almost sold out of the Yorkshire Favourites already," he added. That was the name they'd given to the three chocolates that paid a unique homage to the traditional local cuisine. As well as the rhubarb and custard flavour that Nina had sampled in her blindfold taste test—that now had a stronger, more emphatic tang of rhubarb—they also had a Yorkshire curd tart chocolate, its filling comprising creamy curd cheese, plump raisins, and a dash of nutmeg, and rum truffles whose rich centres were made from the dense oat and black treacle cake known as parkin. Nina knew Oliver had been especially pleased with these creations. Their inspiration had been taken from his grandmother's handwritten recipes for cakes she'd baked for Sunday afternoon tea. She knew how important it was to him that the spirit of Honeyman's was kept alive in some form, and these chocolates had managed that.

"I can't believe how well it's going," Nina replied. "You know we couldn't have done this without you, don't you, Daniel?"

"But I must thank you for giving me the chance. There aren't too many people who would have entertained a crazy Belgian who wanted to make chocolate with chilli and tamarind and lemongrass."

At that point, Oliver came to break up their mutual admiration society to let Daniel know he was needed to answer some question about his balsamic strawberry recipe, and it was only once More Than Vanilla had closed for the night that the three of them were again able to discuss the success of their venture.

The blinds had been pulled down over the windows, and they stood in the centre of the shop floor, surveying the half-empty display cases with satisfaction.

"And tomorrow it starts all over again," Daniel muttered. "Nina, we'll have to take stock of what we're low on."

"Let me know and I'll get on to the suppliers," Oliver said, "but before we start worrying about those details, I think we really need to celebrate." He disappeared into the workshop, returning a moment later with a bottle of champagne and three glasses.

"I put this in the fridge at lunchtime," he said. "It should be nicely chilled by now." He popped the cork and poured each of them a glass before raising his own in a toast. "To More Than Vanilla."

"May people never get tired of good chocolate," Daniel added.

As Nina sipped at her champagne, Oliver asked, "Don't you have something to show Daniel?"

His words sent an excited shiver through her. She'd known this moment would come, ever since Oliver had walked in on her sucking Daniel's cock in the workshop. Just as he'd promised, he'd punished her for her naughty behaviour, using her own wooden-backed hairbrush to spank her backside. Then he'd admitted how sorry he was that he hadn't been able to watch their friend dominate her, and had promised to rectify that. Now, she began to realise just how serious he was about the idea.

"Yes, Sir."

"Then now would be the ideal time to do it, don't you think?"

"What, here, Sir?"

"Of course here. Where else?"

Nina looked around to satisfy herself that no passers-by could see into the shop. Even at this time of night, the street outside would still be busy with people on their way to the nearby pubs and restaurants. There was no way she'd be able to explain to anyone looking in what was about to happen, and why she was completely happy with it.

Taking a deep breath, she unbuttoned her blouse and removed it, then pushed her skirt down off her hips. Daniel's eyes widened as she revealed what she had on underneath.

The corset she wore was a rich purple shade, very similar to the shop's walls, and decorated with scalloped black lace. It left her breasts bare and pulled her waist in tight, giving her an exaggerated hourglass figure. She wore no panties, and the lines of the suspender straps that descended from the bottom edge of the corset and were hooked to sheer black stockings served only to draw more attention to her bare sex.

"You've been wearing that all day?" Daniel asked. When she nodded, he said, "If I'd have known, I'd have been hard all day, wanting you."

"I did think Nina should dress like this for the opening—no skirt or blouse, just the corset. Can you imagine it, Daniel, my beautiful little submissive walking round with her tits and pussy on display to everyone?"

"Mmm," Daniel replied. "And if we'd made her hold trays of chocolate samples, she wouldn't have been able to stop anyone who wanted to from stroking her body, playing with those glorious breasts and finding out just how wet she was..."

All just fantasy, she knew it, yet Nina responded strongly to the images the two men had planted in her head. Just like Oliver, Daniel seemed to know exactly what to say to turn her on, priming her for whatever act he might wish her to perform.

"You know, I bet she's wet right now," Oliver said. "Why don't you do the honours and find out?"

"Thank you, my friend, I would love to." With that, Daniel thrust his hand between Nina's legs. She made no move to stop him as he stroked his fingers over the wet terrain of her cunt. He gave a little 'ah', and she realised he'd found the piercing in the hood of her clit. He rolled the ring with his thumb and forefinger, and she groaned at the sensation, widening her stance a little farther to give him better access.

"Sounds like she's ready," Oliver commented. "Back in a mo."

Ready for what? Nina wondered, as Oliver returned to the workshop. She saw him open and shut the fridge door again, but she couldn't see what he took from it. When he returned, the grin on his face had a devilish edge.

"I bought you a new toy, Nina," he announced, and held it out for her to see. He clutched a sleek dildo, thin enough to penetrate her front or back with ease. It was of an undulating design that tapered to a point at one end, and was made from stylish red and purple glass.

"It's beautiful," she admitted.

"And just like the champagne, it's been chilling for a while," Oliver told her. Her face must have registered her shock at his statement, for he laughed out loud. "Daniel, would you like to test it out?"

"I'd be delighted." He took it from Oliver, admiring its design just as Nina had done. A table stood by one of the display cases, having been used earlier in the day to hold plastic cups of wine for the attending members of the press. In all the hustle and bustle, no one had found the time to put it away. Now, Daniel bent Nina over it, encouraging her to take hold of its rim on the far side. Her bare breasts pressed against the smooth wooden table top and she could only take shallow, excited breaths, her ribcage constricted by the tight caress of the corset. At his command, she parted her legs wider.

"Whatever happens, I want you to stay in position, okay?" he said. "But if you have a real problem, then the safe word is 'red'."

"Yes, Sir," Nina replied in a small voice, but she had to struggle to obey his instruction as the chilled surface of the dildo slid over her juicy cleft. When it teased the entrance to her pussy, she cried out.

"Should I—?" she heard Daniel ask Oliver, clearly concerned by her reaction and wondering whether he should withdraw.

"No, she's fine, aren't you, girl?"

"Yes, Sir," Nina replied. The toy felt like nothing she'd ever experienced, but as Daniel slid it up into her cunt, cold glass meeting hot, vital flesh, she couldn't deny it added a whole extra level of sensation. This time when she gasped, the sound was one of pure pleasure.

Assured of her comfort, Daniel worked the dildo in and out of her pussy in a slow, steady rhythm. He broke off for a moment, leaving her empty and strangely bereft, then the strokes began again, deeper and more powerful than before. With every thrust, her intimate piercing made hard contact with the edge of the table, the pressure of the metal stimulating her clit and building her need to come.

She was aware of something happening behind her, tearing noises and motion, but much as she wanted to turn her head in the direction of the sound she knew better than to disobey Daniel's instructions to stay in place.

Again the toy was withdrawn. "More, please," she begged, afraid of being taken to the brink and left hanging.

Something butted at her opening again, but now, instead of the slender glass cylinder, she felt the fat, domed head of a cock, sheathed in latex. That explained the noises. Someone had been undressing and fitting a condom. And that someone, she knew with certainty, was Daniel. The penis sliding into her was thicker than Oliver's, stretching her wider than she'd become used to. Which meant that they must have switched places the first time the dildo had been removed, and the person who'd been fucking her so forcefully with it had been her master.

He'd planned this so well, and she loved him for it, she thought, as Daniel began to thrust into her. Almost before he'd got into his stride, though, Oliver had walked round to the other side of the table. Naked now, he was fully hard, and a drop of pre-cum glistened on the tip of his dick. Nina licked her lips, wanting to stick out her tongue and swipe the salty pearl away.

"Open wide," he ordered, and when she obeyed he stuck his cock into her mouth without ceremony. Now she was full above and below, in a way she'd never been before, skewered by two hot, virile cocks.

Oliver's eyes met hers, and the adoration he felt for her in that moment was obvious. He'd arranged this so he could watch and enjoy as she was royally fucked by Daniel, while making sure he got his own share of the fun.

Daniel gripped her hips hard, holding her steady as the two men settled into a rhythm that suited them both. His thrusts pushed her onto the fleshy column that filled her mouth, and as she relaxed the muscles of her throat she found herself taking more of Oliver's length than she ever had before. Every nerve ending seemed to sing with pleasure as her dominant lovers took her simultaneously, using her as a vehicle for their own lusts and only serving to inflame hers further.

The scents of chocolate and sex assailed her nostrils, too intoxicating to ignore. Vanilla and cocoa, sweat and her own musky juices. Nina breathed in, imprinting the moment on her memory forever. Daniel's groin slapped into her bum cheeks as he jerked into her for the final time before orgasm overtook him. He held her close till his excitement subsided, while Oliver kept on ploughing his shaft between her lips. When it became obvious that her master couldn't hold back any longer, Daniel slipped a hand down to Nina's pussy, rubbing her clit in fierce, quick circles. His timing was almost perfect. Oliver's seed jetted into Nina's mouth, moments before she came herself, held in the arms of the man who'd helped their dream of a haven for chocolate lovers come true—and had helped turn it into a kinky playtime for the three of them after hours.

"So," Oliver said, as he and Daniel guided Nina into an upright position once more, "we've still got plenty of champagne left. Why don't we all go upstairs, I'll make us some dinner, and we can discuss what happens next?"

Nina was certain he wasn't referring to the ordering of more stock in the morning, or the need to replenish their display of truffles and pralines. Now Daniel had become part of their BDSM relationship, she knew Oliver would be planning new ways to dominate her, and more games they could play together. And from now on, his armoury of toys wouldn't just include paddles, crops and cuffs. He'd seen how much fun Daniel and Nina could have with a bowl of whipped cream, and if he could find a way of using chocolate to enforce his brand of discipline, well, that would only make all of their lives the sweeter.

SATISFYING DESIRES

Victoria Blisse

Dedication

To my readers, you inspire me to keep on writing and to my author friends, without you I'd go completely crazy!

Chapter One

I lay in bed after a long and boring day where I'd watched far more daytime TV than is good for a person. I'd eaten soup—tomato and basil for lunch, and carrot and coriander for dinner. I'd struggled to brush my teeth, wash and jump into my pyjamas for bed.

It took a while to get comfortable, hauling my arm into position, propping it up on a pillow. I shut my eyes, no longer tired. My brain ticked over and I wondered about getting back up, but what would I do if I did? There was always the old standby, the one thing that was guaranteed to send me off to sleep.

I wasn't feeling particularly horny but I knew an orgasm would work. I pushed my left hand into my bottoms and sought out the fantasy that always pushed my buttons. I imagined a tall, thick-set man with large hands and a straight jaw commanding me to bend over his desk. It wasn't a fancy kind of fantasy, it was pretty run of the mill but it would help me come and get me to sleep which, at that moment, was all that mattered.

I bent over the imaginary desk and felt the unreal touch of my master peeling back my skirt and caressing my cotton covered buttocks. As I fantasised I slid my finger between my lips and struggled to get the angle right, to touch the places I like to touch. I tried to concentrate on the dream. It was my best bit, the anticipation of the first strike.

I played it out, waited for it and gasped when the ghost hand struck my ethereal buttock. The spanks continued and I felt the curling of desire deep inside. My fantasy played on, knickers removed, bare arse spanked, then his cock was forcing into me, his pelvis bouncing off my reddened buttocks, the pain highlighting the pleasure. I tried desperately to come, I really wanted to, I was desperate to but I just couldn't find the rhythm and my wrist ached so much that in the end I gave up in frustration.

The annoying thing was I didn't even break my arm doing anything dramatic. I was walking up the stairs to my office and managed to miss the top step. I caught my toe on it and tumbled forward—I broke the fall with my hand and crack, my wrist gave way. I don't know how it happened and I maintain I was not staring at my male colleague's bum at the time.

Not only did my wrist break, it exploded. When I got to hospital and was X-rayed, it showed my poor wrist had been well and truly shattered. I had to have surgery to pin it all up. I felt sorry for the poor surgeon having to put that bone jigsaw back together! I was kept in hospital for a night then sent home with a sick note. I'm completely right handed and my job depends on me typing. I can't type with one hand.

I was glad to be home at first, even if my arm ached despite the fact I was rattling with the painkillers they'd given me. It was when I had to feed myself that

I really came to see how difficult it is to do things with one hand. I was going to have beans on toast but have you tried opening a can with one hand? And buttering toast is equally as challenging. I was useless. I couldn't put any pressure on my bad arm, and I couldn't pinch together my fingers so I couldn't even open a packet of crisps. I ended up going down to the corner store and picking up a few of those pots of soup. I could just about manage to peel back the tab if I propped the pot against the wall beside my toaster. I ate my soup from the pot, which I put on the coffee table and leaned over. In my small flat, it was the only table I had.

I got by and, for a few days, it was nice to lounge around in my pyjamas watching telly and eating soup, but there's only so many antiques programmes and reality shows you can watch before you long for something more stimulating. The night of the frustrated wank was the last straw, the next morning I woke up determined to go outside and do something for a change.

I washed as well as I could and brushed my teeth. I'd worked out how to get the toothpaste on without having to hold the brush—a lot of it ended up all over the sink but at least I managed it. The real challenge came when I had to get dressed. I decided on a skirt and a blouse. I wasn't happy but I decided to forgo the bra. I just couldn't work out a way to put it on and fasten it by myself. I'd never go out with the ladies unhitched under normal circumstances—they're big and wobbly and need some support—but my choice was go out without a bra or stay in, and I really couldn't face another day inside.

I put my arm into the sleeve of the blouse then reached behind me with my good arm to put on the other. I didn't feel quite so clever when I had to do up the buttons one-handedly but on the second attempt I managed to get them fastened correctly. It had taken me nearly an hour but I had succeeded in getting dressed.

It was a little cold out for a skirt and slip on shoes but I shrugged on my black, long-lined coat and it gave me another layer of warmth. It felt strange having the coat sleeve dangling where my arm should be but I was just glad to be out. And who would I see? No one who'd know me, so who cared if I looked a little unkempt? My hair probably wasn't combed as well as it should have been, my teeth could have been whiter, but I was outside in the fresh air so I didn't worry about anything else.

It was a crisp day at the early dawn of spring. The air was cold, there were grey clouds in the sky but the trees had buds and the starts of green leaves poking from their branches and the world was all but ready to leap back into life again.

I walked down the main street, past the corner shop and the launderette. I carried on past the post box and turned the corner to head towards the park. My stomach rumbled when I caught the scent of freshly cooked bacon on the air. I had eaten an apple for breakfast, it was all I could manage one handed. I'd tried cereal one day but dispensing it was challenging and the mess and effort simply wasn't worth it.

I ignored my tummy. As much as I longed for something proper to eat I also didn't want to actually interact with anyone. I was out for a bit of fresh air and exercise, nothing else. I couldn't face people with my loose, swinging boobs in my inappropriate-for-the-time-of-year clothing.

I walked on past. I wouldn't have been able to manage a bacon butty anyway. Sandwiches are tricky,

I was sure all the bacon would splurge out and I'd end up looking a fool. I continued on to the park and admired the peeking heads of crocuses in purples, whites and golds. Even the daffodils were raising their heads, blooms protected by green crinkly leaves that looked like wrapping paper. It wouldn't be long until they opened and trumpeted the arrival of spring to the world.

The park isn't incredibly big. It has a small play area for the kids and a huge field with both rugby and football goals on it for those who liked to chase balls of all shapes and sizes. It's a pleasant green space in such an urban area, but it's not exactly Hyde Park. It took me less than ten minutes to walk all the way around it once, so I did it again just to waste time.

It was relatively quiet—a little late for the dog walkers and a little early for the post-lunch mums and toddlers. After the second lap I was mostly warm, though my exposed legs were not. I decided to head back. I had a thrilling pot of soup to look forward to. I walked back past the café, the scent of bacon still strong, and I nearly made it all the way past but something made me stop and look at the menu on the door.

A guy in blue overalls stepped out and held the door open, I smiled and entered, unwilling to walk on in the face of such gallantry. The interior was clean but dated. Formica topped tables were matched with plain plastic chairs topped by those squashy, plastic almost-cushions stuck to their seats.

The colour scheme was red and white—the top of the serving counter was the colour of candied cherries. I smiled at the guy behind it and sat down at one of the tables. I struggled to undo the buttons on my coat and shrugged it off my shoulders. I then reached out for the menu in the centre of the table.

"Would you like a hot drink, miss?" A deep, lightly accented voice asked from behind the counter. I looked up and nodded.

"A cup of tea, please," I asked.

"Milk and sugar?"

"Just milk," I replied. "I'm sweet enough."

His smile made my tummy flip. He was a very attractive man, tall with broad shoulders and big hands. His eyes were piercing blue and his hair was dark, black as treacle and messily pushed back from his face. It was spiked up randomly as if he'd just run his fingers through it. It was too long to be considered cut short, but too short to be considered long. It was right in the middle, comfortably scruffy.

He wore a white apron over a navy blue T-shirt, and faded denim jeans. When he turned to pick up a mug I ogled his tight arse, pert and curvy, cupped by the old, faded material perfectly. I wanted to squeeze it to feel its ripeness. I was glad I was sitting just where I could see between the gap in the counter or I'd have missed that sexy show.

I shook my head briefly. I didn't know the guy's name, I shouldn't have been thinking about sexually harassing him, even if he was the hottest guy I'd seen in weeks.

"What happened?" he asked when he put the mug filled with tea down on the table before me.

"I tripped, landed badly on my wrist and broke it."

"Ouch." He scrunched up his face in sympathy. "You right-handed too?"

I nodded.

"Nightmare."

"It is," I sighed.

"Have you decided what you'd like to eat?"

I looked back to the menu and everything required cutting or holding and I wasn't confident I could do either of those.

"Erm, no, I think I'm okay with the tea, thanks."

I hoped he didn't hear my stomach growl in protest over my words.

"Okay." He smiled and picked up a discarded mug from the next table then wiped it clean with a cloth he had tucked in the front pocket of his apron.

"Just shout if you change your mind, I can whip something up for you very quick." He winked.

"Thanks." I lowered my gaze and heat flushed in my cheeks.

"Stop flirting with the pretty customers, Lucas and come take my order." A gruff but good natured call came from the corner.

"All right, Frank, I'll be over right away."

Lucas smiled at me and winked. "I have to go look after my best and most annoying customer, his addiction to bacon keeps me in business, you know."

Frank guffawed and his whole body shook with it. I could just see his grin peeking out from a beard that seemed to be eating his face. I smiled politely and picked up my cup as he moved away towards Frank's table. I held the white mug in my hands, enjoying its warmth but knowing the contents would be too hot to sip just yet.

I watched Lucas go about his business. It was good to be somewhere different and be talked to as a person, not a patient. I suppose most people have visitors and friends and family to take care of them after an injury like mine, but I didn't. I was an only child, my father died when I was a baby and my mum passed away when I was in my twenties. I had no other family and I'd never been good at making friends. I'd worked for years in the same office and although I knew many people by name, I'd never spent any serious social time with any of them.

Most of the time I'm happy to keep my own company. I'm not quite a hermit but I certainly don't mind keeping myself to myself. Which is all well and good when I'm in work and interacting with people all the time. I found being alone all day every day to be very wearying.

I wondered if I was reacting to Lucas so viscerally because I was lonely and horny. Would I be so attracted to him under usual circumstances? He was certainly good looking, well-proportioned and incredibly masculine. The conversation we'd shared seemed to indicate he was personable too.

I watched Lucas cooking. He seemed to be preparing far more than a bacon butty but I didn't think too much about it. He was singing along to the radio and his deep tone vibrated pleasantly as I sipped at my tea, which was very well made, just strong enough for my liking.

"Here you go, Frank, enjoy." Lucas passed his customer a plate on which tottered two sandwiches filled with bacon. I licked my lips and felt my stomach rolling with jealousy. I was surprised when he continued to walk over and he placed the other plate he was carrying on the table before me.

"I didn't order this." I waved my hand in front of me.

"No, but you want it," he replied. "Eat up."

I looked down and an array of fried delights greeted my sight. A fried egg, two slices of bacon, a thick sausage, beans and a couple of slices of toast. Everything cut into bite sized pieces.

"Oh, wow, thank you." I smiled, tears pricking at my eyes because I was so touched by his kindness.

"You're welcome." He grinned. "I knew when you came in I needed to look after you."

I dug in with great relish. It was the first real food I'd eaten in what seemed like forever. It was such a sensual delight—there was texture to my food, crispness and velvety smoothness. I dug in with gusto.

Frank left sometime between me starting on my fried egg and finishing the last of my bacon.

"How's your food?" Lucas asked, moving to remove Frank's plate from the table.

"Heavenly," I moaned. "This is the first proper food I've eaten in days."

"I knew it." He nodded, put the plate down in the sink then walked over to me. "You need someone to look after you."

"I do." I was caught up in the bright blue of his eyes and brave enough to say the truth.

"I will look after you." He reached out and covered my hand with his. I couldn't respond, my brain went completely blank. "Come back here at five and I'll give you a meal."

"Oh, no, you don't have to."

"No I do, I do. Food is so important for healing." His hand was still over mine and his touch burnt against my skin.

"It's very kind of you"—I smiled—"but you must be so busy."

"I close at two, in five minutes in fact. So don't you worry."

"Oh, now I feel even guiltier about it."

Lucas shook his head. "No, no. I am offering because I want to do it, I would be sad if you refused."

"Well in that case then, I guess I should just accept your generosity."

"You should" — he squeezed my hand tightly — "by the way, what is your name? You know mine."

"I'm Sally," I replied. "Lovely to meet you."

"And you," he responded. "So how exactly did you hurt your arm, was it long ago?"

I told him the story, leaving out mention of the guy with a nice arse and the whole time he kept a hand on mine. It was both comforting and arousing. I wanted to feel his fingers all over me.

"And no one is looking after you?"

I shook my head. "I live alone," I explained. "I've been looking after myself."

"Well, no more." He squeezed my hand again.

I looked into his eyes and smiled. He seemed so close to me, had I moved closer to him? Could I push a little nearer and would he accept the press of my lips on his? I didn't have to make a decision in the end because Lucas pushed forward and kissed me.

I stopped thinking and just kissed him back. Our hands stayed entwined as I felt the pressure of his plump lips against mine, making my nerve endings tingle and sending pleasure signals to my brain and all over my body. I wanted to squeeze closer, push my body to his, all the pent up sexual frustration from the night before bubbled just below the surface, waiting to be set free.

"Sorry" — he pulled back and pursed his lips — "I shouldn't have taken advantage."

"No, don't apologise, I liked it."

"You're just so beautiful, I can't help myself."

I felt the heat of a blush creeping up my chest to my cheeks.

He kissed me again with much more confidence and I groaned my delight when his tongue slipped between my lips. I knew it was crazy, in fact I did wonder for a moment if it was all just a painkiller induced hallucination, but I didn't care, I was too busy enjoying it. Lucas pressed a hand to my side and his thumb caught the underside of my breast. I moaned and the vibration moved through me to him and he responded by pushing harder against me. I was so caught up in the moment that I leaned too far over and my bad arm slipped down off the table and cracked against my knee.

I pulled up with a wince and Lucas shot out a hand to rub along my plaster.

"Are you all right?"

"Yes"—I tried hard to smile through the blossoming pain—"I'm fine."

"I'm sorry, I will have to remember to be gentle with you."

"Not too gentle." I squeezed out a cheeky wink.

"Really?" He growled, and I giggled, which shocked me as I'm not much of a giggler under usual circumstances but then, I wouldn't normally snog the face off a stranger either, so it was a day of firsts and unusual occurrences.

"Oh, well, I'll have to remember that."

I was contemplating saying something else out of character, like 'tie me up and spank me' or 'fuck me now' as I stared into his eyes and saw the light of kinky experimentation there, but the phone rang.

"I better go," I said with a reluctant sigh.

He nodded and spoke to me as he turned to answer it, "Okay, I'll see you at five, yes?"

"Yes," I tossed back. "See you later."

I wandered back to my flat in a daze. I wondered what would have happened if that phone hadn't rung. Would I have had sex right there over the café table, with the open sign still on the door? I probably would've done. I could have blamed it on the meds or cabin fever, but really it was just Lucas. He addled my brain and not in a bad way. I would've done anything for him, or at least I would've given it serious contemplation.

Why? Well clearly he was hot and clearly he was kind and there was definitely some kind of chemistry between us. He'd said I was beautiful, I'm not sure I'd ever been called that before.

It might have only been a few hours to wait but it seemed like forever. My arm ached but I didn't care — I didn't want to take any more medication, I needed my wits about me. I wanted to enjoy whatever happened to the max.

I must have changed my mind a thousand times about going back to the café. I'm a savvy, single woman and so I knew going back to an establishment once it was shut to meet a man I barely knew was risky. However, my gut told me that I'd felt the most safe, the most comfortable in Lucas' presence and there had to be a good reason for that. He wanted to look after me. He didn't want to hurt me. I had to follow my instinct.

I didn't leave my flat until five o'clock. I watched the time for half an hour and I kept thinking about leaving before time, but I knew if I did, I'd end up on his doorstep really early and I didn't want to seem too eager. It only took three minutes to get to the café, so I was barely late when I knocked on his door.

I waited. The time lagged and I contemplated if maybe I was wrong, maybe I'd come back at the wrong time. The seconds rolled into minutes, I wondered if I had conjured it all up in my fevered dreams. I was just about to walk away when I heard the rattle of a bolt then the click of a key in the door.

"Sally." Lucas smiled. "Come in."

"Hiya," I replied and squeezed myself past him.

"I will just lock the door after you, okay? You have to be so careful these days."

I nodded. Lucas pushed back a top and bottom bolt, giving me a great view of his buttocks straining against the tight denim of his jeans. He then turned a key in the door and slipped the jangling bundle into the pocket of his jeans.

"I'm just finishing the vegetables," Lucas said. "Would you like to join me in the kitchen?"

"Sure, but I'm pretty useless as an assistant right now."

"No problem" — he winked — "just stand there and be beautiful. You can do that without effort, I'm sure."

I giggled again, the light, musical sound feeling foreign to me but also exciting and pleasing to the ear. I didn't laugh enough.

"Let me take your coat." He stepped forward and I struggled to undo the buttons with my one useful hand that, rather counter-productively, was shaking with tension.

"Here, I'll help." Lucas popped open the top button and I dropped my hands to my side. He continued to undo each one.

"I'm useless with my arm like this," I commented. "I feel like a little kid."

Which I certainly did on one level. I was embarrassed to need such help from a sexy man who smelt of spice and leather, but my more visceral reaction was certainly very grown-up indeed. I didn't want him to stop taking my clothes off. I wanted him to strip me naked.

"Oh, Sally, you certainly do not feel like a child." He skimmed his hands down inside my coat and over my breasts, still loose under my blouse as I'd not worked out a way to get on a bra and I didn't have any other clothes that were so easy to put on. I gasped.

"No, you feel all woman to me." He squeezed my waist and winked. "Now, I have to go check on the vegetables before they burn, come join me."

I followed him into the kitchen, my skin tingling and my mind whirling with imaginings. I shook my head and tried to concentrate on what was happening and not on fantasising about him revealing my breasts and sucking on them, leaving my arms tangled in my coat behind my back.

Lucas threw my coat over a table as he walked in. Coming back to the here and now, I became aware of the mouth-watering scents.

"Oh, it smells delicious in here."

"Thank you." He smiled. "I've made you my favourite meal, moussaka, it reminds me of my mum."

"Ah, so you do have some exotic heritage then."

He nodded and turned to the oven.

"Yes, my mum was Greek. She moved here when I was a little kid. So not that exotic."

He picked up a plastic spatula and pushed some carrots around in a frying pan.

"You have a distinctive twang to your accent," I said. "I wondered what it was."

"So you, where are you from?"

"Lived here all my life," I responded, watching him confidently shake a pan of asparagus. "Rather boring really."

"No, no." He shook his spatula at me as he spoke and was so vehement in its stabbing movement that it slipped from his fingers and clattered to the floor. "You are not boring and you should not be so quick to put yourself down."

He bent to pick up the implement and threw it into the sink.

"Sorry," I apologised. "It's a bad habit."

"Very bad," he said. "You should never give people opportunity to say bad things about you, should never think it in your mind. That is my key to happiness. You are the best you there will ever be, so be proud of that."

I nodded.

"Could you open the drawer beside you and pass me a clean spatula and a wooden spoon?"

"Sure." I turned slightly to the side and looked questioningly at him. He nodded as I pulled at the handle closest to me. I dug out a spoon and a flat, wooden spatula then passed them both over.

He put the spatula onto the side and used the spoon to stir the veg, then he turned the heat off under them.

"Okay, so, I think you need to learn a lesson."

"What lesson?" I felt the pressure of my blood rushing around rising in my ears.

"To respect yourself and to not make me so angry I drop my cooking implement."

I dropped my gaze and looked at my toes.

"What do you think, Sally, do you need a lesson?"

I nodded. I wasn't sure what was going to happen next but I was curious enough to find out.

"Look at me."

I lifted my head again and met his piercing stare.

"Do you deserve to be punished?" he asked.

I gulped. The time had come. We were at the point where the dynamics flipped. I either handed him complete control or I didn't. I could live out a favourite fantasy or I could chicken out and maybe lose Lucas in the process.

"Yes," I gasped, mouth dry, body numb, heart racing.

He nodded and walked towards me. "Correct answer. Now turn and lean over the counter, please."

I faced the counter and looked out over the sea of empty tables. The blind was down in the large shop window but I wondered if our silhouettes showed through.

"Hold on." Lucas grabbed a hand towel from where it hung by the sink, folded it and placed it on the counter top. "Put your bad arm on there, and if it hurts or any of this becomes too much, just shout out 'moussaka' and I will stop right then. All right?"

"Yes, thanks." I rushed the words out, eager for him to know I was ready and willing.

"Okay, now from here call me Sir, and speak only when I tell you to. Do you understand?"

"Yes, Sir." I let the words tumble out breathily.

"Good girl. Bend over now and ready yourself."

I leant forward and placed my plastered arm onto the towel. The other I rested opposite, and I pushed my breasts to the cold top which chilled me through the light cotton of my blouse.

I felt like a bomb about to go off, just waiting for that trigger to be pressed. I was primed, ready and eager for something. I'd never been spanked before — my previous relationships had been good but definitely not kinky. I'd enjoyed some fantastic sex with my boyfriends but none of them had ever suggested anything like this, and I'd always been too shy to admit it was what I wanted.

I couldn't tell what Lucas was doing. He didn't touch me for a long time, or so it seemed to me, and when he did I jumped a little as his hand rested on my buttocks. He gathered the material of my skirt and hauled it up to expose my arse. I had struggled into an attractive pair of knickers before I came out, black and satiny at the back with a panel of lace and pretty sparkles to the front. He folded back the skirt and tucked it under my waist band. I was exposed.

I tried very hard not to worry about what he'd think of my thighs, or if he could tell I'd not shaved my legs for a while. I tried not to worry about my arse and how big it was, but it's very difficult to break a lifetime's habit in a moment.

"Gorgeous," Lucas crooned and gently stroked my arse. "Just perfect."

I felt the doubts melt away and suddenly I was back to anticipation. I fizzed with it, vibrated imperceptibly with the pent up energy inside that just ached to be released. I pulled in a deep breath. It felt like my lungs were completely empty, maybe I'd forgotten how to breathe at all. As I let it out slowly, I felt the weight on my bottom lift. I braced to feel it land but it didn't.

I stopped, relaxed a little and wondered what was going to happen next. I should have known because a split second later his hand hit my flesh. The light covering of my knickers seemed to provide no shield. I squeaked as the pain blossomed. I felt embarrassed for uttering such a weird sound but I didn't have time to linger on that because he spanked me again a second later. The sharp slap first crashed with cold intensity then mellowed into a blossoming heat. The initial sting really hurt but the warming sensation seemed to seep through to my pussy and pushed me towards orgasm.

I had only felt the flat of his hand twice and I was already desperate to come. I wanted to feel more, even though the first slap really had stung.

"Ouch," I exclaimed as he rained several lighter slaps on my arse, one after the other. Then I received a much harder one that knocked me forward against the top and exploded a pain that made my eyes sting with water.

It stung and I panicked then almost used my get out of jail free card, but Lucas stopped as if he sensed I'd taken all I could. He stroked my bottom gently and the harsh sting toned down to a more gentle throb, and once again I felt the white hot heat—it seemed to be centred somewhere between my stinging buttocks and my plumped clit.

"Are you okay?" he asked.

"Yes," I whispered, "yes, Sir."

"Good because now, these come off."

He grabbed my knickers and yanked them down, flaring the pain in my backside once more.

He spanked me again, once, twice and three times. I yelped, squealed then moaned. I surrendered to his control.

"Okay, I'm going to use the spatula now. Just a few swats but remember, sweetheart, why I do this. You are the best you there is. Do not put yourself down."

I listened to the chastisement and waited. I was warm, the counter below me was also warm, sweat pricked at my face and as I heard the noise of the spatula rattling against the top, I jumped. I didn't want him to hit me with that hard, wooden thing. His hand had hurt so much, the wood had to be worse. However, below my logical reaction I was curious. I wanted it. I needed his punishment. I wanted to feel what that pain was like.

I found out seconds later. The wooden square impacted on one cheek and the crack hurt most at the middle, but the rest of my arse seemed to prickle with sympathy. I screamed because it was extremely painful. I squirmed, lifted up on to my tip toes. He waited for me to settle, left a moment — I wonder if he was checking if I'd say my word — then he brought it down again on the opposite buttock.

It stung. It wasn't pleasant. Almost everything in me yelled that I didn't like it, that I didn't want it and that I should run away, but there was something deep inside that gloried in the pain, craved it, needed it. I held still after my knees sagged and I straightened them. I waited for the next impact.

When it came, it crossed both buttocks and where the edges overlapped with the imprints already there it felt like I was ripped open, but as soon as that sensation hit it passed into an intense pleasure that shook through me. I rubbed my thighs together and luxuriated in the pleasure that replaced the agony.

"Good girl," he whispered and leaned over my back. "Can you feel me?"

I nodded. Even through the thick denim I could feel the ridge of his erection pressing into the cleft of my smarting bum.

"I want to fuck you." He gathered my hair in his hand, stroked it, then held it back from my ear. "Can I fuck you, Sally?"

"Yes," I gasped. "Oh, please, yes."

He pulled back and slapped my arse again. I yelped.

"You forgot to say 'Sir'."

"Sorry, Sir," I moaned.

"Don't let it happen again."

He slid his fingers down and cupped them into the warmth between my thighs. He split my plump lips and his middle fingertip caught the very underside of my clit. I whimpered with desire. My arse was on fire but my pussy was in desperate need, I was crazed with desire, I had to come.

Lucas removed his fingers and I moaned. I felt bereft. I tingled—the spanking had brought me so close to completion but I knew I needed more, needed him inside me.

His belt clicked, his zip whizzed and the jeans clunked to the floor. I heard a drawer open then the crinkle of a packet. I whined and rubbed my thighs together in anticipation.

"One more moment, sweetheart," Lucas soothed, "I'm just putting on a condom, then I'll be inside you."

Now that was one prepared chef. I wondered whether he kept his condoms with the condiments. All silly thoughts were wiped from my mind when he grabbed my hip with one hand and guided his erection between my butt cheeks with the other. I spread my thighs and he pushed forward, his tip covered with a cool layer of protection pressing into me. My groan vibrated along my spine and down to my pussy. He gradually sunk deeper.

"You're so wet," he gasped. "Naughty girl, you loved your spanking, didn't you?"

"Yes, Sir," I responded, eagerly grinding back against him. He stretched me so perfectly. Lucas moved back then plunged forward and picked up a rhythm that carried me away. He banged against me with ferocity—my hips bumped off the counter edge but I didn't care. I just wanted to come. I felt so alive with him inside me, my bottom flared with pain, my pussy contracted around him in pleasure.

With one hand he held onto my hip tightly and he hooked his other arm around me until his fingers rested over my pubis. He pushed them down into the heat of my folds and when he reached the plump hump of my clitoris, he rubbed at it in time with his thrusting.

"Yes." I repeated the word over and over as the ecstasy within me built. I got louder and louder and Lucas grunted and moaned with equal gusto. When I came, I roared with the orgasm that ripped through me — like there was just too much to exit from my clit it needed to rip through my mouth, too.

Lucas gently withdrew his fingers and ran his hand down my back. He stepped away and I straightened up. It was only then I remembered my arm. It held me down with the weight of plaster and I had to work to lever myself up. I'd been so focused in on Lucas, my spanking and the glorious sex, I'd completely forgotten about my injury.

"Erm, Lucas," I said hesitantly.

"Yes?"

"Could you help me pull up my knickers, please?"

They were tangled around one of my ankles and I wasn't sure I could trust myself to bend down when I was still lightheaded with post orgasmic bliss.

"No," he replied. "Just kick them off, you don't need them."

I did as he'd directed and before I could pick them up, he had. He winked and put them in his pocket. He did, however, untuck the skirt from behind me so at least my bare buttocks had some kind of protection.

"Sit down over there, I'll bring your food in a moment, it just needs plating up."

One of the tables was covered in a white cloth and a small vase of flowers sat in the middle. Knife, fork and spoon were arranged around little circular cork mats.

I listened to the clink and clack of preparation and smiled. I felt so content and comfortable. I didn't question what had happened at all. It had been a good thing and I was quite happy to follow his commands. It had felt so good to lose control, but that wasn't quite it. I hadn't lost it…I'd passed it willingly to him.

"Okay, here we go." He brought over two plates full of food. Mine contained chopped up asparagus and carrots and a large rectangle of cheese, meat and veg, divided into four smaller pieces.

"This looks and smells so delicious," I commented, picking up my fork. "And thank you for cutting it up for me."

"I told you I'd look after you," he replied and sat opposite me.

I wiggled in my seat and felt the blossom of pain that still lingered there. "And you have"—I winked cheekily—"you really have."

Lucas laughed heartily and dug into his moussaka.

"It was my pleasure, Sally."

The meal was as delicious as it looked and conversation flowed between bites. We found we had many things in common—food likes, music preferences and even a love of reading the same kind of books.

"It's so nice to have a proper conversation for a change," Lucas said and lifted my plate from the table when I'd finished. "I talk to people all the time here but we never really say anything, you know? It's so good to have a conversation."

"I know exactly what you mean." I nodded. "I'm exactly the same. I talk a lot at work but then I get home and I'm on my own. I can't remember the last time I had such a fun evening with such entertaining company."

"Me neither." He dropped the plates into the sink. "I will wash those later, now it is time for dessert. I thought I'd go for something very British." He pulled out a dish from the oven.

"Oh, that looks good, I've never met a pudding I haven't liked, you know."

"I love my sweet stuff too, and this is my favourite — apple crumble and custard."

He served up two bowls full of the crumb-covered fruit dessert then carried them over to the table. He went back and transferred creamy custard to a jug.

He poured some out onto my dessert for me then coated his own. I dug in with enthusiasm. The soft melting apple and the crunchy, butter topping melded with the rich, warm custard blanket. I was in food heaven.

"Glorious," I commented.

Lucas nodded, his mouth was still full. He chewed first then he answered, "Yes, British puddings are the best. My mum used to make them all when I was little. This was the one she loved the most."

"My mum was an awful cook," I shared. "One day she made rock buns and we ended up using one as a door stop for a while.

He laughed and shook his head. "My mum taught me to cook. I was crap at all the academic stuff in school but I rocked home economics. The other guys teased me at first, until they realised I was the only boy in a class filled with very hot girls who found it charming that I could actually cook."

"Oh, yeah. The way to a girl's heart is through her stomach."

"I learnt that early on in my life. Went to catering college, saved up, got a huge loan and took on this place. I've not looked back. I love my job."

"I don't love mine." I sighed. "Boring clerical work. I spend most of my time looking at a screen, wishing the photocopier would hurry up, or passing on meaningless messages to colleagues."

"What would you like to be?" he asked.

I shrugged.

"Well, what did you want to be when you were a little girl?"

"I wanted to be a teacher. I'd spend hours setting up my dolls and showing them how to spell and do sums." I chuckled.

"Then why don't you teach?"

I shook my head. "I was going to but when I hit eighteen my mum became really ill. I couldn't leave her to go to uni. So I stayed with her, got an office job and cared for her until she died. Then I felt like it was too late to change."

"It's never too late to change, Sally. You should chase your dream."

I was about to say something about doubting I was clever enough when I looked at him and I realised that wasn't what he wanted to hear.

"Maybe I should." I nodded. "It's kind of scary though. I'm not sure I could go back to school now, I'm a bit too old for it."

Lucas shook his head. "You are still young and it is never too late. A friend of my mum's went to university when she retired. She'd always wanted to study English Language, so she did. You are not older than that, are you?"

"No." I laughed. "About half of retirement age, give or take."

"Well then, you should go for it."

He was probably right. My life was so boring, so empty because I didn't strive any more. I didn't dream. I was depressingly stuck in a rut.

"You're so damn chipper, Lucas, how do you do it?"

He chuckled and shrugged his manly shoulders. "I was born like this I guess, and my mother, she told me that if it weren't for hope the heart would break. So very true."

"Your mum sounds like she's a lovely lady."

"She was" — his face relaxed into something approaching a frown — "she was always my rock."

I smiled gently. I knew there wasn't anything I could say to make his pain go away, so I sat in silence. I knew what he felt. I finished my last mouthful of pudding and flopped against the back of my chair.

"Wow, I'm full." I moaned. "Thanks so much for that."

"You're welcome." He picked up my bowl and carried it over to the sink. "I'll just wash these then I'll walk you home."

"There's no need, really, I only live around the corner."

"No, no. Not at night, not in the dark. A lady should not be alone after dark. I will walk with you."

"Okay." I realised he wasn't going to be argued with, and night had fallen — I could see nothing but black under the pulled down blinds. He helped me into my coat when he'd finished cleaning up and, after locking the door behind us, he grabbed my good hand and clasped it in his.

"Will you come by tomorrow for breakfast?" he asked.

"I don't know..." As tempting as it was, I was aware I'd already imposed myself on him quite a lot.

"Oh, come on, Sally. You know now I want you to."

"Well, when you put it like that…"

"Good." He squeezed my hand again. "I will look forward to it."

When we reached the door of my block of flats we stopped. I let go of his hand and fished my keys from my pocket.

"Thanks…" I smiled nervously. "I've had a lovely time."

"Me too." Lucas kissed me. Our breath steamed between us as we pulled back, the clear night cold around our mutual heat.

"Look, do you want to come in?" The words stumbled from between my lips.

"I shouldn't, I have to be up early."

My look of anticipation dropped into one of disappointment.

"Oh, okay."

"But as you asked so nicely, I will, yes."

On the way up the stairs I was thinking that the one good thing about being armless was that I'd been capable of making very little mess in my flat. Yes, my bed was unmade, my kitchen bin was stuffed with empty plastic pots and the floors needed a bit of a sweep, but I hoped he'd not notice those little details.

He followed me into my apartment and when we got in he took off his coat and again helped me to undo mine. He hung it on the hook behind the door.

"Would you like a drink?" I asked, like I'd been taught good hosts should.

"No," he replied. "I'd like to fuck you again."

His blunt answer brought a flush to my cheeks and my eyes widened with shock. Before I could reply, he pushed his mouth to mine and pressed me up against the wall. My stupid cast arm caught between us and he pulled back a little to relieve the pressure.

"Come," he beckoned. I followed him. It was weird—he was in control even in my home. He strode across the lounge to the door opposite, which led to my bedroom. He signalled for me to sit as he closed the door. I sat at the end of my bed and waited.

Lucas pulled off his T-shirt, and I admired the planes and dips of his chest. The soft caramel colour of his skin and the puckered peaks of his darkened nipples under the rolling curls of dark hair that covered his chest in a sparse mat. I wanted to run my fingers into it, to rub my naked breasts against his hardness.

He kicked off his shoes and unfastened then pushed down his jeans with his boxers and revealed his cock, which was fattening into an erection under the heat of my gaze. I waited patiently for his next command. He walked over to the corner of the bed.

"Kneel," he told me, pointing to the floor. "Rest your arm on the bed, angle your head to my dick."

I followed his instructions, feeling a warmth of gratitude for him remembering my arm. I scooched up to the corner of my divan. I rested my arm on the mattress and sat on my heels, anticipating what he'd ask next.

"Good girl." He stroked my hair with a strong hand then grabbed a fistful and pulled my lips to his straining erection.

I didn't wait for an explicit instruction, I didn't need one. I licked out and tasted his flesh. I ran my tongue up to the tip of his cock and tasted the pre-cum there before I sunk my mouth around him and pushed my head down to envelop his shaft.

He hissed his pleasure as I wiggled my tongue, testing and tasting his width. I drew my lips up again then bobbed up and down in small, rapid strokes. He tightened his fingers in my hair and I heard his breath hitch. I loved the switch of control. I had his arousal in my grasp, well between my lips in fact. I could dictate when he would come. Except after a few moments, he pulled me off his cock and I was once again waiting for his instruction.

"You're good with your mouth," he said. "Another time, I'll fill your mouth with my cum but now, now I want to fuck you. Stand up."

He stepped back to allow me to press down with my good arm on the bed to lever myself up.

"Let's take these off." He undid the buttons on the front of my blouse, his wide fingers surprisingly delicate and deft at releasing the tiny fastenings from their holes. When the garment hung open, he guided it down off my shoulders, careful not to jolt my bad arm.

He moved down to my skirt, yanking it past my hips and leaving it pooled around my ankles. I kicked off my shoes and I was naked, bar the plaster anyway.

"Beautiful," he gasped.

I felt it under the heat of his gaze.

"Lie on the bed."

I did. I sat at the end and wriggled back. Even getting into bed is a challenge with a dodgy arm. Lucas paused before following me, and when he did, he had a couple of small, square packets in his hand. He put them down on the bedside cabinet then turned back to me.

"Can you lift your hands over your head?" he asked.

"I think so," I said and moved them back. The right one pulled on my arm muscles more than the left.

Lucas took some time to move pillows to cradle my arm so that it didn't hurt to hold it back above my head.

"Are you comfortable?"

"Yes, Sir," I replied.

"Good, then stay still."

He got up off the bed and walked out of the room. I wondered what was going on, but I lay still like he'd directed even as I heard clanks and squeaks from my kitchen. Surely he wasn't making himself a snack! When he came back, he held a cucumber in one hand and a pot of chocolate spread in the other.

"I'm hungry," he explained. He put the cucumber on the bedside table then sat next to me. He unscrewed the cap of the chocolate spread, dug his finger in then offered it to me.

I opened wide and accepted his chocolate-laden digit between my lips. I sucked it clean.

He dipped back into the pot, and when he withdrew it again he took it down to my chest and drew a line down between my breasts. The he took the finger to my nipples and painted the chocolate over the puckering nubs.

I bit my lip and waited for his next move. I arched my back as much as I could with my arms above me, and encouraged him the only way I could to lick off the mess he'd made.

"Nothing better than a hot, naked girl," he said. "Except for a hot naked girl covered in chocolate."

He dropped his lips to my tummy then ran his tongue directly up over my breastbone, gathering the chocolate in one sweep. I giggled—it tickled and the giggle melted into a moan as my skin tingled with the attention of his mouth on me. He continued to lick, smearing chocolate all over me and over his lips and my body.

I writhed beneath him and the pot in his hand dropped with a thud to the floor, neither of us concerned for its safety as Lucas sought out my chocolate coated nipples. One then the other, he sucked with sharp, intense movements. One then the other and back until I was dizzy with lust and aching all over, eager for release.

As he sucked, he pulled the cucumber down from beside the bed. He sat up, picked up a condom then slipped it down over the vegetable. I wondered if it was a vegetable or if it was one of those weird ones that actually classified as a fruit. I was interrupted from my strange pondering by the trail of the cold, condom-covered cucumber that Lucas dragged down over my stomach, through my pubic hair and laid it just over my clit.

I spread my thighs and Lucas scrambled down the bed then clambered over one leg to rest between them. He moved the cucumber down between my lips and pushed forward. It was cold and chilled my insides as it stretched me wide. I yelped and wiggled—the intense chill made me want to move away from it, like when someone tickles you, you might love it but you want it to stop...it was just like that, torture and delight.

Lucas didn't let me pull back, he held the natural rod deep inside me. I looked down over my body and he was looking at where the cucumber split me wide. I couldn't see what he could see, but I could imagine how lewd it must have looked.

He pulled it back a little then pushed back in. He continued to scrutinise the fucking action and I wondered if he was also imagining his cock in its place. The cucumber was hard and unrelenting in a way that a hot, human erection couldn't be. I loved it, especially when he took one hand and fingered my clit as he pumped me. I felt an orgasm gathering deep inside.

"Wait, wait," he cooed. "Not yet."

I whimpered. I wanted to come. The sensation of being stretched combined with the manipulation of his fingers and the extra frisson of naughtiness of knowing he was watching it all so closely, drinking in every detail, was overloading me with pleasure. I didn't think I could hold on any longer.

"Please, Sir," I begged, rocking up and down on the bed in frustration. "I need to come."

"Not yet," he whispered.

"Please" — I humped my hips desperately — "please, please, please, Sir."

"Come for me," he said it calmly, slowly, but my orgasm was the direct opposite. It ripped through me and rocked my whole body. I gasped and curled up, everything within me throbbed. I panted and moaned my pleasure. Lucas removed the cucumber, prompting another flash of pleasure as my stretched walls contracted once again.

He knelt up between my thighs and reached over to grab up the other packet. He ripped the packaging and slid the condom confidently over his dick. He smiled at me and shuffled forward.

I had just experienced an incredibly intense orgasm but I craved more. I was insatiable. I wanted to feel the heat of him inside me. He butted up against my pussy lips and shifted his hips to prod against my opening. He sat there and I strained to feel him slip into me.

He laughed and I rocked my hips against him, the last chuckle turning into a moan as I managed to jiggle him a bit deeper inside. I saw the delight in his eyes as our gazes met and I knew this was a fight for supremacy. I would have to work to get him inside me. He wanted me to make him lose control.

I accepted his challenge without a word. I knew I had to keep my hands above my head. I really wanted to drop my left hand to where we nearly joined and guide him in but I just knew he'd think that was cheating. So I braced myself and wrapped my legs around his hips. He strained against me as I tried to pull him tighter in.

I struggled to grip him, to push him deeper and he simply smirked. It was all at once infinitely annoying and completely alluring.

"Ask me nicely," he whispered.

"Please?" I begged. I wasn't too proud. I wanted him inside me.

"Nicer than that." He relented a little and his cockhead pierced me. I arched with the pleasure and asked again.

"Please, Sir."

"What do you want?" he asked, sliding a little further inside me. His gaze never breaking away from mine.

"Please fuck me, Sir." I gasped the words falling over each other in their eagerness to leave my lips.

He nodded once and with a forceful shove he filled me. I cried out as I was gifted with his hot erection. My pussy greedily sucked him deeper, I wanted to hold onto him but he pulled back and when he thrust in again and his body came forward, he put a hand above my head and grasped my good wrist with the other.

He held me down as he fucked me. He didn't once look away from me. I wanted to close my eyes but I couldn't—the challenge had changed, I had to look, I had to watch the desire dance in the blue of his eyes as we joined so intimately. I had to let him see the rawness of my lust. I had to let him in completely.

I came again, not once or twice but several times, a string of pleasure pulses throbbing through me and in the end I had to close my eyes. I wondered if he'd punish me for it later. I hoped he would. Then he came and stilled within me.

"Sorry I made a mess," he said, "I will clean it up before I go."

"Don't go," I pleaded, grabbing him with my good hand as he rolled to his side next to me. "I've been so lonely."

The sheer depth of our love making made me bold enough to tell the truth.

"Okay, okay, I will stay, but I have to be up early in the morning."

"I'm sure I can make sure of that," I purred as he curled up against me.

"I'm sure you can," he replied with a light chuckle, then he leaned in to kiss me.

"You know"—he propped his head up on his hand—"I reckon this was all a ploy to get yourself breakfast in bed."

"No comment," I smiled then giggled because he tickled my exposed tummy.

"I knew it"—he sighed dramatically—"I've been used."

"Yes," I replied. "I don't hear you complaining."

"No, complaints here, sweetheart. I told you I would look after you and I will, as long as you'll let me."

I was stunned by the depth of emotion in that light word play.

"As long as you cook and make me come, I'll let you look after me."

He nodded. "I will satisfy all your desires, Sally."

"All of them?"

He nodded.

"You don't even know what they are yet," I teased.

"No, but I will enjoy finding out."

"So will I."

He kissed me. I felt so relaxed, so perfectly at ease with him. It felt like I'd found home, not just a place to lay my head. My flat had always been a place to stay—it had no life, like I had no life. I did the same thing day-in, day-out just because I always had and I was too scared to try anything else.

Lucas, in less than twenty-four hours, had helped me to see that. He'd shown me that I was the best me there was and I had to live life to the full. Apparently, self-discovery starts with a greasy fry up and a masterful man. Who knew?

FIVE COURSES

Ayla Ruse

Dedication

This story is for anyone who has ever had chef-inspired fantasies.

Chapter One

Mike sank onto the couch with an audible sigh.

"Nothing catching your eye tonight, either?" Trent asked.

Mike turned his head and studied his best friend and business partner. He didn't answer. He didn't have to. They both suffered from the same problem. Wanting a woman they couldn't have.

The music pumped loud through their favourite club, the lights dim except for the stations. Mike crossed his arms over his chest and watched one sub being spanked, another being flogged and still another kneeling before her Dom.

"This sucks," Trent commented without heat. "I've never had it this bad for a woman. I look around and all I see is Melissa."

Mike nodded his head in agreement. "I don't know whether to thank you or punch you for talking me into having her rent the middle loft."

"I didn't have to talk you into shit, Mike. She had nowhere to go. You would have offered her the loft by the end of that night if I hadn't mentioned it first."

Mike grunted at the truth in Trent's words. That impulsive decision to give temporary aid to a woman in need had led to their four-storey building being infused with the sights, sounds and scents of a woman they couldn't touch. Amend that— —*wouldn't* touch. In the months she'd been living with them, she'd shown herself to be trustworthy, fun, spontaneous, dependable and of course, sexy as hell. Even when she raided the industrial-size refrigerator in the middle of the night sporting that ratty-ass robe of hers that covered every inch of skin, all he wanted to do was strip it off and feast on her delectable body.

Mike set his hands on his thighs. He liked control. Savoured it. Commanded it. But the constant thoughts of the woman out of their reach made him antsy, which irritated him to no end.

Trent interrupted Mike's thoughts. "She seemed happy to see us go tonight. Makes me wonder what she's up to?"

Mike sat back. "Shit, Trent, we have it bad. As far as Melissa, she's no doubt fast asleep."

"I wonder if she ever dreams of us?"

Mike laughed. "Okay, I think you have it worse than me. When has she ever given any indication that she's attracted to us? Not only that, she seems too vanilla. Remember the asshole she was engaged to? That was the kind of man who wants a quick fuck on Wednesday night from the wife, but gets nasty with any hooker he can find on the weekends."

Trent scrubbed his face, calling Mike's attention to him once more. "Fuck, Mike. This isn't working tonight. I know it's early, but I'm ready to head home."

Mike agreed and followed Trent outside. The cool air felt good as they made their way to the car.

"There's the Crewson job coming up next week," Mike commented, forcing his mind away from Melissa. "When we get home, I think I'll work on those new crêpes."

"Sounds good. I'll probably whip up a batch of gelato. It'll take my mind off Melissa."

Mike chuckled. "Do you think she knows?"

"What? That we're Doms?"

"Yeah. She's submissive through and through, yet she sees us as nothing more than a couple of roommates."

"I know. But then we've never put her in a position to force her submissive side, have we?"

Mike shook his head. "No." He tapped his foot and looked up to Trent, adding, "It'd be sweet, wouldn't it?"

They shared a smile before they climbed into the car to make the long drive back to their building.

Tuck it away, Mike, he told himself, almost like a mantra, preparing to go home to a woman they couldn't touch.

* * * *

Melissa ducked and twirled to the song, loving the way the beat surrounded her. She held a slice of pizza in her left hand and danced towards the refrigerator, glancing at the clock as she moved. Ten o'clock. She easily had another couple of hours before Trent and Mike returned. Plenty of time to finish her forbidden late-night dinner, clean up and tuck herself away in her third-floor flat. Feeling smug, she belted out the chorus, looking over the cluttered countertop. Every Thursday night she indulged, like a naughty girl when the parents were away. And even though Trent and

Mike weren't her parents, they were well-known chefs-turned-caterers who guarded their large kitchen like a pair of pit bulls.

Oh well, the kitchen—heck, the building—might belong to two of the hottest chefs-cum-caterers in town, but when they disappeared mysteriously every Thursday night, the place became hers. At least, that was her reasoning. On those nights, she'd made a ritual of bringing home pizza from the corner pizzeria and junk food from the grocers. Basically, if the pair had classified a food as off-limits, Melissa indulged in just those items. Then, because they were good to her and had saved her from being jobless and without a home, she'd clean the place, knowing they'd never find out.

She smiled wistfully and swayed to the song playing over her MP3. She'd been living in their building nearly six months. She'd become an employee for their front office almost two months ago. But she wanted more. She wanted them. Unfortunately, they scared the crap out of her. Not because they were ugly or mean. Just the opposite. The men she lived and worked with were buff, built and kind. The only ones she'd ever known to give a crap about her. When they came too near her, she had to work not to stutter or freeze. To say they intimidated her would be an understatement.

Another of her favourite songs came on and goosebumps pricked her skin. She sang loudly to a song touting the joys of BDSM. At the top of her lungs she belted out the refrain, exclaiming how things like canes and whips turned her on. She bet she made a sight, but she didn't care. No one home but her, and she loved being able to let loose, to do something so seemingly mundane—yet sexy—like bumping and grinding to the beat while munching on pizza. She stopped, tipped up her beer bottle and found it empty, then danced over to the refrigerator for another. Only her second one that night. Knowing her, this would be her last and she'd carry the rest upstairs with her later.

With the pizza in her left hand, she opened the door with her right. Just before she plucked out another beer, she spread her knees and shimmed into a low crouch before working her way back up. The words of the song rushed through her, making her wonder what it'd be like to be loved rough. To have a lover want to tie her up, or spank her ass, or…or…hell, she didn't really know what all kinds of naughty stuff could go on, but just the thoughts heated her blood. Especially when she imagined Trent or Mike taking charge and doing these things to her.

Nothing could stop the huge grin at these thoughts as she turned and hip-checked the door closed.

Then something to her left caught her eye. She turned her head and shrieked.

Oh shit. Busted.

Trent and Mike stood at the end of the long kitchen. Trent wore a silk suit minus the jacket, and Mike had on leather pants and a vest. No shirt. She'd spied them leaving earlier dressed like this. Similar to how they dressed every Thursday night. She lifted her wrist to her mouth to make sure she wasn't drooling.

Even though they stared right at her, she knew they saw everything. Wincing, she darted her eyes around the kitchen at proof of her wrongdoing. A greasy, open pizza box, a plastic grocery bag ripped open with store-bought chocolate chip cookies spilling out, crumbs littering the counter and floor. And her, guilty as charged. If that wasn't bad enough, she suddenly realised with embarrassment, all she had on was a pair of blue silky tap pants and a matching cami top.

Oh, crap.

She glanced at the men again and wanted to disappear. To say they looked pissed off would be an understatement.

Please don't let them fire me, she prayed fervently. *Or kick me out of the building.*

"Um, hi. I wasn't expecting you," she said brightly, her mind working feverishly fast for an excuse. "I, um, am expecting some friends over. That's all. Sorry." She immediately put her pizza back in the box, closed the lid and began working to bag everything up. "I'll have this cleaned in no time. Okay? I would have, um, taken this straight to my flat, but I was too hungry to wait. You'll never even know I was here. Promise. Go on." She shooed her hands at their stoic, arms-crossed-over-very-well-built chests stance.

As the last chords of the sexy, incriminating song faded away, the distinctive repetition of letters seemed to echo through the room. She flushed toe to neck and hurried her cleaning. Her hands shook and she cursed herself fifty different ways. Why wouldn't they say anything? Why wouldn't they leave? *Oh shit, oh crap. Oh heck.* She was in *so* much trouble.

"Melissa, stop."

Mike hadn't raised his voice. If anything, he'd lowered it, and the rumble coursed through her like a distant thunder. She stilled immediately. They were to her left, but she wouldn't—couldn't—look at them. She clenched dirty napkins in one fist while sweeping up crumbs with the other.

"How many people were you expecting to entertain…in our kitchen?"

She squeezed her eyes shut. "Oh" — she tried for a nonchalant laugh — "you know, just a few. But they should have been here by now and since they aren't, I don't think they're coming. Besides, I wasn't going to entertain in your kitchen."

Footsteps clicked on the ceramic floor and a warm hand grazed her neck and trailed down her bare shoulder. "And just *who* were you expecting to entertain," Trent whispered across her ear, "dressed like this?"

With her head already bowed, she glanced down at herself and blushed again. She'd never left her flat wearing so little. At least, not when these two were home. She'd always come downstairs dressed head to toe, or wearing her favourite old floor-length robe.

She straightened her spine, and despite her painfully erect nipples, she stepped out of Trent's reach and turned around.

"Trent, Mike, I am very sorry. I know you don't like anything store-bought in your kitchen. I know this space is sacred to you. Being in here like this is wrong of me. I have no excuse. Please let me clean up. If you want me to leave, please give me at least a few days to find another flat."

The music had shifted to another song and the beat seemed too loud. She reached to turn it off, but Trent's hand over hers stopped her.

"I like this song," he explained. She glanced at him and blinked. His face was inches from hers and despite the firm line of his mouth, his eyes looked excited.

She trembled. She wasn't very experienced, but she'd seen that look on the face of other men, looking at other women. Did he want her? *Oh, no, no, no.* He couldn't want her. He only wanted her in *her* fantasies.

She didn't know what the hell to do with a man like Trent. Or Mike, for that matter. She peeked past Trent and saw that Mike had stepped close and the same desire shone in his eyes.

Mike, too? She shivered. They intimidated the crap out of her. If they wanted her, what would happen? Would they make her choose? While the fantasy part of her relished that idea, the reality part of Melissa shrivelled in fear. These men reeked of experience and knowledge. She'd never even been taken doggy-style, for heaven's sake! What the heck would these two expect her to know?

Mike opened a drawer and fingered several cooking utensils. He picked up a flat, solid spatula. "How's this one look, Trent?" he asked.

"I think that one will start us off pretty good. It always makes me think of an oversized crop."

"Me, too," Mike answered before turning to her fully. "Melissa, I appreciate your understanding of how important our kitchen is to us. I appreciate that you apologised for your error in judgement tonight. But tell me, have you done this before?"

She bit her lip, and curled her hands around the counter's edge, her knuckles turning white. She wasn't afraid of being hurt by them, but she was afraid of the unknown. Would they beat her? She didn't think so. Would they chew her out and tell her to leave? Would they fire her? God, she hoped not.

"Your silence is telling us your answer must be yes," Trent murmured, and cupped her cheek in the large palm of his hand.

"I believe you're right," Mike agreed. "It's all adding up now. For several weeks I've noticed odd little things. A stray bit of crumbs in the corner, a crumpled-up napkin from that frozen pizzeria, shoved in the trash. A lone bottle of cheap beer stowed in the back of the bottom shelf of the fridge. Not to mention having sexy dance parties here, in our kitchen, instead of her flat."

"So tell me" — Trent took over, crowding her against the counter — "do you defy us in our own place to spite us? Or because you want us?"

The latter truth of his words shot through her body and she knew her face confirmed his suspicion. Before she could make one sound, Trent growled and crushed his mouth over hers, licking at the seam until she opened with a surrendered moan. He darted his tongue in fast and swept over hers, exploring her beyond what any man had ever done.

He placed a hand over one of her fists gripping the counter, and slid his other hand to the back of her head, holding her still for his onslaught. He stepped even closer and she trembled when his erection pressed against her belly. *Oh God, this cannot be happening.*

She lifted her free hand to his waist, but a stinging slap to the back of her hand made her cry out into Trent's mouth. Mike's voice cut through the sexual haze burning through her.

"You don't move unless we give permission, Melissa."

Trent finished his soul-stirring kiss with a long lick over her swollen lips. He lifted his head, but he didn't back away.

"We are going to take you, Melissa," Trent informed her, his eyes boring into hers. "We will use you, pleasure you, fuck you until you can't walk, then we'll do it again." He stepped back three steps and stood next to Mike, who still held that spatula. Despite his brutal language, she could see the excitement in their faces.

Mike added to Trent's words. "You have ten seconds to make up your mind. Your choices—you can run up to your flat. We'll clean up, you promise to never invade our kitchen such as you have tonight, and we'll forget the entire incident. Tomorrow it'll be like this never happened."

"Or," Trent continued, "if you're still standing here when Mike reaches ten, you're ours. From that moment on, until we tuck your exhausted, passed-out body into bed, you agree to do exactly as we say."

"One," Mike began. He paused. "Two." Pause.

Melissa's mind scrambled. She could stay here and who knew what could happen? She had no doubt they'd make love to her as they'd said, but could she handle two men? How did that work anyway?

"Three." Pause. "Four." Pause.

On the other hand, if she walked upstairs, no harm, no foul. Sure, she'd be embarrassed for a little while, but they were always true to their word.

"Five."

She'd also probably never have another chance to have her body rocked like she could only imagine they'd do.

"Six."

She stared from one man to the other. Mike slapped the flat side of the spatula against his palm and just that quickly, she understood why he'd taken it out. He planned to use it on her. Her blood heated and her pussy grew damp.

"Seven."

Crap. She glanced behind her, towards the corner where an alcove led to a set of back stairs. She could be snuggled up in her bed in no time.

"Eight."

And she'd be alone. Forever alone.

"Nine."

Screw it. It was only one night after all, right? If it turned out bad, she wouldn't have to guess anymore.

"Ten."

The song blasting out spoke about how sexy it was to have his woman kneel at his feet. Jeez, she'd never realised how many, um, controlling songs she had. She returned their stares and other than the incriminating lyrics, silence descended.

Chapter Two

What now? Melissa wondered.

Mike and Trent both smiled and seemed to relax, if that were even possible. "Thank you, Melissa," Mike told her. "We'll take good care of you. But first, we need to go over a few things."

"Huh?" What, were they going to lecture her, or screw her?

"First, have you ever submitted to anyone before?"

"I...I don't think so?"

"I didn't think you had," Mike commented, "but I wanted to make sure. We will require you to submit to us tonight. We'll tell you what to do, and you'll obey. If you do not, you will be punished. Do you understand?"

Worry puckered her brow, but she nodded.

"You'll also have an out, if anything gets too much for you. Use the word 'spoon', and we'll stop. Everything will stop. We won't be mad, but if you use the word 'spoon', our night ends immediately. You have to make sure, before you think of using this word, if you're just nervous, or if you're truly frightened. Understand?"

"I, um, think so."

"No. You either do, or you don't. We don't play with hesitation or mixed signals."

She shifted her feet. "I get it. I say 'spoon' and that's it for us."

"In the sexual aspect, at any rate," Trent said, his lips quirking up to a grin.

"Now what?" she asked. She liked how they spoke so clear-cut, but at the same time, would they treat her like a toy? Would they use her up, without regard to things maybe she'd want? At least with the word, if she wasn't having any fun, they could stop.

"Now, our naughty little Melissa," Mike said, his voice dropping, "turn around and lean over the counter."

She blinked at his tone, at the subtle growl that bled out from the words. What had come over him? Why did she feel compelled to obey, and why was her pussy growing moist, just from this one command?

"Now," he barked. She spun with a jump and leaned her chest down on the stone counter. She felt more than heard him approach her. He ran a heavy hand down her back and over her ass, making her jerk in surprise. When he cupped her butt and squeezed, she felt as though he were testing her out.

"Do I pass?" she muttered sarcastically.

Mike's hand met her ass with a stinging slap.

"Ow!"

"You do pass," Mike answered. "But you don't take that tone with me. Understood?"

She nodded even as her eyes widened. Had she really signed up for this? He resumed his caresses, even sliding his hand up under the loose bottom edge of her tap pants to stroke her bare bottom. *Oh, that feels so good.* She laid her head on the counter and enjoyed his exploration. When he smoothed his fingers down her crease, then lower to stroke through the moisture of her pussy, she moaned, but tightened up at the same time. It'd been so long since she'd been touched by any man, and never like this. She wanted to be wanton and give herself over to Mike's touch, but inexperience made her tense.

A quick thwack of the spatula over the back of her thigh made her cry out.

"Relax, Melissa. It's just us here, okay. We won't hurt you. Unnecessarily," he added softly, using his fingers to open her swollen outer lips. He caressed her with firm, sure fingers, and she pushed back, wanting more. "You are so fucking wet," he murmured, sounding pleased. She softened against him, thrilled that he was happy.

"But, Melissa," Mike continued, "despite your apology, you have messed up here tonight. You'll have to be punished."

Swift hands pulled her silky tap pants down and off her legs before she registered what had happened. Before she could comment on Mike's statement, he brought the flat side of the spatula down on her butt. Hard. She cried out and jumped. It didn't hurt so much as surprise her.

"Easy," Trent told her, coming around the huge island to stand opposite her. He leaned over onto his elbows then reached out and stroked her cheek. "Now I have a few questions for you," he started. Mike, meanwhile, was taking the spatula and swatting her rear. Not hard, but enough to send little stings through her nerve endings. Amazingly, this attention turned her on. She tried to squirm, tried to rub her thighs together, but Mike had growled to keep still. And now Trent wanted to ask her questions?

"Really? N...now?" Her breath was beginning to hitch and she curled her fingers against the stone top.

"How many lovers did you have before your ex-fiancé?"

Oh, he must want to know about disease and stuff, then. "No one," she answered honestly. "And after I left him, I was tested and everything came back clean. I haven't been with anyone else. I'm also on the pill," she added, then moaned when Mike took the utensil and rubbed the flat side over her now-heated backside.

Trent chuckled. "Good to know. So your ex was your only lover, hmm? If I remember his type, he probably only fucked you missionary, in the dark, on a schedule."

Melissa bristled under Trent's spot-on conclusion. She spoke up, not because she had any need to defend the asshole, but because it made her sexuality seem like a joke. "No. Not...all the time." The hard, knowing look in Trent's eyes had her looking away.

"Is she telling the truth?" Mike wanted to know. She peeked at Trent to see a barely imperceptible shake of his head. The next thing she knew, Mike struck her bottom harder than he'd done so far — and with his bare hand this time!

"Ow!" she cried out and jolted up. Mike must have expected that because her back slammed into his palm and he shoved her torso back down.

"Never, ever lie to us."

Trent held her eyes as he spoke, until she nodded.

"We wouldn't ask these questions if it weren't important to us. Don't be afraid to open up."

Melissa saw the sincerity and truth in Trent's eyes and she nodded again. She knew these men. Heck, she'd been living with them for half a year. She'd seen them grumpy and put out, happy and mellow. They deserved honest answers from her. Especially as the wrong ones apparently led to bad consequences. She'd always considered herself a fast learner.

"Tell us how it was, Melissa," Trent encouraged.

She swallowed. Trent held her hands, his thumbs over her palms while Mike had taken to caressing her stinging backside. Comfort and excitement at the same time. Conflicting, yet she wanted this and more. She had no choice but to confess what she now saw was the ugly truth. "Yes, it was like that. He wouldn't even sleep in the same bed with me. Even after I moved in. We'd…we'd make love, then he'd leave. He'd said he was saving that for when we married." Her face flamed as her spoken words brought to light how badly her ex had treated her.

"Asshole," Mike muttered behind her. "The man didn't know the meaning of the word love." She heard the spatula being laid on the counter, then Mike stroked his fingers across her swollen pussy again, making her moan. "Thank you for being honest," he praised her.

The microwave dinged and Trent pushed himself up then walked away. "Have you ever been eaten out?" he asked.

Dang, he was blunt. "Um…well…"

Mike stroked her pussy again. "Honest answer. Believe it or not, we like that you don't have a lot of experience."

"Really?"

"Really," Trent answered, moving in front of her again and stirring something thick, smooth and pale in a bowl. "Everything will be new to you, which is exciting for us to see. Plus, we have the ability to show you how we like things done."

"Ohhh," she groaned. Mike sank his finger between her folds and deep into her channel. Her muscles gripped him hard and when he wiggled the digit, she felt every twitch through to her toes.

"Open your eyes, sweetheart," Trent whispered. He rested back over the counter, the bowl now between them. He raised the spoon and let the pale mixture pour slowly back into the bowl. "I take it you've never sucked a guy off either, have you?" His whisper caressed her skin and she shivered even as she went up on her toes. Mike pumped his finger in and out of her—feeling Mike behind her while Trent talked right in front of her was screwing with her brain. She'd never been so sexually open. And under bright, industrial lights, too.

She shook her head while staring at the late-night stubble on Trent's jaw, and she couldn't help but reach out to touch him. He allowed one stroke before turning his head to capture her forefinger between his lips. He nipped the tip, then spoke again. "Keep your finger out. Yes, just like that."

Trent drizzled the mix over the tip of her finger. Then he sucked it into his mouth, closing over her knuckle and swirling his tongue against her. Melissa couldn't have held back her moan if she'd been ordered.

When Trent released her finger, he'd eaten all the syrup off. "Now you try it," he told her, extending his forefinger towards her. She opened her mouth. "Wait," he said, and dribbled the syrup over his finger. The entire finger. "Lick the glaze from my finger. Use only your tongue."

She stuck her tongue out and with the tip, tentatively swiped at the glaze. She tasted it, and a sweet, tangy lemon flavour burst over her tongue.

"Melissa." Trent sounded exasperated. "Open your mouth and lick. The syrup. Off. My. Finger. Then you'll get to do it from my cock."

Melissa sucked in a breath.

"Problem?" Trent asked.

"I'm not used to the way you talk," she admitted, hoping they'd use more user-friendly terms, like 'private parts', or something.

Mike had dropped to his knees behind her and his hot breath fanned her inner leg. "She's like a faucet down here, Trent," Mike announced, his voice sounding like he was beaming with pride.

"I imagined so," Trent answered, before sucking the glaze off his finger, smiling at Melissa and addressing her comment. "I like to be blunt. Less room for confusion. So you're not one to talk dirty, hmm? That's okay. Mike and I'll do it enough for you as well."

A devilish gleam lit his eye and the corner of his mouth twitched. He pushed the bowl out of the way and captured her chin in his hand. His voice lowered. Not into a whisper, but into another timbre. "Mike's about to put his mouth on your *pussy* and eat you out. Pretty soon, you're going to wrap that pretty little mouth of yours around my *cock* and *suck* me off until I come. We'll *fuck* you in your *cunt* and we'll *fuck* your *ass*, and you're going to take it all, begging for more while you come over and over."

Trent emphasised every naughty word and she flushed with each mention. She'd never felt so exposed and, despite the part of her that wanted to say his words were wrong, she craved what he promised. Mike had pushed her legs farther apart and pulled her hips back. Yeah, she could think those words all day long, but to hear them said shocked the heck out of her.

"Fuck, Trent, I don't know what you're doing or saying up there, but her pussy's become a flood gate." Mike ran his tongue up her inner thigh and she shuddered with delight.

Trent chuckled and pulled back, bringing the bowl between them once more. "Go ahead, Mike. Enjoy her."

While Trent spoke, he drizzled the warm glaze over his entire finger again, then held it out to her.

"Tongue only," he reminded her.

She opened her mouth this time and as soon as she took her first lick of the syrup on Trent's finger, Mike pressed his tongue into her pussy. She would have jumped if he hadn't clamped down on her hips. "Aahhhh," she stuttered, sucking in a deep breath and readying herself for more.

So wicked. So naughty. And darn if she didn't want more. She must have said something out loud because Mike barked out a laugh before tilting his mouth against her and running his tongue up and over her slit, circling tighter and tighter.

"Focus," Trent reminded her. She tried to, she really did, but she'd never had anyone put their mouth down there and her brain was turning to mush. Feel, that was all she wanted to do—feel.

"Stop, Mike. Can you hear me?"

"Um-hmm," Mike murmured below her.

"She's losing her focus. We're going to play red light, green light. Remember that game?"

Mike chuckled. "I do. Just make sure you speak loud enough."

"Will do."

"How do you play?" Melissa wanted to know.

"You'll find out. Now lick."

Chapter Three

As soon as she touched his finger, Trent called out, "Green light." Mike ran his tongue over her pussy. She shivered and repeated the movement.

She tried to focus on Trent, but what Mike was doing to her felt so delicious, she forgot to lick the glaze.

"Red light," Trent called out. Mike stopped eating at her.

She groaned and moved towards Trent's finger again. When her tongue touched him, he said, "Green light," and Mike resumed pleasuring her.

Ah, so that's the game, then. When she licked Trent's finger, Mike would lick her pussy. When she stopped, Mike stopped.

She smirked at Trent. "Clever."

He nodded his head and grinned back.

"Full power now, Mike," Trent announced, and Melissa wondered what the heck that meant. "Melissa, suck my finger clean."

She took his thick finger into her mouth at the same time Mike pushed a finger inside her pussy and swiped his tongue over her swollen clit. She moaned around Trent's finger as Mike increased his pleasure to her.

As Mike licked, she found herself mimicking the movements and sucking on Trent's finger. She imagined Trent's cock in front of her and she moaned all over again, wanting to know what a man's flesh felt like between her lips. Heck, she was curious as to what it looked like up close and personal. Her ex had only taken her in the dark, so she'd never had a chance to see a penis in person.

The images spinning through her head, combined with Mike's mouth on her, his finger in her, Trent's finger in her mouth and his eyes boring into hers made her belly quake. She threw her head back, letting go of Trent's finger, and whimpered loudly. "Trent, there's... What's... Oh. My. God!" She cried out as the orgasm tore through her. Trent pushed his finger into her mouth once more and she clamped her lips around the digit.

When she came down, Mike pulled away, stood up then leaned his body over hers where she sprawled over the counter.

"C'mon, baby. You're made of more stamina than this. We've not even started," Mike said, turning her and lifting her in his arms.

"You've not started?" she managed to say, wondering again what the heck she'd got herself into.

Mike took her over to one of the long, benched tables. He sat down and cradled her in his lap while Trent handed her an open bottle of water. Trent stroked her hair as she swallowed.

"Go get a couple of cushions, will you Trent?" Mike asked. When Melissa handed Mike the water, he capped it and placed it on the table, then jostled her in order to pull off her cami top. The cool air hit her nipples and they tightened instantly. She instinctively tried to cover up, but he captured her wrists.

"Keep your hands down, baby, or I'll have to keep them out of my way. Got it?"

She nodded, then crossed them down over her belly.

"Good girl." He looked down to her breasts and under his gaze, they seemed to swell. "Beautiful." He grazed her nipples with his knuckles, playing his touch over before capturing one between his fingers.

Trent returned carrying a few thick cushions and set them on the table behind Mike.

"Bring me that glaze you were using, Trent. I need to see if you used the right amount of sugar this time."

Trent chuckled. "Asshole," he returned the slight, but brought over the bowl. He pushed her arms out of the way and set the bowl right over her mound. The warmth felt good.

"If you tip the bowl," Mike warned, "the consequences will be severe."

He didn't sound exceptionally threatening, but she knew now these guys didn't mince words. Besides, the bowl wasn't large and it seemed to be nestled pretty good between her belly and legs. She should have no worries.

Then Mike picked up the spoon and lazily drizzled a bit of syrup over one of her breasts. She jerked as the heated liquid made her nipple pucker. He kept applying the warm mixture, bits of it running down the globes and into the valley between her breasts.

Mike had no sooner finished then Trent knelt down and sucked the entire nipple into his mouth. She inhaled a startled breath and stared down at him in amazement, delight and residuals of shock that these two men were loving her so much.

"Tilt your head back and open your mouth," Mike instructed while Trent continued to lick and nip at her flesh. "Not so much, more like you're whispering. Good." Then Mike lifted the spoon, watching the glaze trail over her mouth, letting a small stream slip between her parted lips. "Don't lick it," he warned when she stuck out her tongue. He kissed her then, their lips slippery, wet and sliding back and forth as Mike deepened the kiss. At the same time, Trent had moved to her other breast while he plucked at her bare nipple.

She moaned into Mike's mouth and tried to shift. The bowl tilted in her lap and made her still quickly.

Mike chuckled against her lips. "That's right, baby. You can't move." He kept kissing her until she could barely breathe.

"I'm ready for the second course," Trent announced, getting up and removing the bowl from her lap.

Mike lifted his head and smiled at the slumberous gaze in Melissa's eyes. Her chin and upper body were sticky, her lips swollen, her nipples tight and flushed. *Perfect, just perfect.* He and Trent had wanted this woman ever since she'd walked into the first appointment she'd made with their catering business over eight months ago. The night of her ex's surprise party, when the jerk had stumbled into the house with a hooker on each arm, they'd felt her pain and had desperately wanted to kick the shit out of the guy. They'd found her, crying in the pantry, and she'd told them that she'd been new to the area and had nowhere to go. Trent had immediately offered her the use of the middle flat of their building.

The shock mixed with immediate desire still flooded his blood when he remembered how, not an hour ago, he and Trent had ditched their club to come home, way earlier than normal. They'd planned on playing with some recipes, a favourite way they each had found eased tensions. Instead, they'd come to home to find luscious little Melissa bumping and grinding and singing about how she'd love a little pain with her pleasure.

He grinned with an idea. "I want her knees on the bench," he told Trent, handing him the precious bundle of woman before hurrying over to the deep freeze. "This is a good time to see if that new recipe I made for that birthday party worked out."

Mike pulled a tray of long slender moulds out, and working with warm water, he wiggled free a homemade ice pop. He licked the treat and smiled. *Yeah, this is good.* It'd be even better dripping with Melissa's juice.

When he returned to the table, Trent had Melissa kneeling on cushions he'd placed on the bench. He grinned when Trent coaxed her to bend over. Her round ass, still pink, filled Mike's view and his cock pulsed hard beneath the tight leather. Trent had placed her near the end of the table while he stood at the head with his bowl of lemon glaze nearby. While Trent opened his pants and removed his cock, Mike ran the tip of the ice pop down Melissa's spine. She arched and bowed under the cold, yelping at the frozen contact.

He didn't stop, but trailed the frozen treat slowly down the crease of her ass, pressing as he went. "What?" she stuttered, but Trent called her attention back to him. Mike slipped the ice pop down farther and slicked it through her pussy lips and up over her clit. She cried out and squirmed until he swatted her ass. He loved seeing his handprint on her flesh, and he enjoyed even more the way she submitted to his physical command.

Then he pressed the slender treat into her cunt. Slowly, so slowly, and she whimpered and tensed with every slide. "I like ice play," he informed her, his cock twitching, wanting that mix of cold and heat that it would soon encounter. Her sounds were muffled now, as Trent had coated his cock with glaze and Melissa was working diligently to lick him clean.

As he pumped the frozen treat in and out of her body, he noticed how quickly it melted. When it was almost down to the plastic stick, he pulled it out and sucked the rest into his mouth. Sweet, tart, cold and hot mixed on his tongue, and he couldn't wait another minute. He yanked open his pants and, with trembling hands, sheathed his cock in a thin condom. "Get ready, Melissa," he warned, positioning his aching dick at her entrance. He started to move and even through the condom, the freeze sank into his flesh. He shivered and closed his eyes, sliding into her with clenched teeth. "Damn. Your cunt is so fucking tight, Melissa. I love it."

She moaned her response, Trent's dick now stuffed between her lips.

He continued to push into her channel, and the mix of temperatures he moved through drove him crazy.

He sank balls-deep and thrust his groin against her, doing his damnedest to fit every single inch of himself inside her body.

"I don't think I've ever seen that look on your face before, Mike," Trent commented.

Mike opened his eyes and smiled. "You have no idea. Just wait, you'll find out. Melissa, thank you. I think you're the one who's going to kill me and take me to heaven."

He pulled out and pushed back in, loving the way her walls tightened around him, but he wanted more. Needed more.

Considering her body was angled towards the end of the table so she could take care of Trent, Mike helped her out. Still buried inside her body, he lifted her left knee and placed it on the table. As soon as he did, he slid another inch inside her and she groaned around Trent's cock. "Damn, I bet that feels fantastic, too," he told his friend.

"Oh, yeah. She may be innocent," Trent said affectionately, brushing back a curl from her forehead and smiling down at her, "but I've never had head so good."

Mike grunted his approval, straddling the bench so the three of them lined up evenly. He gripped her hips and started to fuck her with intent. Slow at first, to get her used to him and because the hot-cold sensations still battered his dick, then increasing in speed until his thrusts shifted her body hard enough that her mouth fucked Trent's cock at the same speed.

A ripple squeezed his erection, alerting Mike to her impending orgasm. "You'd better come soon, Trent," he warned, "or your cum will be all over the floor."

Trent nodded. "No problem." To Melissa, he said, "I know you've never done this, but do your best to swallow. I'm about to... Ah fuck, yes!"

Mike stilled his movements, allowing Melissa to focus on Trent. When she became more experienced, she'd be able to handle anything they did to her at any time, but for now, she was still learning. He couldn't begin to imagine all the sensations they were infusing into her body. He smiled. When he'd told her she'd pass out, he'd not lied. He imagined they'd keep at her until she was worn out.

And he'd do his damnedest to make sure she went with a smile.

He waited while Melissa sputtered and even gagged once, but she managed to swallow Trent's cum. Some women liked to swallow, some didn't, but both he and Trent were firm believers in having to try things at least once.

"I'm so proud of you," Trent praised, running his hands through her hair. He leant down and kissed her lips before he stood up as if revived. "Fuck her well," Trent told Mike. "I'll be back. I've got an idea I want to try."

Mike shrugged off Trent's words and turned his focus to Melissa. "Look at me," he whispered, and she turned her head, which she'd laid on the smooth surface of the table. Her lips were red and puffy yet her eyes were excited. "Having fun?" he asked, not because he needed to know, but he wanted to see her expression.

She didn't disappoint. Her eyes widened and she smiled shakily at him. "I don't know how to answer that. I'm not used to any of this at all. But I..." She pushed back against him. "I still need you."

"I know, baby. I know. Face forward and brace yourself."

She did as he'd asked and this time when he gripped her hips, he didn't push into her so much as he yanked her back over him. Hard and fast, he drew her cunt around his cock. Her walls rippled hard and she mewled and whimpered, the sounds skating up his spine and mixing, adding to his own impending orgasm. There was so much surprise and amazement in her voice, in her discoveries of pleasure. And the sounds came because *he* worked her body, he made her body sing, and that alone was heady.

He picked up his pace and angled her hips, his eyes focused on the glistening slide of his cock into her pussy and just a bit up, her little puckered hole. His balls tightened. Before the night was over, he'd get in there too, and damn if he couldn't wait.

"Oh, Mike. It's too much. Not enough. I don't know…"

He knew. He changed the pace and reached around her hip, brushing his fingers over her swollen clit, and fuck was it ever puffy. Just little touches, circles, trails of his fingertips across the wet surface. She tightened around him and began bucking back against him, lifting her hips to meet his every thrust and crying out for more.

When sensations started tingling through his balls, he touched her with a more firm hand, and sliding her clit between two fingers, he pinched the bundle of nerves tight. She pushed against him, arched beneath him and screamed out as she came around his cock. He gritted his teeth and groaned long and low as his orgasm tore through him.

"God, baby, that was so good," he finally managed to say. "I can't wait for the third course."

"What?" came her faint, exhausted reply.

Mike chuckled as he slid out of her heated body, giving her ass a smack as he moved away. Damn, his handprint looked good on her ass.

Chapter Four

Trent smiled when Melissa's screams reverberated through the room. He stirred his thin concoction once more, dipped in his pinky for a quick heat test, then lifted the digit for a taste test. Spicy. Hot. Perfect.

He turned off the heat and transferred his mix into a small bowl, then swirled it gently and blew over the surface to cool it down. He smiled wickedly, imagining Melissa's response to his special concoction of cinnamon and vanilla essential oils. He'd tweaked it over time, adding a dash of this and a dash of that until he'd created the perfect blend to dot on sensitive spots of the skin that would warm then heat up the area. Combined with their lovemaking, Melissa wouldn't know what to do.

"This is gonna be sweet," he murmured. Whether Melissa knew it or not, she was now theirs. Both he and Mike had wanted her for so long, but they'd promised themselves they wouldn't make a blatant move. Okay, so maybe tonight they were being pretty damn blatant, but who could blame them? The way her tits had swayed under that silky top and the flashes of pussy she showed from under the loose little tap pants she'd worn when she did her bumping and grinding would have sent any man over the edge. Especially them. Especially tonight.

They used to love going to their private club—a club exclusively for fetish life. Their fetish—they loved food and they loved to share their women. And they loved to be in control. But lately, easily the last month, their weekly visits had become burdensome. He couldn't remember the last time he'd had a good scene. Every sub seemed tired and old, even though that was far from the case, but not one of those women stirred his blood anymore. All he could see in his mind's eye was Melissa. Every sub who knelt before him made him wish their flatmate was there instead. He knew the same disillusionment was plaguing Mike.

He glanced around the corner and watched Mike cuddle Melissa. So innocent, he still couldn't believe it, and knowing she'd given so much to them—and still would—made his heart lift and his cock harden.

"Mike," he called out softly, leaning against the side of the fridge, still swirling the contents of his bowl. He waited for his best friend to raise his head. "How about we take her upstairs. I think she'll be more comfortable."

"Sounds good. I'll take her to yours, since it's only one floor up."

Trent chuckled easily because Mike lived on the fourth floor with Melissa taking residence on the third, between them. Surrounded by them, just as it should be.

"I have some water in my fridge," Trent added, seeing Melissa's eyes half closed and those beautiful lips parted slightly, still panting to catch her breath.

She shuddered in Mike's arms and Trent grinned, knowing her body still experienced aftershocks.

"Hey," Mike called from over his shoulder as he walked towards the back staircase. "Bring that bag of cookies."

"What?" Trent curled his lip and pointed behind him to the crinkly bag still on the counter. "That store-bought crap?"

Mike's wide grin made Trent's blood heat up. Not for him directly, but knowing Mike had something wicked planned. "Yeah," he told Trent. "She still has a lesson to learn. Maybe after your course?"

Trent's laughter shook his shoulders as Mike disappeared with Melissa. Testing the mixture in his bowl, he nodded. The temperature was perfect. He switched off Melissa's music and glanced around their kitchen. It made his skin crawl to see the condition of their favourite room in the house...and that he was about to walk away from it. He knew he and Mike would be down later to scrub everything clean, but still. Despite his anal need to clean up the counters, Melissa was waiting upstairs. He grabbed the bag of cookies and with one final, shuddering look at the mess he was leaving, he turned and headed up the stairs.

Soft laughter met his ears when he let himself into his flat. He followed the sound to his bedroom where Mike and Melissa were snuggled together, as if sharing secrets. Mike stroked over her body with a wet cloth, no doubt wiping away some of the sticky glaze. Trent smiled at the picture they made, and felt instant acceptance and connection. He'd never once known jealousy with Mike, and he felt pretty sure the feeling was mutual. He couldn't imagine any other man holding or touching Melissa. With sudden insight, Trent knew this woman could make their lives complete. At this moment, he indulged in his fantasy that they'd remain together, but time would tell. Perhaps tomorrow, when she woke, she'd regret everything about this evening, but looking at her smile and glow now, he doubted it. Besides, if she even hinted at regret, he and Mike would surely show her the error of her ways.

Giving Mike time to wipe Melissa clean, Trent thought back over the past year. He and Mike had become fast friends with Melissa, and he knew in his heart it was always leading up to this — to the time when they'd be able to celebrate their lives, wholly, together.

"Are you planning to join us anytime soon?" Melissa teased, cutting into his daydreams. Her voice had become husky with their continued loving, and he fleetingly wondered if they'd be able to make her lose her voice before the night was through.

"You make such a pretty picture," he admitted, stepping closer to the bed. Keeping his gaze on Melissa, Trent handed Mike the bag of cookies. "Missed a spot," he said, leaning over to suck her lower lip between his teeth.

"Trent, is that what I think it is?" Mike asked, indicating the bowl Trent held. Trent grinned and gave a curt nod. "Fuck, you and your spicy shit," Mike said, but the comment was filled with mirth.

"Hey, you like your cold shit. I like spicy. Nothing wrong with that."

Melissa glanced from one man to the other. "Excuse me, what are you guys talking about?"

Trent smiled and kissed her again. "You'll find out in a minute. Why don't you lie down?"

Mike helped arrange Melissa flat on her back in the middle of the bed. He scooted to her left side while Trent knelt on the bed and moved his way up between her gorgeous legs. Watching her pussy lips part and open as he spread her thighs was like a welcome home for him.

"Wait," Melissa said. Trent blinked up at her.

"What is it?" Mike asked, his hands on his pants, working them open to free his cock.

"Do you two always—you know?"

Trent chuckled. "Spill it. Know what?"

"Um…" She bit her lip and darted her eyes between the two. He wanted desperately to fall down on top of her and nip that lip she dared to bite. "Do you two always make love dressed?"

Mike and Trent stared at one another before they both broke out laughing. "No," Mike answered between chuckles. "Not always. I guess we've never really thought about it."

"Can you, for me, be naked too?"

There was so much hope in her question, Trent knew he couldn't refuse. Then another thought hit him. "Melissa, since you said your ex had been your only lover, and that he fucked you in the dark, have you ever seen a naked man in real life?"

She shook her head. "Only the parts of you I've seen tonight."

"Fuck," Trent breathed out, the curse punctuated with stunned joy. "Mike, we can't disappoint the lady."

"My thoughts exactly."

As the men climbed off the bed, a thought struck Trent. "Wait, man," he told Mike, reaching out a hand to stall his friend. "If you want us to strip, Melissa, you have to do something for us."

"Like what?"

"You have to touch yourself. Your breasts, your nipples…your pussy. Nothing timid either. I want to see you pleasuring yourself while we take off our clothes."

Mike added his own conditions. "Imagine us already around you, in you, as you watch us. When we're done and climb back into that bed, you'd better be wet and ready, or I'll have to punish you."

Trent smiled to see her eyes widen at Mike's threat.

Melissa shook her head, then nodded quickly, agreeing to their demands. Heck, she'd do just about anything to see them completely naked.

"You start," Mike said.

Melissa looked around and snagged pillows to make a prop for her lean against. If she had to touch herself, she'd better get in a position to be able to watch the show, too.

"Open those legs back up, sweetheart," Trent admonished. "I want to see all your lovely cunt." When she'd made herself comfortable, she'd naturally closed her legs. Keeping eye contact with him, because this connection thwarted her shyness, she lifted her knees and spread her legs wide. Cool air hit her pussy and she shivered at the sensation. She wrapped her hands around her breasts and stroked over the globes. This part was easy so far. She remembered how Trent had sucked her nipples and they tightened under her fingers.

Mike took off his leather vest and tossed it on the chair behind him. She'd already been ogling his chest all evening, but now she could see the whole thing. Strong pecs, a light matting of hair, and all hers. He shifted to his pants and the muscles along his arms flexed and bulged at the simple act.

Then she caught sight of Trent. He'd finished unbuttoning his shirt and was in the process of removing it when both men stilled.

"What?"

"You stopped touching yourself," Mike reminded her.

Shit. She screwed up her face but began caressing her breasts again. She'd thought having more than one lover at a time would be easy. No way. It took too much thought process. How the hell was she supposed to remember to play with her body when two veritable gods were getting buck naked right in front of her?

At almost the same time, they unzipped their pants. As if they'd practised it, they opened the front of their pants and started to push them down their hips. Again, they stalled.

"Crap," she muttered under her breath, realising her hands were completely still.

"Play with your pussy now," Trent directed her. She snaked a hand down her chest, over her belly and through the short hairs at her mound. She did this every night, worked herself into an orgasm—she stopped that thought with a silent snort. She'd never had an orgasm in her life, according to what Mike and Trent had made her experience so far, and three times tonight, no less. Still, it was one thing rubbing her body when she was laid out in her own bed with the lights out. Another thing to be under full lights with two gorgeous men looking on.

"Melissa, if you don't start touching yourself like you mean it, Trent and I will stop right here. Nothing else off."

"Okay, okay." But apparently her flippant answer wasn't right because both men frowned at her. "What?" When their lips pressed into a hard line, she thought back over everything this evening and she mentally backed up and sobered her response.

"Crap. Sorry. I mean, okay, I will touch myself."

"You still have to learn about how you will talk to us when we're together, but for now, because of your attitude, you can tell us exactly what you're doing, as you're doing it."

She almost came back with a 'what the heck?' but quickly decided it was in her best interest to do as they'd asked.

Double crap.

"Okay. I'm sliding my fingers down my, um, labia."

"Go on," Trent encouraged, letting his slacks fall down his legs. He wasn't wearing underwear and his cock sprang free. Thick and hard, it made her mouth water. She ran her tongue over her lips and remembered how he'd tasted.

"This is wicked," she murmured as Mike dropped his pants. His cock was darker than Trent's, but just as beautiful.

"Yes, it is," Trent said.

"I mean, it's hard to look at both of you at once. I love what I'm seeing. Thank you."

"You're so welcome, but you've forgotten yourself again."

She bit her lip and ran her fingers through her folds, surprised to find her pussy drenched. "Wow. I'm so wet."

Mike chuckled. "Perfect. That's just the way we want you." He wrapped a fist around his cock and Melissa's eyes stayed to glued to his erection. "Speak, baby," he reminded her.

Her fingers fumbled around herself until she dared to slide one inside herself. "I'm...I'm putting a finger inside me."

"No, baby, say, 'I'm putting a finger in my pussy."

Her eyes shot to his. *Damn.* "I...I'm putting a fingerinmypussy." She hurried the last part of the sentence and dropped her voice to a whisper. Her face heated and she closed her eyes.

Chapter Five

Mike climbed onto the bed, chuckling softly. "You'll get used to it. Thank you for trying. You've been very good, Melissa." He pushed her hands above her head then pulled the pillows from behind her before tossing one to Trent, who had moved between her legs.

"Lift your hips," Trent instructed, tucking the pillow under her when she did.

"Hold up, Mike," Trent said, stalling his friend. Melissa looked to the left where Mike sat on his knees, his heavy cock seeming to strain towards her.

Trent distracted her once more when he lay over her, causing her to suck in air and her pussy to leak. His strength, his size, his naked body touching all of hers sent sparks shooting through her entire system.

He kissed her then, hard and deep, and her mouth went soft beneath his. Her legs tightened against his hips and his cock throbbed along her slit. She shifted against him, wanting more, needing him to fill her up.

He pulled back, but set a finger over her lips. "When you started working for us, you told us you had no food allergies, right?"

Melissa furrowed her brow. "Right."

"Good." He rubbed another finger over her lips, tracing them, spreading something wet across her mouth. "Don't lick it yet. It's going to get warm. And in a minute, when you go down on Mike, it'll warm his cock."

"Oh."

Trent smiled at her even as Mike groaned. The sound made her think Mike wasn't too keen about the upcoming heat. Her thoughts were confirmed when Trent said, "Yeah. See, I like it hot, and Mike likes it cold. Next time," he told his best friend, "let me get to her pussy first."

Melissa smiled at their banter and pursed her lips to keep from running her tongue over them. She didn't know what Trent had put on her, but it smelt great.

As Trent rose from her body, he rubbed that oil across her nipples. The heat there reacted faster and her nipples throbbed with the sensation.

"I gotta admit," Mike commented, "that's pretty."

"Isn't it?"

She wanted to lift her head to see, but Mike had his hand across her forehead.

"Shh," he told her. "Relax. Feel. Enjoy. We're about to send you through the roof. Breathe while you still can."

His smile reassured her even as his words sent shivery excitement through her nerves.

Trent had sat up. She could feel him shift between her legs.

Mike lifted his hand from her head and leant down to pull a nipple deep into his mouth. "Irresistible," he murmured as his lips caressed her breast. The oil Trent had rubbed over her nipples radiated out, and when Mike sucked, the temperature became almost unbearable.

She gripped his head, unsure if she wanted him to stay there or go away.

"Take your hands off me," he growled. "Tuck them behind your head if you have to, but if I feel them again without permission granted, I'll tie you to the headboard."

Melissa shot her arms up and away. She wasn't afraid of his words or his growl — they turned her on more — but she knew he was serious.

While Mike pleasured her breasts, Trent had run his hands up and down her legs, over her mound and across her pussy. She jerked at his every touch, half afraid he'd use more of that warm oil stuff.

Then he did. With a slick finger, he gently spread the oil around her outer labia, her inner folds, then her swollen and overly sensitive clit. She cried out and bucked, resulting in both Mike and Trent pushing down on her hips to keep her still.

"Aaaahhh!" She cried out again, the heat rocketing immediately. She felt like her pussy had burst into flames.

She squirmed beneath them, crying almost incoherently, things she didn't understand. It was burning hot, but it also created an unquenchable need for more. More of their hands, their mouths, their cocks. She was at the brink of an overwhelming climax. And she wanted to come. Desperately. She begged them to get her off.

Instead, Mike ordered her to lick her lips. As she did, heat spread over her tongue. She'd barely savoured the flavour when Mike scooted close, turned her head, and pushed his cock into her mouth.

They both groaned at the contact. Melissa sucked on his length greedily, her tongue lashing over him and her cheeks hollowing out as she sucked him furiously.

Earlier, when she'd taken Trent into her mouth, the act had seemed like a sexy adventure. Now, as she panted for breath around Mike's erection, it seemed as though a storm had swept through her. No control, no play. She could only surrender to the desires they'd created in her.

To top it off, Trent took just that moment to slide a finger deep into her body. Damn the man, he'd oiled the digit and now the fire burned everywhere deep inside.

Heat. Lust. Fire. It all threatened to consume her.

Mike grabbed the back of her head to still her movements. "Easy, baby. There's no rush. Besides, I'm surprisingly enjoying the added heat from your lips and tongue. You're scorching me."

She moaned as he pulled back until the rim of his crown rubbed back and forth over her lips. Then he pushed deep, making her gag. "You can take this, Melissa. Breathe. Relax. It's okay."

She was choking, what the hell did he mean? But he continued to speak easily to her and she finally listened, relaxed the muscles in her jaw and throat, and breathed through her nose.

After several minutes of Mike's guidance with the ways he wanted her touch, she heard him say, "She's ready now, Trent. Do your worst."

She peeked up and saw a huge smile cross Mike's features. She'd learnt by now that that kind of smile meant an *uh-oh* moment for her. She braced herself, but got her thigh slapped in the process.

"Don't tighten up, Melissa," Trent told her. "At least not yet." Then he set his mouth right over her clit.

Even with her eyes closed she saw stars. His tongue... She couldn't keep track of what his tongue was doing. Licking and sliding and pushing over her, in her, around her cunt. She bucked, despite the hands that held her down. She forgot all the things Mike had told her to and she panted, losing air. She didn't care right now what they said, she couldn't take it. Too much. Heat everywhere. Her lips stretched, her mouth was on fire, her nipples plucked and twisted and those burned, too. Her pussy — dear God — her poor pussy felt like it was being bathed inside and out with a flaming torch.

Yanking her arms from behind her head, Melissa used one hand to push Mike away and the other to push off Trent.

She expected to fight them, she half worried they wouldn't pay attention to her, she was afraid they'd kill her in unbearable pleasure-pain.

Everything stopped. Mike slowly removed his cock from her mouth, but kept the tip pressed close to her lips. Trent removed his finger, but his lips whispered kisses along her inner thighs.

"Baby?" Mike asked softly. "Take it easy. Breathe a little, okay?"

Melissa looked up into his eyes and felt moisture run down her temples. He brushed the few tears away and smiled reassuringly at her.

Could she take any more from them? She looked down to Trent and met his gaze. He trailed his fingers up and down her thighs, but he remained silent. Patiently waiting.

Spoon. The word was there on the tip of her tongue. She'd been loved so much tonight. She imagined most women didn't get fucked like this in their whole life. Did she take what they'd given her and let that be it?

Earlier they'd told her that if she said the word, they'd stop. Everything. Forever. Tomorrow would be another day and tonight would be a one-time memory.

Even now, their touches were full of care and pleasure. They hadn't hurt her outright, and even though she still burned inside and out and wasn't sure if she could take any more, she didn't want their affair to end already. They'd spoken to her as if this would be the beginning of more fun together. She'd dreamt—okay, maybe not of taking them on at the same time—but she'd had more than her share of fantasies involving these men.

"Sweetheart," Trent called, "either we're not doing something right with all the thinking you're doing, or you have something very important to tell us."

Damn him for hitting the nail on the head. How did he do that? He caught her eye. She licked her lips, noticing how the flare of heat wasn't as potent anymore.

"It fades," Trent explained, again seeming to know what she was going through. "I know what's on your mind, Melissa. I know we've overwhelmed you tonight. But we wouldn't have even begun to take you on this journey with us if we didn't think you could handle what we demand. If there's something you want to say, a word, think hard before making that decision."

She nodded then looked up at Mike, who continued to caress her face, and she knew her answer.

With a blooming smile and a hoarse voice, she said, "You guys are such pushovers if you think I want to give all this up."

Both men chuckled and the earlier worries she'd felt melted away. She didn't have to give them up. They would listen to her. They would give her time. With her hands still on each of them, she stroked Mike's hip, curling her palm around his cock. She threaded her fingers through Trent's hair and tugged him back up to her pussy. Words weren't needed as they each took their time resuming their pleasures with each other.

Her nerves burst with small shots of pleasure under their ministrations. The oils still warmed her various body parts, but she was either used to the sensations now or the feelings were fading, because the heat intensified her desires for a higher peak instead of wanting to burn her to a crisp.

Mike had allowed her hand to remain around his cock and had even let her take over the blow job and explore him, for which she was grateful. She peeked up at him and wondered at the picture she made, her mouth stuffed with him, her eyes hopeful. He smiled and brushed his hand through her short curls. Encouraging her, praising her.

She didn't want anything to stop, but as they had all evening, they dictated the order of events.

Trent picked his head up, his breath coming out in short gasps. "Damn, Melissa, you are fucking delicious. My cock is throbbing right now, wanting to be deep inside your pussy. Mike, I'd say it's time for the main course."

"Hell yes," Mike answered with a whisper.

Chapter Six

Melissa had no idea what was coming next, but she smiled to see their flurry of activity and the way their naked bodies moved and flexed around her.

First, Trent tugged the pillows out from under her and tossed them to the side. Mike pulled her over while Trent made himself comfortable in the spot where Melissa had lain. Mike tossed over a condom and each man spent a few seconds encasing their cocks in protection. Her eyes darted from one man to the other. She desperately wanted a camera, or for them to move at half speed. Their bodies, their actions, hell, just being here was sexier than anything, and she wanted to capture the moment forever.

Wrapping his hand around his cock, Trent pumped it a couple of times before calling her over to join him. She rose to her knees and came closer. With a jerk, he yanked her down over his massive chest, making her gasp at the contact.

"Straddle me," he ordered, and she did so clumsily. He was so freaking big she felt stretched just trying to place her knees on each side of his hips.

"What do you want me to do?" Melissa asked, wondering if she should try to work his erection inside her.

"You're doing exactly what we need you to do, sweetheart. Mike, it's in the left drawer."

She glanced over to see Mike rummaging through Trent's nightstand. Now what was up with that? Before she could find out, Trent slipped a hand around her head and brought her down for a bone-melting kiss.

Aahhh. She sighed into his mouth, loving the way he took and demanded from her. She loved how, when she met each touch of his tongue, he wanted more. She thrilled with the sensation, like she was progressing. Every time she could match him, he changed the rules, letting her learn and catch up. Then he'd move her head or nip at her lips and swirl his tongue around hers, every time showing her something new and exciting.

She held him back as tightly as he held her and her blood heated from the inside out. She'd never had any man touch her, hold her, kiss her, love her like these two did. She wasn't just lucky. She was meant for them, and they for her.

So lost in Trent's kisses, Melissa didn't pay too much attention to Mike at first. She knew he was there behind her. He caressed her ass and played with her pussy and even her rear entrance. She pushed back against him, craving his touch. When he slapped her bottom, she jumped, but returned to her position, as if asking for more.

His earlier spankings had shocked her at first, but after the initial surprise, she'd been almost embarrassed by how much the sharp stings had turned her on. Even now, as he struck her in a rhythmic pattern, she moaned with pleasure.

Cool liquid ran down the crack of her ass and she welcomed the icy feel after the burning torture Trent had put her through. When Mike focused on her puckered hole, she felt pretty sure she knew what was coming.

"Trent, need your help a minute."

She heard Mike's voice as though through a tunnel. When Trent nipped her lips and pulled back, she lay her head down on his chest and tried to catch her breath, which was hard now that Mike kept pushing her nerves higher.

Mike spoke to Trent first. "Grab that over there for me, would you? Thanks. Melissa, turn your head to me." He'd pressed his body against hers and his cock felt overly huge nestled in the crack of her ass. She looked over her shoulder, then laughed. He held out a chocolate chip cookie.

"You're wanting to feed me? Now?"

"No, baby." There went his wicked grin again. "You did a very bad thing in bringing this kind of food into our kitchen. You know that, right?"

Uh-oh. "Um, yes," she answered carefully.

"You want cookies, you let us know. We'll make them for you. Hell, from now on we'll be sure to keep fresh batches available. That, or you keep this store-bought, preservative-filled, substituted-ingredient crap in your own cabinets. Am I clear?"

She swallowed, not liking the firm tone and hard stare. But she understood. She'd known even before now, it just sucked that she'd been caught. "Perfectly," she answered honestly.

"Good. Now, because you broke the rules—and we all know you knew better, here's what's going to happen. Trent and I are going to fuck you at the same time. He'll screw your pussy while I take your ass."

Melissa had figured that was what would happen, but hearing the coarse words, the blunt language and the definitive way he spoke made her flush from head to toe. But she couldn't concentrate on her body yet, Mike still demanded her attention.

"You are to hold this cookie between your teeth while we take you. We're going to go nice and easy and take our time. If you bite the cookie, we take you hard and fast. If the cookie falls, we take you hard and fast. You will gently hold this thing, with your teeth, until I tell you that you can let go. Any questions?"

She stared at him in disbelief. "You're kidding, right?"

He sniffed the hard cookie, wrinkled his nose and shook his head. "No. Serious. Now open up."

She glared at him, but opened her mouth as he wanted. He pushed the cookie between her teeth until the offending dessert pressed halfway in.

"Bite gently. Good girl, just like that. Remember, don't let it fall, and don't bite it off." He smiled and pushed her head away from him. She looked down at Trent, whose eyes laughed back at her, and she glared at him for good measure.

This time, when Mike played with her bottom, everything within her responded, as if her body knew and wanted the dangerous excitement to come.

The cookie tasted sweet on her tongue, if not a little hard. She wanted to lick at the chocolate, but knew that if she did, she'd probably want more, then the cookie would fall and that'd be all she wrote. She squeezed her eyes shut.

Trent ran his hands over her shoulders and back, reaching down to her ass and pulling her cheeks apart for Mike. More cold liquid poured down her ass and this time Mike succeeded in pushing a large finger into her backside. Sure and steady, he didn't stop, even though her muscles protested. Melissa whimpered at the strange intrusion and tilted her head back, hating that they'd made her just about immobile.

When Mike pushed a second finger inside her, her ass clenched down and she shook her head. *Too much. Too much.* Her refusal to let him in earned her a hard slap on her bottom. She cried out around the cookie, but blinked hard in amazement because when her ass settled his second finger was able to slide right in along the first.

Trent rotated his hips, making his cock rub over her pussy, and the added play relaxed her muscles even further. She closed her eyes, thinking this wouldn't be so bad. The sensations building in her were new and she wanted to chase after them to see where they would take her.

His fingers left her ass, but no sooner could she relax than the broad head of his penis was pushing through her tight ring of muscles. She didn't want him in her, but at the same time, she did. She groaned, the action tightening her jaw, and she felt the hard press of the cookie against her teeth. *Shit.* She'd better stop thinking about what Mike was doing and focus to keeping the cookie in one piece.

True to his word, Mike worked himself into her ass in small increments. He'd push, stop, run his hands over her back and hips, telling her with words and actions how tight she felt, how great she was taking him, how he loved how her back dipped or the flare of her hips or the way he'd made her ass such a pretty pink colour. Trent did his part, kissing her neck and shoulders, mixing with Mike's hands on her body, and always rubbing that delicious cock over her engorged clit.

Her ass burned and her virgin muscles fought his entry, but soon he'd seated himself fully. With a final shove, his groin bumped her ass. Mike let out a long, low groan, as if he'd just run a marathon. Melissa let her throat work to match him, knowing the feeling was mutual.

She wanted to talk, to lick her lips, to eat the damn chocolate morsels teasing her tongue, but according to what Mike had said, they were only halfway done.

Now that Mike was tucked snugly into her backside, he lifted her hips, causing his cock to move and slide inside her, while Trent reached down, set his crown to her entrance and pushed hard yet steadily to insinuate himself into her pussy.

"Oh, God," Melissa muttered around the cookie between her teeth. Words were forcing themselves from her throat whether they had meaning or not. She wanted to rest her head on Trent's shoulder, but she was afraid she'd bump and break the cookie. As Trent worked his cock in, a lot faster than Mike had pushed into her ass, the feeling of being stuffed took on an entirely new meaning. Every nerve ending went taut and her body battled to figure out if these sensations were pleasure or pain.

She closed her eyes and breathed hard through her nose, doing her best not to scream and grit her teeth.

"Fuck, yeah," Mike said from behind her. He stroked her hair, turning her so she could see him over her shoulder. Sweat beaded up on her brow and her nostrils flared. *What now?*

"I am so proud of you, Melissa." He touched the cookie. "You can let go, unless you want to try to eat it."

She opened her mouth and let it fall into his hand. Pain shot through her jaw and she took a few seconds to work it open and shut, then in circles, until the muscles there began to relax. She laid her head on Trent's chest as they allowed her these moments to get used to them. No words were said, but Mike was the first to move. He slid back, the drag of his cock inside her making her tense. When he shifted and pushed back in, Trent eased away. Slow at first, then gaining speed as her body eased around their actions, the men worked in tandem, one sliding out while the other thrust in. Back and forth, as if they were taking turns in their efforts to please her, they became the tools to stir her body to life.

She reached down and trailed her nails over Mike's hips. The flex of muscles as he worked himself in and out of her rippled under her fingers. She dropped her arms and touched Trent, loving how both surrounded her.

Melissa had thought her orgasm would build slowly, especially with as many times as she'd already come tonight, but her body had different plans. One minute Melissa was all about touching her men and enjoying the new feelings they were providing her, and the next minute, she was thrashing between them. Their cocks stirred her inner nerves to life, as if they'd shot pure adrenaline into her system. She grabbed onto Trent, onto the bedsheets, onto anything her fingers could claw around. Her moans came louder and turned into fierce cries, begging them for more, for release.

How long can they keep this up? she wondered frantically. She wanted to laugh and shout, but the signal became tangled somewhere between her brain and her tongue. Incoherent words, phrases, sounds, were her way to let them know how much she loved every thrust and pull.

When her orgasm hit, she lost track of everything. Shot up in a spiral dance, Melissa zipped through the universe and never wanted to come back down. Trent and Mike each followed with their releases, and the pulsing cocks nestled deep inside her set off a ricochet effect of pleasure heaped upon pleasure.

And true to their earlier word, when Melissa's body exhausted itself completely, she laid her head on Trent's shoulder and drifted off with a heavy, satisfied sigh.

* * * *

Melissa roused when the men tugged her up and into the large shower. They washed her head to toe and everywhere in between, then carried her back to Trent's bed and snuggled her close between them.

"Umm," she murmured, "I don't think I've ever felt so amazing."

Trent's broad chest heated up Melissa's back, and Mike's easy breaths stirred the bangs around her face. They ran their hands softly over her body, keeping her nerves at a simmer.

"Thank you, guys," she said sleepily. "I've never had a better night. I can't wait to sleep, sleep, sleep."

"Oh, you can't go to sleep yet, baby," Mike corrected. "You haven't had dessert yet."

She frowned. "I'm too full for dessert."

"Too bad," Trent said from behind, giving her ear a nip. "We want our sweet ending, and no five-course meal is complete without one."

She huffed, but otherwise didn't respond. At this point, she wanted to say to hell with it, why not, but thought her flippant answer might set them off with another demand. This time, she was too exhausted to even contemplate fulfilling anyone's orders.

She dozed as they kissed their way down her body—Trent along her back and Mike along her front. When they got to her legs, one of them lifted her top leg and held it high in the air. Good thing, because her body was so lax it'd probably fall on one of their heads.

Wait. What were their heads doing down there?

"Ah, ahh, ahhh," she mustered the energy to cry out when they swiped their tongues over her exposed flesh. Mike slicked his over her pussy and clit, playing with her softly and gently. Trent circled her ass and he used the tip to flick at her hole.

A part of her wanted to push them away, but their taking of her this time was sweet and easy. Light. Tender. They didn't hurry or press. There were no requests for more. Simply gentle lapping and soft sucking.

Melissa sighed and sank farther into the mattress, her body now needing what the men were doling out. And this time, when her orgasm came, it swept through her body like smooth cream. Heavy, sated and delightful. Her body undulated softly through the passing of the pleasure, and when she drifted back down, Trent and Mike took their time easing away from her, as if they knew not to interrupt the roll.

She smiled as Trent and Mike returned in their spots, surrounding her.

"I love you two," Melissa murmured on a whisper. Their returning answers of the same topped off her night, as she slipped into sleep.

SUBTERFUDGE

Normandie Alleman

Dedication

To My Loving Husband.

With special thanks to my father—who really knows how to mess up a pie.

Chapter One

Ashley snuggled down under the lofty comforter. Sunlight floated in lazily through the bedroom window, the yellow light blending with the cream-coloured walls of the old Victorian tenement. Lounging around on Sunday mornings, curled up in her Egyptian cotton bed sheets, was when she felt the most cosy and secure.

She and Roger shared the newspaper—he read the business and sports pages, while she perused the comics and the lifestyle section.

Ashley sipped her coffee daintily. She pretended to be reading an article about the latest colour trends, but took a sly peek over the top of the paper to observe the man she loved. He sat next to her, reading. That broad, muscular chest, those deep blue eyes...he was everything she could want in a man. Watching him caused her heart to skip a beat.

But lately, Roger had been acting a bit off. *What is with him? He seems restless. Wonder what it is...*

Roger's coffee mug made a clinking noise when he set it on the bedside table. "Darling," Roger said, looking up from his newspaper, "I'd like you to learn to cook."

"Cook? Me?" She arched an eyebrow in his general direction without completely turning her head.

Out of the corner of her eye she saw Roger give her that benevolent, indulgent grin she loved so much. The one that told her he adored her. She softened.

"Yes, you know? Cook. Prepare food," he teased, running his hand through her hair, mussing it up. He winked at her. It made her insides go all mushy, and she felt a tingle of delight between her legs.

Ashley hesitated, but only for a moment. "All right." She had never tried cooking before. This was unchartered territory for her. She hated to admit it, but she felt uncomfortable with something so foreign to her. What if she was a flop?

But a sub's job was to make her Master happy. To comply with his requests, to serve him. So she agreed. *Anyway, lots of women do it. How complicated can it be?*

In her everyday life, Ashley was a professional equipped with all the assertiveness that required. She could stand toe to toe with anyone in business, or in any sort of dealings for that matter.

But at home, behind closed doors, Ashley had no greater desire than to please her man. In her relationship, she had chosen to be submissive to him. She needed a take-charge man in the bedroom, one who could dominate her and make all her fantasies come true.

Two years ago, some friends had introduced her to Roger. At first Ashley had thought he might be too buttoned up for her. The serious investment banker had come across as too staid for her free-spirited, artistic nature. But behind closed doors, Roger surprised her. He wasn't a bit boring, and they'd turned out to be a great match.

He became her Dominant in a short time. He gave his heart to her completely, and he cherished her. In return, she gave him the gift of her submission. Ashley prided herself on how she took care of Roger and met his needs. She had never trusted anyone the way she trusted Roger. He was a better man than she had ever dreamt she could have, and she was thankful for him every day.

They'd moved in together a year ago, settling into a quaint, if unconventional domesticated existence. With some whips and handcuffs thrown in for good measure.

Their life together was so...complete. *Why bring this up now?* It caught her off guard. *I thought he was happy with the take-out and frozen dinners.*

"How do I learn?" She furrowed her brow. "To cook, I mean."

Roger handed her an ad he'd torn out of the newspaper. 'Culinary Class' was printed at the top in large letters. There were some dates, times and a phone number along the bottom.

"I'll call and sign you up. Looks like it starts tomorrow. I'll see if I can secure you a spot."

Ashley's heart sank. *Tomorrow?* She had a full day planned with things *she* needed to do Monday. She worked for herself, basically, as a freelance graphic design artist. Sure, her schedule was flexible, but if she had to go to a cooking class the next day, she'd have to put off her most high-maintenance client.

She realised she was frowning and forced herself to brighten. "I'll call, don't you worry about it," she said. She took the scrap of paper. *I'll handle the client, do all that other stuff on Tuesday.* After *I learn to cook.*

"That's my good girl." He reached over and stroked her face.

He kissed her and the rest of the world melted away. The scent of his aftershave pierced her senses and she was rocked with an ardent desire to have him inside her.

"It would mean so much to me for you to make meals for us. It's a great way for a woman to show her man she loves him." His tone was low, sexy.

"They say the way to a man's heart is through his stomach." She giggled.

"There are other ways." He laughed and pressed her hand to his erection.

She chortled and squeezed his appendage gently.

Roger slowly peeled back the designer camisole and tap pants she slept in, kissing every inch of her bare skin as it was revealed. She sighed—his lips were magic, invigorating her senses.

"Right now I want to show *you* how much I care for you," he told her.

Ashley was naked now except for her blue silk and white lace panties. Roger set the newspaper aside and laid her flat across their bed.

After a moment of rifling through her bureau, he drew out some of her softest silk scarves. The divine feeling of the sumptuous fabrics running over her body invigorated her skin. Gliding the silky-smooth material over her supple curves, he teased her to arousal. Then, he bound her wrists and ankles to the four posts of the bed. Her taut limbs stretched and exposed her, confining her movement.

"What are you going to do to me?" she panted.

"You should know better than to ask questions, my dear. I like to keep you guessing." His eyes glistened in the sunlight. "I know what you *need*. Don't I?"

"Y-y-yes, Sir." Ashley had known he wouldn't give her the satisfaction of an answer. But she couldn't help but ask. When he tied her up, her heart got all poundy, she got anxious.

What would happen next? She had no control over his actions, and she couldn't move her own body. It was as maddening as it was arousing.

After excusing himself for a minute, he returned with an implement from the kitchen.

"Do you know what this is?" he asked.

"A spatula?" She wriggled in her restraints.

"That's right." His tone was matter-of-fact. "Something you should become familiar with now that you will be spending more time in the kitchen."

She closed her eyes. It was easier that way.

The first strike was on her lower leg. A light tap.

Then another. And another.

The taps grew more firm and they travelled up her leg.

The delicious smack of the spatula warmed her thighs. It smarted, but she liked it. After the initial blow, the way her skin throbbed as it recovered was delicious. A moan escaped her lips.

"I told you I know what's good for you."

He ran his fingers up her other leg and traced the edge of her panties. She lifted her hips to meet him, encouraging his touch. She thought she'd go mad with desire.

"What an insatiable little cunt you have. I shall have to punish you for that."

"No, please no, Sir!" Her voice shrilled.

The spatula slammed down on her panty-clad pussy. *Ouch!*

"No!"

"No, what?" he asked, a smirk in his voice.

"Please, no, Sir."

"I don't believe that hurts, darling."

He stopped anyway. Roger respected her limits. He struck her other leg with the spatula. Her flesh stung, the blood rushed to the surface. Nerve endings came alive.

Ashley squealed.

"You've always been such a noisy sub."

He swatted her with one hand while he sneaked his other hand under her panties and stroked her stunned pussy lips. She gyrated to greet his attentions with her hips, her pussy dripping wet. She wanted him. Roger was right, she had a voracious appetite, and she ached for a release.

Climbing onto the bed next to her, Roger cradled her head to his chest. "Dearest Ashley. You are such a good girl."

He untied her feet. Grateful for her newfound freedom, she wrapped her legs around his waist as he entered her. Rocking into her body, back and forth in a sensuous motion, he bent his head and caught a nipple between his lips. He worked it with his tongue and teeth, and she whimpered until her lust became a raging fire.

When she could hold back no longer, she came all over his cock, her walls pulsing and grasping snugly around him. She shuddered and collapsed, spent.

Roger lifted her hips and thrust deeper. He clasped both hands underneath her ass, holding her as he pulsed hard and fast into her. Ashley clasped her ankles together behind his back and held on tightly as he ravaged her juicy pussy.

Roger pushed one final time before he collapsed on top of her.

"Oh, Sir," she said, "that was intense." She nibbled on his ear and held him close.

"Yes, it was," he agreed. His mouth found hers, both of them hungry to seal the pact their bodies had just made.

Chapter Two

The next morning Ashley asked Roger about his favourite foods. If she was going to do this, she meant to start with a bang right out of the gate.

"Turkey," he said. "The kind people eat at Thanksgiving."

Ahhh. A large hen, not some sliced up meat from the deli.

"No problem," she assured him, and scooted him out of the door, offering him a peck on the lips as he said goodbye.

After closing the door, Ashley sat down at the kitchen island with a cup of coffee to contemplate her next move. When it came to the gastronomic arts, she knew most girls inherited their skills from family members. Ashley's mother had been first-rate in the kitchen. But she had never taught Ashley anything, and she had never thought to ask her mother about how to prepare a meal.

Seems kinda stupid now. Wish I'd taken advantage of that time when I had it. She propped her chin up with one elbow. But her mother had catered to Ashley and her father. It had been her way. Then she had died in her late forties and Ashley's father had introduced her to the world of frozen food and take-out she knew today.

She picked up the phone and dialled the number for Roger's class.

The woman on the other end of the line answered in an ancient, raspy voice. She seemed to have a hard time understanding Ashley and kept asking her to speak up until Ashley was practically screaming into the phone. Not a good sign.

The class was being held at the stodgy old lady's house. Hmm. She didn't relish being trapped in a stranger's house all day. Creepy. She'd thought the class would be held at a community centre or someplace like that.

Plus, what if the old lady had cats? Ashley was terribly allergic.

She sneezed just thinking about it.

Okay, not taking the class. Crumbling up the ad, Ashley tossed it in the wastebasket.

Then she decided to do what anyone of her generation would do—she turned on her Wi-Fi.

She watched Internet videos on cooking turkeys until she almost fell asleep. When the last online video came to an end, Ashley yawned and snapped the laptop closed. It didn't look that tricky. Basically, all she had to do was throw the turkey into a roasting pan and pop it into the oven for a few hours. She made a phone call to her client, emailed her some files then headed off to the store.

Hours later, Ashley stood in the kitchen staring at the turkey and all her groceries.

To make life easier, she had also bought refrigerated mashed potatoes. A lady at the grocery store had told her nobody would be able to tell the difference between those and the kind made from scratch. She had purchased canned vegetables, frozen rolls and a pre-made sweet potato casserole.

Was she cheating? Well, maybe a little, but Rome wasn't built in a day…the turkey was already going to be a monumental task.

It was time to tackle the bird. Ashley put it in the sink and began cutting the wrapper off with scissors. Copious amounts of pink juices flowed everywhere. "Eeeeeeewwwwwww!" Ashley shrieked and jumped back, dropping the turkey in the sink.

Gathering herself, she approached the poultry again. She picked it up and finished removing the rest of the wrapper. Then she remembered from the videos that she was supposed to remove the neck and some other parts from inside the bird. *Ugh. Okay, here goes.* Sticking her hand down into the neck area of the bird, she found there was something down in there.

She grabbed hold and tugged. It didn't want to budge.

Huh.

She tried again.

Nothing.

Hmm. She considered the matter.

Maybe if I fill the cavity with hot water like when you have a ring that's stuck on your finger…

She turned the water on. While it was heating up, she washed her hands and put away the rest of the groceries.

After the warm water had run over the turkey for several minutes, Ashley yanked on the slimy internal packet one last time, and it finally gave way. *Hooray! Goodbye neck.*

She turned the bird over and winced as she removed another large package from the other end. Who knew what was in that? She didn't want to. Something about giblets, but she was skipping that part. So far, the whole thing was disgusting.

She rinsed, then salted and peppered the bird before placing it into the roasting pan. She shoved an onion and some celery into the open cavity then placed pats of butter onto the breast and onto the legs. Then she set it into the oven at three-fifty and made a note of the time as per the instructions from the video she had seen.

Several hours later, the apartment smelt divine, the aroma of a homemade meal wafting through the air giving the apartment a cosy feel that made Ashley beam with pride. It should be time to remove the turkey from the oven. Having forgotten to buy oven mitts, Ashley ran around searching for towels to use.

She prepared the other dishes and waited impatiently for Roger to come home. How exciting that he was going to try her dinner, the first one she had ever made.

While she waited, she tried to distract herself with magazines and television, but the twenty minutes until he arrived home seemed like two hours. When she finally heard his key in the lock, Ashley jumped up to greet him at the door.

"It smells delicious in here!" Roger's enthusiasm washed over her.

"Thank you, Sir," she said, basking in his praise.

"You made a turkey?"

Her lips widened from one ear to the other. "I sure did."

"Is it ready to carve?"

"Yes, Sir. It's all ready. I've been waiting for you."

"How wonderful." He tucked a stray strand of her hair back behind her ear. "Let me wash up and I'll do that."

A few minutes later, Roger was in the kitchen with a carving knife and a huge fork cutting up the meat. Ashley fixed them some drinks.

"Ashley, dear. Come here."

She joined him at his side with their cocktails.

"Feel this meat."

"What?"

"Put your finger here. Inside the turkey." He pointed to the middle of the bird where he had made the incision with the carving knife.

Confused, Ashley did as she was told.

To her horror, the meat was ice cold.

"I-I don't understand."

"It's not cooked. It will have to go back in the oven." He sighed and put the turkey back into the roasting pan. "Probably for another hour at least."

"But then everything else will get cold!" Ashley wailed.

Roger frowned, his forehead wrinkled. "Well, we'll keep it warm in the oven…"

He began to put the other dishes into the bottom of the double oven on a lower temperature. He shot her a sidelong glance.

"You didn't check to see if it was done?"

"Well, I thought it was…I pulled it out when it said it would be done!" She was incredulous.

"When *what* said it would be done?"

Was he patronising her now? Sheepishly, she answered, "The Internet."

"The Internet? Really?"

With a grimace, she nodded.

"What happened to the class?"

"Oh, um, I think that lady has cats, and it's at her house. Sir, you know how allergic I am. I couldn't *possibly* have gone there." She gave him her most pitiful look, and batted her big brown eyes at him, hoping to stay out of trouble.

"Well, regardless of the cats and not taking the class, darling, you have to check the meat *yourself.* You can't just read instructions or listen to the Internet. Do you understand?"

She felt the heat rise on her face. "Yes, Sir."

"Go kneel on your blocks for ten minutes."

Her shoulders drooped. *Not the blocks!* But she nodded and did as she'd been told.

One of the punishments she hated the most was the blocks. They were children's 'ABC' blocks, with a letter from the alphabet embossed on each individual block. She set them out, all in a square then knelt on top of them. Her weight made it uncomfortable. Not exactly painful, but certainly it was something she didn't like to do.

It was the kind of punishment that worked well as a correction, and Roger knew it. He often sat in the same room watching television or reading where he could observe her on the blocks. He had a touch of a sadistic side to him, just a touch. Real pain wasn't a big part of their play, but he got his needs met in other ways.

While she knelt on the blocks, Ashley's mind wandered to how they had got to this point in their relationship. Every couple had to find their way, whether it was a Master/sub type relationship or a 'regular' one. Heck, all relationships are tough. Just living with another person had compromises you had to work through.

Once, at the beginning of their relationship, Roger had tried to give her a punishment and she had set her foot down. Okay, that was putting it mildly. She'd gone *ballistic* on him. She bit her lip to keep herself from laughing thinking about it.

Ashley had been up for a big job and she hadn't got it. In hindsight, she probably hadn't been aggressive enough, hadn't pulled out all the stops. She might have got the assignment if she'd been bolder about her interest. When she'd told Roger about it, he'd wanted to punish her for not getting the job!

Ashley had been outraged, her feelings had been hurt. She'd cried, ranted and raved at him for his insensitivity. Roger had been stupefied. He hadn't understood. In his mind, a Master was always supposed to punish or correct his sub when she made mistakes. It had taken some educating on Ashley's part to help him understand that sometimes a sub needs love and understanding more than discipline.

When Roger had come around, he'd felt like a perfect ass. As the blocks' raised areas began to dig into her flesh, she grimaced. *Men need training, even when they are your Master. Roger does love me. And he knows what is best for me. But there are times...* Now was not one of them. Even though she didn't like the blocks, she knew they would help her remember to check the meat next time.

Yes, her friends would have thought she was nuts to submit to kneeling on blocks, but to Ashley, submitting to her Master's punishments was sexy. And in truth, she herself was wildly undisciplined. Having him discipline her occasionally worked for her.

After the ten minutes were up, Roger called her to him. He beckoned her to sit in his lap. Ashley curled into him and wrapped her arms around his neck.

"I'm sorry I wasn't more careful with the food. It won't happen again, Sir."

"I know you are. Everyone makes mistakes, love. It's okay." He kissed her. Nothing felt better than when they came back together. She knew that her punishments were a bit of a game. He didn't mean her any harm.

Holding each other close and snuggling, they made out like teenagers on the couch until the turkey was ready — the second time.

Roger helped Ashley get all the food out of the oven. He carved the turkey, and this time it was too dry. *Gosh, I can't catch a break! Not cooked enough, then cooked too much*, Ashley thought. But they heaped their plates high and ate more than their fill that evening anyway.

When they crawled into bed that night, they were so stuffed they fell sound asleep right away, their arms around each other, legs intertwined.

Chapter Three

Ashley strolled down the baking aisle at the grocery store. She reached for the box of brownies with the best picture on the front.

Even though her first attempt at cooking had been a horrific bust, she was not going down without a fight. Ashley wanted to create something yummy today. She was determined.

Reading the back of the box, she thought, *Brownies don't look that complicated.* She looked at the list of ingredients and added everything from it to her cart.

On the way home, Ashley checked a voice message Roger had left saying he would be home late. *Good, plenty of time to bake the brownies.*

At home, Ashley set the groceries out on the counter then cleaned up. She read the box's instructions, and turned on the oven to preheat. After finding a bowl and a big spoon, she got to work mixing the ingredients. Only a few bits of eggshell fell into the batter. *Pretty sure I fished out most of them.*

She coated the pan with cooking spray.

I'm starting to feel like a real chef! She grinned.

After pouring the batter into the pan, she popped it in the oven. *I'm making brownies. All by myself.* She bopped around the kitchen, humming as she danced about.

While the brownies baked, Ashley went into the bedroom to check her emails.

Click, click went the mouse. She cleared spam from her inbox. The apartment filled with the powerful aroma of chocolate. Ashley smiled to herself. When Roger came home he would be so proud of her. He loved sweets. He would be so thrilled that she was taking care of his gastronomical needs, he would take her into his arms, kiss her and want to spend the entire evening pleasuring her. Her mind wandered.

Wait! What is that smell*?*

Her nostrils were assaulted by a crisp, burning odour.

Burning… Oh no!

What about the timer? Oh crap! She'd forgotten to set a timer!

Ashley sprinted to the kitchen and threw open the oven door. Damn! Those brownies were way too dark for their own good.

She had to get them out. Fast.

She touched the pan with her fingers. *Y-y-ouch!*

Plunging her scalded finger into her mouth, she tried to think.

Oh, double crap! She had forgotten to buy oven mitts again today. *Ugh! I am so stupid. Where are the towels I used last night? Think, think, think.*

She ran around until she found them.

With the towels wrapped around her hands, she reached in and grabbed the pan of scorched brownies then set them down. The hot pan sizzled and hissed at her as it hit the sink's wet surface.

"Damn!" Tears of frustration rolled down her cheeks.

She grabbed some air freshener out of the pantry. *Spppptttt! Sppppptttt! Sppppptttttt!* The smell of cinnamon apple over burnt chocolate left an odd bouquet in her wake. Setting down the aerosol can, Ashley wiped her eyes. She quickly snatched her coat and purse off the couch, and headed out of the door.

* * * *

An hour later, Ashley fumbled with the key to her mailbox in the basement of the apartment building. She balanced a box from the bakery with one hand as she attempted to retrieve her mail with the other.

"Hey, girl! What are you up to?" The voice belonged to her eternally effervescent neighbour, Lance.

"Not much. Just picking up my mail…" She tucked a stack of envelopes and catalogues under her left arm, clutching the newly purchased baked goods in her right.

"What's in the box?" Lance pointed to it, eyebrows raised.

"Oh, brownies. Roger wants me to learn to cook, and today I burnt some brownies. So I bought these…hoping he won't know the difference." She shrugged.

"Is *that* what I smelt earlier?"

She nodded grimly.

"How did you do that?"

A sense of gloom crept into her bones. "I don't know. I guess I forgot about them."

"Don't you have a timer?"

"Yeah, I do. Guess I didn't hear it or something. I got busy in the other room and the next thing I knew I smelt something awful."

Lance shook his head. "You poor thing. Maybe you should try something in a slow cooker. Those things are almost fool proof."

"That's a good idea, thanks." She smiled at him.

"You're welcome. And let me know if you need help. I know my way around the kitchen."

Lance was an apprentice chef at one of the city's most touted restaurants. Ashley made a mental note to remember that Lance might be a good resource for her. She waved to him as she walked up the stairs.

Back in the apartment, Ashley arranged the store-bought brownies on a plate and covered them with plastic wrap to keep them fresh. She broke down the telltale bakery box and hid it at the bottom of the kitchen trashcan.

Exhausted, she put on her nightgown and crawled into bed. After reading only a few pages of the latest bestseller, she fell asleep.

"Mmm." Hands on her. A warm body clutched hers, moulding itself to her, rousing Ashley from her slumber.

Opening her eyes, she realised it was still dark. It must be night time.

As consciousness flooded back, she became aware of Roger's hard body pressed up against hers. *Nice.*

She scooched her ass backwards into him, feeling his erection lodged up next to her.

"I'm sorry to wake you, baby. But you were just too tempting." His lips touched her neck, nibbling, kissing the spot she loved the most.

"Are you kidding?" she murmured. "You can wake me up like this anytime."

He reached his arm around her body and hiked up her nightgown. Searching between her legs he found her wet little cunt and inserted his fingers deep inside her aching hole.

"Mmm. You're ready for me."

"Always."

He pressed his thumb into her clit and fucked her with his fingers. He caressed her sweet, swollen bud with his thumb. She groaned, arching her pelvis towards his hand, meeting him stroke for stroke.

"Sir! You have the most amazing hands."

He chuckled softly.

She held her breath and focused on her orgasm. Her muscles clamped down around his fingers and she shuddered all over. When he loved on her, everything was right with the world.

"Are you ready for a good fucking now?" He growled.

She nodded, then realised he couldn't see her in the dark. Plus, a sub needed to answer her Master properly. "Yes, Sir. I would like a good fucking, please." Sometimes passion made her forget the rules.

Lying on her belly, she inched her nightgown up all the way above her breasts and lifted her ass in the air. An invitation.

"Oh my," he gasped. "You are a tempting little sub, aren't you?"

She giggled. "All for you, Sir."

He entered her slowly, and it was her turn to gasp. Anticipation made her heart race and his teasing aroused her all the more. She wanted him to hurry and fill her.

Roger held her hips in his hands as he crushed into her. She rose up onto her elbows so that her nipples scraped the bed sheets with every thrust. Each trip, more pleasurable than the last, brought her closer to that highest peak. She clutched the sheets tightly.

Loud cracking sounds echoed through the room as Roger slapped her bottom. The first strike surprised her. Ashley tensed her muscles, bracing for more spanks. As the blows became more rhythmic, she relaxed and let the pain wash over her.

He grabbed her hair up into a ponytail and pulled her head back. Wielding her locks as reins, he rode her as though he were breaking a wild mare. Aflame with a torrid lust, her body exhilarated at being the instrument of Roger's pleasure. When the slick thrusts of his hard cock pounded against her cervix, her heart thumped in unison, sending her mind into orbit. Giving up control and letting Roger enjoy her body and use it how he saw fit sent tight spasms of orgasm through her. Her cunt twitched as she came again, dripping her juices all over his cock.

Drops of sweat fell on her back. His breathing changed and she heard a catch in his throat when he stilled inside her. They both collapsed onto the bed. Ashley snuggled up under his arm and shifted her body against his.

"I love you," she said, catching her breath.

He sighed. "I love you, too. And by the way, those brownies were delicious."

"Oh? Thanks." She smiled to herself in the dark and hugged him close. A pang of guilt nudged at her gut, but she willed it away. *Score one for the subbie.* With that thought, she drifted off to sleep.

Chapter Four

With her laptop opened to Pinterest, enticing images screamed, *Pin me, pin me* from the screen. Ashley shook her head and tried not to get distracted from her mission. While sipping her coffee, a steamy picture of a hot couple caught her eye—a man with a chiselled physique bent over a doe-eyed beauty, his hand was wrapped in her long tresses, he was grabbing her and... *Oh my!* Ashley clicked 'like' so she could show the image to Roger later. She loved giving him ideas about what turned her on.

No more of that. She heaved a sigh. *I can't get sidetracked. Must focus.*

She typed the word 'crockpot' into the Pinterest search engine and pressed 'Enter'. Her reward was an endless page of recipes for slow cookers. All with images of scrumptious-looking meals.

After looking up half a dozen recipes, she decided on a pizza casserole. *Roger and I love pizza, and this looks easy.* The instructions said she basically had to throw a bunch of things into the crockpot and turn it on. Lance was right. This was the way to go.

In the late morning, Ashley ran some errands. She visited the dry cleaners to pick up Roger's suits and the local superstore where she bought all the ingredients she needed for her dish, as well as the invaluable crockpot.

Back at home, she pulled up the recipe on the computer then dumped the ingredients into the slow cooker. Pursing her lips together, she vowed, *No way I'm burning this.* Hands on her hips, she stared down the new appliance. Ashley set her phone to sound an alarm when the food was done, and took it with her into the bedroom.

Engrossed in her design work, she didn't hear Roger come in. All of a sudden, his warm hands were on her shoulders, massaging them gently. He bowed his head and whispered in her ear, "It smells like an Italian restaurant in here, my love. What are you making?" He left behind a trail of kisses on her neck before he stood and loosened his tie.

"Pizza casserole." She glowed. His compliments made her feel all warm and fuzzy inside.

"You made the meal, how about I serve us? Ready to eat? I'm starved."

His helpfulness was endearing. *I'm so lucky to have him.*

"Sure, that would be nice." Looking at the app on her phone, she said, "The timer says it's done."

Ashley joined Roger at the kitchen table. He poured them both a glass of merlot and heaped their plates with the contents from the slow cooker.

"Ashley, I appreciate the effort you're making." He smiled at her.

Ashley returned his smile as she lifted a forkful into her mouth. Hmm. Still hot and the flavour was delightful, full of tomato, basil and garlic. She chewed and swallowed. Pride filled her head with grand visions of her preparing delectable dishes, friends and relatives fawning all over her...

Her thoughts were interrupted by Roger sputtering. His face screwed up and his jaw made crunching noises.

Oh dear. She hadn't accidentally poisoned him with her cooking, had she?

Roger's eyes grew large. He reached for his glass and took a big gulp of his wine.

"What is it? Are you okay?" Ashley asked, alarmed.

He cleared his throat before taking another swig of his drink. Once he'd regained his composure, he said, "The noodles. Try the noodles."

After that display she was afraid to. "Why? What's wrong with them?" She eyed him suspiciously.

"Just try them."

Knowing it was always better to do what her Master asked, Ashley tentatively took a small bite of mostly noodles. They crunched between her teeth.

Uh-oh. That is not *good.*

After she had finished her bite, she glanced nervously at him. "They're crunchy."

"Yes."

"I'm sorry. I'm not sure how that happened...I read the instructions. I did it all just like they said... I don't get it..."

Roger picked through his plate and continued eating. "It's good if you don't eat the noodles."

Mortified, Ashley took another bite.

They ate in silence for the next five minutes.

"Some of the noodles are cooked, you just have to find them," she offered feebly.

"I appreciate the effort, dear, but"—his eyes twinkled—"you may need to be punished for this little blunder."

Ashley's eyes widened. "A punishment? Not again!" Whenever he talked about reprimands, a part of her felt like a little girl again. Her gut churned and she furrowed her brow, worry filling her head. Her temperature rose, her fists balled in defiance. Another part of her, the grown-up woman inside her, became excited, and her nipples pebbled with arousal. The combination of emotions was heady, intoxicating.

Roger eyed her as an eagle spies his prey before swooping in for the attack. "You'll see when the time comes."

"Yes, Sir." Her stomach did a flip. That was the end of her appetite. "Think I'll do the dishes." She drained her wine glass and got up from the table. She took her plate into the kitchen and dumped her latest glop of failure down the garbage disposal.

She felt him before she heard him. Their bodies were so in tune with one another, she could sense him. He wrapped her up in his big, strong arms and held her close.

"Sir, I feel badly about dinner…" she began.

"Shhh!" He put a finger over her mouth. "Come over here." He walked her over to the refrigerator.

"Take off your clothes," he growled.

That mixture of fear and arousal raged through her body, but she removed every stitch of clothing as he'd asked.

"That's it. Now spread your legs for me."

Butterflies flitted in her stomach. A shiver ran down her spine.

Roger pinned her up against the refrigerator. He lifted her hands above her head and held her wrists together.

"Hmm, do I bind you or blindfold you?" He drummed his fingers on the side of the icebox indecisively.

She fidgeted.

"Hold still," he commanded.

"Yes, Sir."

The silky caress of his tie tightened over her wrists as he bound them together above her head.

He nibbled her ear, his lips moist, his breath scorching her tender flesh.

Pulling her hips backwards, he ordered her, "Stick your ass out."

Ashley did her best to obey. His hands grazed her curves as he worked his way from her shoulder to the curve of her hip with his lips. He knelt behind her.

"C'mon. Back that pussy up onto me, baby. I want to see you grind that ass up onto my face."

A combination of shock and pleasure swirled through her. She tilted her pelvis back and felt the delight of his kisses between her ass cheeks. The heat from his mouth was a luxurious change from her cold limbs resting against the fridge.

"Are you clean, baby?"

He meant her ass. Had she cleaned herself for him... "Yes, Sir." She had used an enema an hour or so before he came home. Roger had recently developed a penchant for ass play, and she tried to be prepared for it most of the time just in case.

"Such a good girl. Don't move a muscle, stay right here."

She heard him rummaging around in the kitchen drawers behind her. *Oh Lord, what is he going to do?*

"Ah, this is what I was looking for."

Curious what it was, Ashley turned her head to see. He held a wooden spoon.

"Ah, ah, ah. I said not to move, didn't I?" His voice was stern.

Ashley hung her head. "Yes, Sir."

"I'm going to have to paddle you." He slapped the spoon against the palm of his hand.

"Oh dear," she murmured.

A gentle tap to her naked buttocks. The spoon, smooth against her skin, made a muffled thwacking noise.

Another tap. This one harder, more jarring.

The third time was more of a swat than a tap. Her cheek smarted from the blow. She gritted her teeth.

"Now we're getting warmed up. Darling, how many smacks do you think you've earned tonight?"

"Ten," she answered dutifully. He usually liked to administer ten. She knew his habits by now.

"Ten it is. Please count, my love."

The spoon landed on her ass with a thud.

"Ten."

"Very Good."

Smack!

"Nine."

Smack!

"Eight."

Thwack! This blow landed on both cheeks making a slightly different noise. *Good. It's not as hard as the others.* Relief flushed through her.

"Seven." She'd almost forgotten to count. She tried to focus on her task.

Smack!

"Six." Beads of sweat formed on her forehead.

Swat!

"Five." Her bottom was tender now and she guessed it was quite pink by this point.

Smack!

"Four." Her voice was shrill.

Smack! His strikes now genuinely hurt. She tried to embrace the pain, to let herself go. But she couldn't forget to keep counting. That was the hard part...

"Three!"

"Almost done, my love," he said as he spanked her again.

"Two."

"Last one." He brought the spoon down hardest on the last lick.

"One!" She allowed her body to droop as she released the control she had been so carefully holding on to.

"You've been such a good girl." Roger slowly caressed her sore cheeks with his hands. He knelt behind her and kissed her swollen flesh. She felt a chilled sensation like that of an intimate whisper on a cold, windy day.

Her breathing slowly returned to normal, but her heart still raced. His proximity kept her aroused. She was curious what he had in store for her next. Never having been a very patient girl, she wantonly arched her back.

"You can't get enough, can you?" He chuckled. He glossed over her aching cheeks with his palms, snaking them around the outside of each of her legs then grabbed hold of the front of her thighs. "That's one of the things I love about you — your passion."

Wet warmth crept up her butt crack. *What is that? Oh my God, his tongue...* He held her tight up against the appliance, her hands bound, him controlling her legs.

She was powerless to stop his assault. Of course she *could*, but why would she? He felt magnificent.

Roger explored her nether regions with his mouth. She held perfectly still and savoured the moment. Waves of pleasure reverberated through her.

She felt her ass being spread apart.

There was a pause. She had no idea what he was going to do to her next. Would he insert something into her? Or…or what? It was as frightening as it was exciting. Her adrenaline was flowing now.

Cool breath blew on her anus. She trembled.

Then the warm touch of his tongue lapping around the entrance to her tiniest hole. Primitive sounds erupted from Ashley as he breached that puckered opening. Roger used his mouth to tease her. With his pointed tongue, he played around the outside of her wet opening occasionally entering her, fucking her with it. Driving her wild with desire.

"Please, Sir!" she finally shrieked.

"Please, what?" he asked innocently.

"Please fuck my ass."

He laughed as he stood. "I thought you'd never ask."

"Here, why don't you bend over the island?" He nipped her neck as his erection bore down against her backside, guiding her into position.

Wobbly on her feet, Ashley was so weak with desire that she appreciated his help. She turned her head and captured his lips in a kiss. Their tongues hungrily devoured one another.

The backwards kiss took her off balance. Ashley turned back around to catch herself, almost falling onto the island. She threw her bound arms over it, eagerly awaiting her fucking. "Okay, Sir, I'm ready," she said.

Roger hesitated as he stood back to look at her, admiration in his eyes. He grabbed some lube from the drawer nearby. "Darling, you look so beautiful with your pink ass, so eager for me."

She giggled. "I'm glad you think so, but be gentle, you know how I get nervous about this."

"I do."

Deftly, he worked one finger into her anus. She winced and tried to stay still, hoping the discomfort would ease. She focused on her breathing as he slowly moved it in and out.

Another finger entered her, then she felt a welcome slippery finger on her engorged clit. *Mmmm.* The pain she felt in her ass was off-set by the pleasure he gave her in the front. In fact, the combination was incredible.

If it hadn't been for the island, Ashley would have collapsed onto the floor. Grateful for the support, she melted onto its butcher's block surface.

She squirmed when he removed his fingers and entered her with his cock. *Remember to breathe. In through the nose...out through the mouth. Damn! The things I do for sex...*

She tensed up, went rigid again. Roger reacted to her signals and as he pushed into her quaking hole, he gradually reached around and massaged her tight little button of nerves, helping her to relax.

He leant down and kissed her shoulder. "I love you."

"I love you, too," she managed, her jaw loosening. She tried to focus on the good feelings and allowing her muscles to relax. It took some effort, but she was getting there.

Roger was the first man she had ever had anal sex with, and they had only done it a few times before.

Ashley was determined to get the hang of it, but it was taking some practice. Her butt was so damned tight!

Tonight she had been more turned on than ever by Roger eating her ass. And the way he was thrumming her clit took her mind off the discomfort for sure. In fact, it was amazing.

Of course she couldn't see, but it felt like he was already halfway inside her rear channel, and she was okay. He pumped faster than he had in the past, and it didn't hurt.

He took his hand off her clit and tweaked her left nipple. Pulled on it. A groan of ecstasy rose from her throat. Her arms thrashed as he pinched and worked the hard little bud with his thumb.

He penetrated her deeper, and a guttural noise sprang forth from Ashley.

"You okay?"

She nodded. "Maybe a little slower."

"Okay."

He slowed to a sensuous pace, and returned his attentions to that sensitive button. He rolled her little nub between his fingers, all the while burrowing his cock in her ass, rocking her at the right pace, taking her to a body-rippling place. The combination of having her very core stroked and her ass rammed was too much for Ashley to take. Her body convulsed, her muscular rings tightened around Roger's cock, her pelvis bucked and she shook from her chin to her toes.

Roger continued to pulse into her for another couple of minutes, until she heard the familiar catch in his throat, and he was still.

"My darling, I love you. What would I ever do without you?" he asked as he gathered her up in his arms.

She smiled. "I don't know, but never find out, okay?"

"Okay." He winked at her. "Let me untie my girl." He loosened then freed her arms from his expensive Armani tie, then tossed it to the side.

"You know, I am such a lucky man, to have a girl who will let me do all these things to her."

"Yes, you are." Ashley kissed him on the nose.

"And now one who's a budding chef," he teased.

Ashley felt a cloud pass over her face. "Yeah, that too."

Roger kissed her on the lips then walked over to retrieve his clothes.

Ashley chewed her bottom lip. Her cooking experiment tonight had been a disaster. Why was he so happy?

She didn't get it.

Well, she'd just have to get it right next time.

Chapter Five

Ashley had just sat down to her computer the next morning when the doorbell rang. Special delivery, and the package was addressed to her.

With scissors she opened the box, being careful not to cut into any of the contents. Her heart filled with joy when she pulled a precious, pink and chocolate-coloured polka dot apron out of the box.

A flirtatious little ruffle ran around the edges of the skirt, and the ties were brown and pink striped. *Wow, this is cute! And the fabric feels so good.* She pressed the sash to her cheek. Then she saw Roger's note.

Wear only this tonight.

Ashley blushed and hugged the new garment to her chest. *He is so good to me. Gives me so much attention. I need to make something special for him tonight. Something to make up for that debacle last night. I just can't have a repeat of that.*

She racked her brain. What could they have? Hmm.

Dinner usually involved so many different food groups, and she wasn't trusting that crazy crockpot again. Maybe she'd go back to dessert. She and Roger each had a sweet tooth. What did they love?

She remembered they had shared a heavenly French Silk pie on their first date. She'd try that. Women were always making pies on TV, it couldn't be that complicated.

Subsequent to finishing a few work tasks, Ashley found a recipe online and printed it out. She made a list then went to the market to purchase everything she needed for the pie. She realised she was humming while she unloaded the groceries. *Maybe I have a domestic side after all.*

First, she had to make the crust. Ashley, the proud new owner of a rolling pin, got her surface prepped and pulled out the pastry sheets the recipe called for. They were frozen solid. The recipe said for them to sit out for a few minutes to thaw.

Aha! This is usually the time I would go check email and leave them here too long. Think I'll do something else instead. She read through the recipe a few times, took care of a few dirty dishes then made a quick trip to check some laundry. Once the pastry sheets had sat out for the right amount of time, she rolled them into one big sheet. She used her pie plate to cut around and remove the excess dough.

Lifting and plopping the dough into the pie pan was easy enough, even if it made her heart skip a beat. *What if it all falls apart? Maybe this wasn't such a good idea.* But it landed well in the pan, and she was able to pinch the sides down just like the directions said.

She set the pie plate into the preheated oven to bake then turned her attention to the filling. She grinned. Now for the yummy part!

Once she'd dumped all the ingredients into the big stainless bowl, she turned on the mixer. Droplets of batter splattered on the wall. *Oops!* Ashley took better control of her new kitchen machine, turning it down a notch. Medium speed seemed to work better, less splatter, but it still mixed the ingredients at a frenetic pace.

The oven timer sounded. Ashley set the mixer down and put on her new oven mitts. They were like big gloves, making her feel official. After opening the door to the oven, she took a step back.

What was that?

Her pie crust was sky high!

It looked like a dome. *Huh?*

Instead of cooking down in the pan, it had made a huge poof of a thing. *What in the world?* The crisp, warm scent of the crust wafted under her nose, cueing her brain to remove it from the oven before it burned.

Whirling around to set it on the warming racks she had purchased, tears began to form in her eyes.

*Perhaps it will sink down...*she tried to be hopeful.

But she was beside herself.

She slinked over to the other counter where the chocolate concoction sat. With a frown on her face, she dipped a finger into the batter then sucked it between her lips. *Sometimes chocolate helps.* She sniffled.

The instant her tongue touched the dark brown substance, it rebelled. Ashley stood over the sink spitting out the revolting stuff.

What's wrong *with it? It tastes disgusting! So bitter...*

"I'm such a failure," Ashley said, bursting into tears. She studied the recipe through blurred eyes.

What happened? Tossing the paper down, she ran into the bedroom and threw herself on the bed. Her body racked with sobs.

I'm good at most everything I try. Why can't I get this cooking thing right? This was an unfamiliar place for her to be in.

Ashley had made good grades in school, and had been above average at sports. She'd always been popular with her peers. She'd considered herself blessed, but this cooking thing was kicking her butt. What would Roger do when he found out how terrible she was in the kitchen? Would he end it with her? Her sobs were replaced with a sense of panic in her chest. Her heart raced and she chewed on a fingernail, shuddering as her breathing settled down.

Ashley sat up and squared her shoulders. *I've gone this long without knowing how to cook. I can go a while longer.*

* * * *

That evening, Ashley considered her reflection in the full length mirror that stood in the corner of the bedroom. She had spent an hour with the curling iron, turning her platinum-blonde hair into ringlets that framed her face. Her makeup was light—brown mascara and pink lip gloss. With nothing underneath, the apron highlighted the outline of her breasts, hugging her curves beautifully, and showing lots of leg. She had to admit she looked rather sexy.

The sound of a key rattling in the front door told her Roger was home. She dashed to the kitchen just in time to strike a seductive pose in the doorway. Wearing nothing but her new apron and a smile.

She knew how to obey her Master.

Roger's eyes lit up when he saw her.

"Hello, darling," he greeted her warmly. "You look gorgeous in the apron, and you followed my directions. I knew you would." His arms were full of gifts.

"Oh my! Sweetheart, what do you have? Here, let me help you." Ashley rushed over to him. Not only did he have boxes in his arms, but he also carried a sack from the market over his arm. A bottle of champagne peeked out of the top.

"I brought you some surprises" — he chuckled — "which you will have to earn."

Ashley stuck her lower lip out. "That doesn't sound like much fun."

Roger grinned. "Oh, it will be fun, I promise you that." He set the presents and bags down on the kitchen counters.

"Okay." She brightened. "When do I get my first present, Sir?" She waltzed into his arms and kissed him full on the lips.

He grabbed her ass and squeezed, giving her a firm slap on the posterior as he released her. "What a saucy little sub you are tonight. And here I was, wanting to reward you for your good behaviour…"

Ashley dropped to her knees in front of him. "I'm sorry, Sir. I lost my head. Will you please forgive me, Sir?" She looked up at him with pleading, puppy dog eyes.

His eyes were playful when he looked down at her. "Yes, of course I forgive you."

She knew how much he liked her on her knees. She liked it too.

"Would you like some champagne, sub?"

"Yes, Sir."

"I'll pour. You stay on your knees."

"Yes, Sir."

Roger opened and closed cabinet doors, while Ashley knelt quietly on the floor in her sub pose with her hands clasped behind her back, waiting for further instructions. Roger said, "Ashley, go see if there are any glasses in the dishwasher."

"Sir, there aren't. I unloaded it earlier today."

"Excuse me?"

"I said there aren't any in there, Sir."

"Are you disobeying me?"

Ashley sighed. She hated when he refused to listen to her. She had unloaded the dishwasher. She knew what was in there...*Duh*. Sometimes men could be so annoying...

She stood up and opened the dishwasher.

It was empty, except for two brand new crystal champagne flutes that she had never seen before.

"What are those?" Roger asked.

"Um, I've never seen those before..." Ashley stammered.

"I'm sure you haven't. Pull out the top rack of the dishwasher and bend over it."

Ashley did as she was told. How did those get in there?

He traced the outline of her breast. Ever so slightly. Her skin tingled under his touch. She sighed, relaxing, yearning for him to keep going.

She felt the air conditioner blowing cold on her bum. Then *whack!* He slapped her ass cheek hard. She stiffened.

"That was for disobeying me, sub."

"Yes, Sir. Thank you, Sir."

"Do you think you need another?"

She could hear the leer in his voice. He enjoyed this immensely, keeping her off balance.

"Yes, Sir. Probably."

Whack! Another swat landed on her bottom. She winced. It began to feel warm.

"Thank you, Sir."

He ran his hand over her aching cheeks in a quick motion, lightly touching them. As the burn went away, he massaged them, groping between her legs, searching out her wet spot.

"Mmm, thank you, Sir, that feels good."

"Oh, I have a lot of things for you tonight that are going to feel good."

She sighed. "Thank you, Sir."

"Would you like to have some champagne and open your presents first?"

"Yes, Sir. Thank you, Sir." She winked at him seductively.

"My, my. You are sassy tonight. Well, no matter." He turned and handed her the first box. He picked up the magically appearing champagne flutes, popped the cork of the bottle of Cristal then poured them each a glass.

Ashley tore open the thick, shiny cream-coloured wrapping paper, pushing the golden ribbon to the side, unearthing a box which contained a brushed stainless steel spice rack.

"Oh." Ashley wasn't sure what to say. "Thank you, Sir."

"Do you like it? See, you can put all your spices in there!"

He seemed so excited. Inside Ashley's spirits were sinking. "Yes, dear. It's lovely." She plastered a fake smile on her face.

Roger could hardly contain his excitement. "Here, open this one." He shoved the next box in front of her on the island.

"Okay," she said with as much enthusiasm as she could muster. *I'm a disaster at cooking. What would he do if he knew how bad I really am? Would he leave me? The* thought made her hands shake as she unwrapped the next gift. A knot formed in her gut.

"A knife block." Her voice was flat.

Roger didn't appear to notice. "Yes, you've got twelve different knives. One of the best brands, I made sure. Supposed to be chef quality. They should help you chop easier, well, should make lots of jobs easier."

His face held so much promise, as though he had been dreaming of all these sumptuous meals that she would prepare for them when he bought her these gifts.

Ashley summoned a pathetic smile. "You have been very generous, Sir."

Roger came over to her side of the island and hugged her. "I love you, and I'm so proud of you, Ashley."

She looked into his eyes and knew she never wanted to disappoint this man. "Would you like dinner now?" she asked.

"Later. I have something planned for you right now, my little subbie." He raised an eyebrow. "Go lie down on the table."

She took a sip of champagne. "On the table?"

"You heard me. Don't make me have to punish you." His eyes gleamed.

She hopped right over to the table and scooted the centrepiece flowers over to the end to make room.

"Good idea, we'll want to move those far away," Roger said, the corner of one side of his mouth curling up.

Ashley shifted herself to the middle of the table and lay back.

"Stay right there." He went into the other room for a second. She didn't move—she didn't want to. She only wanted to lay there and savour the thought of what he might do to her when he returned. The anticipation was intoxicating.

He came back with a black scarf, one he regularly used to blindfold her. He asked her to lift her head and close her eyes. *Okay, he's not going to let me see what's coming.*

This was one of her favourite parts of being a sub in a D/s relationship. She trusted Roger implicitly and knew he would take care of her, knew he would never harm her. That trust was what made it okay for her to submit to his will. It was sexy as hell to her to hand over the reins and let him be in charge.

She loved knowing that, at the end of the day, she had a place where she could be dependent, submissive, and that everything was still going to be all right. That was the ultimate relationship to her. Not having to be strong and in control all the time. Being able to let go. It was pure bliss.

"Music, my pet?" His voice interrupted her reverie. He stroked her neck sensuously.

She nodded. "Jazz, if it pleases you, Sir." She craned her neck until he fed her his thumb. She greedily sucked it into her mouth.

"Mmm. Jazz is fine."

She heard the click of the stereo remote, then the velvet voice of Ella Fitzgerald began to croon in the background.

He knows how to set the mood. She wriggled her hips and electric currents ran through her limbs and her cunt, impatient as she was for him to touch her.

Something soft and fluffy drifted up the inside of one of her legs, barely passing over her crotch before it glided down her other leg. It could have been a feather…a frilly, lush sensation. *Yes, please.*

"I know how much you like being tied up...do you think I need to do that to you tonight?"

"Yes, Sir." Her voice quivered with need.

"Good thing I brought these, then." He clutched her wrists and bound her with the familiar cloth restraints that he used with her so frequently. Her hands were confined above her head, their movement restricted to a few inches in each direction.

"Spread your legs for me."

Ashley obeyed. The air in the room was chilly. A sense of vulnerability came over her. It reminded her of that feeling when you're a patient in a cold, sterile hospital room.

Then she felt his mouth on her. She lurched and gasped for air when he buried his face in her mound. Tongue licking, nose nudging, teeth nipping, his hot breath coated her with his own lust. He had her quaking in moments.

She was on the verge of climax when he stopped.

Bastard! He's teasing me. She was breathless, at the peak of arousal. *He loves seeing me like a bitch in heat.*

"I'm going to play with you with some unusual toys. I want you to try and guess what they are. I will help you along, but you give your best guess. Ready?"

"Yes, Sir." She nodded.

Thwack! She felt something on the inside of her leg. *What is that?*

"Keep your legs spread." His voice issued a warning.

"Yes, Sir. Sorry, Sir."

More swats from the unknown implement. *That feels familiar. What is it? When have I felt it before?*

Then a swat to her pussy woke her up. The sting wasn't terrible, but it definitely brought the blood to the surface and made her cry out.

"What am I smacking you with, little sub?"

"I'm not sure…"

He swatted her pussy lips again. That beloved combination of pleasure and pain washed over her.

Ashley moaned.

He smacked her again on her clit.

"Mmm."

He continued swatting her. Just when she wasn't sure she could take any more of the intense sensation, she remembered what it was. "A spatula, Sir."

"Good girl," he rasped. She felt him dip his head to lick and tickle her pounded little pussy folds. The moisture from his mouth felt incredible against her hot, pink flesh. She arched her back, tilting her cunt towards him.

She felt something inside her, probably his finger. Her muscles clenched around it and she urged him on with her pelvis.

"God, you are so wet. Time for the next one."

A light scraping sensation grazed her arm. Hmm. What's that? It feels like a small paintbrush.

The brush-like object moved to her chest and painted shapes and designs on her nipples. Up and down, around her breasts. With each stroke he spurred her fervent desire for him.

She pulled against her wrist straps, wriggling with need. Her pussy was pulsing, aching for him.

"Any idea what that is?" he asked.

"Well, it feels like a paintbrush."

"Close, it's a pastry brush."

Something large pushed inside her. *Finally, something to fill me!* It was solid, like a cock or a dildo, but it didn't feel quite like either one. It was cool and firm, not human or plastic.

She relaxed and allowed her juices to flow. Whatever it was, she trusted him. She wanted him to fill her. *Please, just fuck me with it.*

As if he could read her thoughts, Roger drove the object in and out, piercing her again and again. Sweat beaded up on her skin as she concentrated on the sensation. Roger manipulated her clit and he continued fucking her with the unknown toy, the combination was unbelievable.

"Oh, my God, I'm going to come," she shrieked.

"Not yet. You have to guess what this is, and then I've got one more." He stopped touching her clit. She wanted to cry. Instead, she let out a growl of frustration.

"Don't be such a bratty sub, Ashley. Try to work towards some more self-discipline. You need to trust me. I will let you come…"

She heard footsteps move away, then the sink tap was turned on.

He came back and held one of her bound hands, the object still buried inside her. "What do you think I have stuffed inside you?" He paused. "I forgot to tell you. It is a food."

A food? Wow, is he kinky!

Her mind raced. What did it feel like?

Big, cylindrical, slickish…

"You give up? I know this is a hard one. I have an idea. I'll give you a bite of one. Not the one that's inside you, of course. That should help."

She heard him shuffling in the kitchen, then chopping noises.

Cool pressure against her lips. "Open."

When she did, he placed a small bite inside her mouth. It was almost flavourless. Round, like the one in her pussy, part of it had the same texture. She bit down and chewed to capture the flavour. It was cool, light and crisp.

"Cucumber!" she said gleefully.

"You are right, my darling girl. The next one is an easy one. I'm going to coat my cock with something, let you worship it and you tell me what it is, okay?"

Ashley nodded.

First, he coated her nipples with a sticky substance by dribbling it all over them. Then licked it away, sucking those pebbled peaks, making sure he got all of it, getting her tremendously aroused in the process. The hard little buds screamed for more attention and her hips moved languorously. She wished he would do something that would allow her come.

Heat flowed throughout her body. She whimpered under his touch, and when he climbed on top of her and offered his cock to her mouth, she eagerly took it in to suck.

The substance was sweet and sticky. She knew at once that it was caramel. What a sweetheart. *Roger knows I adore caramel.*

Ashley licked the liquid, sugary substance off his shaft and swallowed what she could. She was at a disadvantage because her hands were tied and he was on top—essentially she was at his mercy. Roger lunged into her mouth until he hit the back of her throat. She gagged once and he pulled out, asking her if she was okay.

"Mmhm." She nodded and opened her mouth again to receive him. Once he had a good rhythm going and she was breathing well, she felt his hands on her cunt again. He began fucking her with that cucumber and flicking her clit with his tongue at the same time.

The oral stimulation in conjunction with being fucked and fingered all together sent her over the edge. Roger kept grinding against her clit as he pumped into her mouth and her cunt. Wave after wave of orgasm flowed over her. Silently, she prayed that he would never stop. She loved being overwhelmed by the helplessness of his cock in her throat and his tongue on her pussy.

A stream shot down her throat then he pulled back, leaving some semen in her mouth for her to swallow. Her body quivered as he backed off her sensitive button and plucked the fruit from her pussy.

"Sir…?" When he withdrew, her skin grew cold, and without being able to see she immediately felt vulnerable again.

He whispered in her ear, "Yes?" He gently removed her blindfold and her restraints.

She gazed at him. "Nothing, Sir. I just… That was wonderful."

He looked at her with kind eyes. "I'm glad you liked it." He rubbed her cheek then scooped her up into his arms. "How would you like a shower before dinner?" Looking down at the traces of caramel all over both of them, they burst into laughter.

"Uh, good idea." Ashley giggled and Roger carried her into the bathroom.

After a quick shower, they dried off then slipped on matching thick, plush bathrobes—luxurious souvenirs they had brought back from a romantic trip to the Turks and Caicos.

Ashley padded back into the kitchen then pulled the food out of the oven. Earlier, when she had gone out to buy a pie to replace the failed one, she had picked up some enchiladas verde at the gourmet shop next door to the bakery. She had put them into her own stoneware and popped them in the oven to keep warm.

She cleaned the table and set their places.

Roger served their plates.

"Thank you, dear," she said as she sat down at table where he had so delightfully ravished her earlier. She was exhausted. And starving!

She took a bite of her dinner. She must have devoured it too fast, because something went down the wrong way and she choked.

Coughing, she tried to clear her throat. Ashley stood up to get something to drink.

"Are you okay?" Roger asked. "This is delicious. Did you make this?"

She nodded, her back to him. Her eyes burned. She still couldn't talk yet. The food in her throat made it hard to breathe.

She held a glass in front of the water dispenser on the refrigerator, then drank it down. Gulp, gulp, gulp!

Wait! I nodded that I was okay, not that I made the enchiladas!

When she stopped seeing red, she realised Roger was saying, "...is delicious, you've really outdone yourself tonight, my dear. I'm impressed."

She nodded at him. "Would you like some water?"

"Yeah, that'd be great. Are you sure you're okay?"

"Fine." Her voice was hoarse. *Why can't I tell him? I'm such a chicken.*

She filled a glass of water for him and brought it back to the table.

"So how was work today?" She wanted to change the subject. To anything but the food.

"Oh, it was fine. Pricewater House is talking mergers and..." He went on about a business deal she only vaguely understood. That was okay with her.

When it came time for dessert, she presented him with a piece of the fluffy chocolate pie. She had been prepared to pass the pie off as her own, but he had unnerved her when he'd given her credit for the entrée as well.

That was an accident. She hadn't intended on saying she'd cooked the dinner.

But he was so proud of her...and she'd been choking. By the time she'd been able to answer him, well, she couldn't disappoint him. Not these days. She was afraid if she failed at this cooking task, he might leave her. He had been acting so oddly in the days leading up to his request. Clearly it was important to him that she succeeded in the kitchen.

She frowned, her stomach knotted. *Great, now I feel guilty.*

A little voice inside her said, *But not guilty enough to tell him the truth.*

Roger beamed at her. He had been so good to her tonight. *I won't do anything to destroy this beautiful evening.*

By the time they were snuggled up together in bed that night, Ashley had practically convinced herself she'd cooked that meal.

Chapter Six

Tap, tap, tap. The pencil hit her shoe. She wasn't getting anywhere with work this morning. Ashley stared out of the window. She couldn't keep her mind off Roger.

He was so good to her, treated her like gold. Last night he had been so focused on her pleasure. A shiver ran through her body. *He must be thrilled with my cooking.*

But it's not technically my *cooking…* She screwed up her mouth, making a face.

Staring at the blank page on the desk in front of her, she uncrossed her legs and stood up. She stretched her arms above her head and decided to take a break. The project wasn't due for another week. It could wait.

What would she 'cook' tonight?

Every time I try to prepare food myself, it's a disaster. I screw it up. And I hate to disappoint Roger. But when I buy food and he thinks I made it, he's so happy! No failure, and he doesn't have to be disappointed – plus, *we both get an edible meal. It's a win-win situation.*

Ashley convinced herself she should keep buying food and placing it in their serving dishes. Or in the oven. It was in both of their best interests. It didn't matter that Roger didn't know she wasn't slaving away all day in the kitchen preparing their dinner.

Occasionally, she'd get a gnawing pang in her gut, but she'd squash it down, never allowing it to surface. Roger deserved a decent meal, for Heaven's sake, not the pitiful ones that she could make herself.

I can get take-out from that little gourmet market...they have lots of delicious dishes Roger and I like – lamb, crab cakes, lasagne, those little gorgonzola tortes. I don't have to tell him I made it myself... If he assumes I did, I just won't correct him.

The following week, Ashley served Roger several delectable, gourmet meals she purchased from the local market. She never actually lied and said she made them. He just thought she did, and she never corrected his inaccurate assessment.

Each evening provided such domestic bliss that Ashley almost believed herself to be an accomplished cook who made delightful dinners every night for her beloved Master. Roger bestowed such high praise upon her that she relished her new role as goddess of the kitchen.

After one such lunch, Ashley lounged in the bedroom reading a magazine. It was a Saturday and Roger had been kind enough to do the dishes and give her a break. Ashley was reading about which star wore what on the latest red carpet.

All of a sudden, Roger charged into the room. His face red, he waved white slips of paper in her face.

"What are these?" he yelled at her.

"Roger, calm down. I have no idea." She sat up straighter in the bed.

"These are receipts from different markets. They're for food, Ashley. Prepared food. Not ingredients. What have you been up to?" His eyes bulged.

She felt heat rise in her cheeks. "Well…I just…some things were hard to make. That's all," she answered, her voice uncharacteristically small.

"Here is a receipt for the chicken cacciatore we just ate." He was breathing hard, hurt reflected in his eyes. It broke her heart. "You *bought* it?"

Ashley tucked her legs up under her and hugged them. Wiping at the hot tears she felt welling up, she nodded, wishing the ground would swallow her up.

"Why, Ashley? Why would you lie to me?" His face was crestfallen.

She hung her head and wept softly.

"Why?" he repeated angrily.

She didn't answer.

He shook her. "*Why did you lie to me?*"

Unable to meet his gaze, she shook her head and whispered, "I don't know."

He turned and barrelled out of the room.

She heard the door to the apartment bang shut.

* * * *

Moments later, Ashley ran after Roger. She couldn't let him go like that. She had to make him understand that she had never meant to deceive him. She'd made a terrible mistake, but he had to forgive her. He just had to!

She pushed the elevator button repeatedly, tears streaming down her face. The thought of life without Roger was unbearable.

Finally the elevator opened. She jumped inside and pressed the button for the lobby.

When the doors opened on the ground floor, Ashley bolted, calling, "Roger, Roger!" She searched for him. She jogged onto the street, looking everywhere.

He was long gone.

Dejected, she made her way back into the building where she bumped into her neighbour Lance.

"Oh me, look what the cat dragged in! What happened to you?" he exclaimed, cupping his hand over his mouth.

Ashley collapsed into his arms sobbing.

"Gracious, girl! Why the waterworks?" Lance gave her a sidelong glance as though he were worried other people might see the embarrassing display, but he patted her back.

Ashley stepped back. "It's Roger." She boo-hooed. "I'm afraid he's left me."

"Left you? Apparently I've missed a lot. Let's get you back upstairs. You're a mess, girl. Mascara's running all down your face." Lance shook his head, shielded her face and hurried her back upstairs.

Once she was back in her apartment, Ashley took some deep breaths and tried to pull herself together. She offered Lance some tea. He accepted and found her some tissues for her leaky eyes.

They sat in the living room, waiting for the water to boil, and Lance threw his arms in the air. "So what gives, sister?" Clearly, he was dying to get the skinny on her emotional breakdown.

"It all started when I tried to learn to cook for Roger."

He nodded, encouraging her.

"Well, basically, I'm a failure. Everything I tried was a disaster. I either burned it or didn't cook it enough or it just blew up somehow. Then I got some take-out that he thought that I cooked—but I didn't. And he was so happy, so proud of me…that I just let him think I made it."

"*Ashley!*" Lance feigned disapproval.

"I know I shouldn't have!" She stuck her bottom lip out. "But I was so *bad* at it, and he liked it so much… It was just easier. So I started buying food and passing it off as my own." She frowned. "Then I got caught," she said, slumping onto the couch.

Lance jumped back on the sofa in dramatic fashion, clutching his hand over his heart. "Oh Lord! How did he find out?"

She sighed. "He found some receipts. They must have been on top of the trash or something. I should've been more careful."

"What you should have done was come to me for cooking lessons, umhmm, that's right." He snapped his fingers and looked at her with disdain, shaking his head.

"You're probably right."

"Well, quit acting like Eeyore and let's get with the program. What did you try to cook? Did you try the crockpot like I said?"

"Yes, and the noodles were hard."

"Okay, well that can be fixed by either adding water, some stirring or cooking longer. Sometimes with a slow cooker you have to play with it a little. I can help you with that."

She wiped her eyes and brightened. "Really?"

He nodded. "What else?"

"I tried to make a French Silk Pie. That was a mess!"

"A *what*?"

"French Silk Pie."

"Girl, you've got to be crazy. You don't try something like that when you don't know how to cook. Why don't you just try to make a soufflé?" He laughed as if that was the most ridiculous thing in the world.

She furrowed her brow, puzzled. "A soufflé?"

"Yes, goose! They're almost impossible to make."

"Oh."

He rolled his eyes heavenward. "I have *got* to take you under my wing, child."

"Would you?" She sniffled.

"Yes. Clearly you need all the help you can get. And I hate to see my favourite neighbour running around looking like the Rocky Horror Picture Show. Do you have any eye makeup remover? Maybe you can go do something about that." Waving his fingers in front of his face, he indicated she had black streaks on her cheeks.

"Okay." She smiled for the first time since her fight with Roger.

The tea kettle sang out from the kitchen.

"I'll get it," Lance offered. "You go take care of that." He shooed her off to her bathroom.

* * * *

A couple of hours later, Ashley heard the creak of the front door.

"Am I in the right place?" Roger asked as he rounded the corner and walked into the chocolate cloud that hovered through the kitchen.

There, Ashley and Lance hovered over the stovetop. Ashley stirred a pot of dark brown liquid. The air was thick with a blanket of chocolate that coated one's nostrils with a sugary sweetness.

"Yes," she said. "We're making fudge. Lance is teaching me." The corners of her mouth turned up tentatively.

"Okay, well, I don't want to interrupt…" Roger started to leave. She couldn't read his expression. *How mad* was *he? At least he's come back. That's a good sign. Isn't it?* Inside, her heart did a cartwheel.

"No, no. I was just leaving. We're about done here," Lance said, looking ill at ease.

"Are you sure?" Roger asked.

"Yes. Ashley, all you have to do is stir it for another two minutes, pour it into this glass pan then refrigerate it for several hours. Call me tomorrow and tell me how it turns out, or bring me a piece. It's easy. See?"

Ashley wasn't sure she *did* see, but she smiled and nodded robotically, nervous about being alone with Roger. She was in so much trouble, and she was too upset to deal with the blocks or any of his punishments right now.

Lance grabbed his coat.

"We'll walk you out," Ashley said, nervous about the prospect of facing Roger by herself. She and Roger followed him into the living room and said goodbye to Lance.

Then Ashley and Roger were alone. Tension hung in the air between them as tight and unforgiving as an old wire bedspring.

"I—" They both spoke at the same time, then stopped.

That eased the awkwardness. Ashley sighed with relief.

"I'm sorry," Ashley blurted out. "I was wrong. I should never have taken credit for cooking something I didn't make. I'm just so terrible at it, Roger, and I hated to disappoint you. But I was wrong."

"I need total honesty from you, Ashley. For a relationship to work, two people have to know that they can trust each other completely. And when you lie to me, I don't know what to think. I have to admit that I was disappointed that you didn't feel you could be honest with me."

She made herself as small as she could. "I know. I feel awful. I'm so sorry, Sir."

"I'm sorry too, Ashley."

Huh? Ashley couldn't believe her ears. What was *he* sorry for?

"I'm sorry that I made you feel like you had to fake things for me. If you don't like to cook—that's okay." His face was gentle, kind.

"It is?" She was confused. "I thought it was real important to you that I become a chef or something…" Her mouth curled into a question.

"Well, it was. At first. I don't know. I was confused myself. Let me try to explain. I've been thinking more about our domestic life lately. And it seemed like a good idea to start eating at home more. Since you're my sub—that's the role you and I have agreed upon for you—it seemed the right thing for you to do. That you'd do the cooking. But if you don't like it, dear—*I* can do it."

"It's not that. I don't mind it. But I wasn't successful with it, Sir, and it made me sad to disappoint you. I hated that. It made me feel like a failure."

He took her in his arms. "Silly girl. I will love you even if you can't boil water. There are lots of things that take a while to learn. Cooking is one of them. I don't expect you to be perfect, or great at everything. And I don't expect you to do all the domestic chores, especially if you hate them. I can help around the house."

"Well, Lance says he'll help me learn in the kitchen. He wants to take me under his wing." She looked up at him hopefully.

"You two looked rather cosy when I walked in. Should I be jealous?"

She thought he might be teasing her, but she wasn't sure. He rocked her body back and forth as he held her.

She pretended to punch him on the shoulder. "No, Sir. Lance has a boyfriend."

"Okay, that's good. Can't have him movin' in on my girl." He kissed her on the lips.

"So, you're not mad at me?" she asked.

"To be honest, I'm concerned that you lied to me. You don't ever have to lie to me."

"I know. That was the worst part. I'm sorry." She hung her head.

"You need to understand that I accept you for who you are, Ashley — warts and all. There is nothing you ever need to hide from me. Do you understand?"

She fought back tears. Had anyone ever loved her so much *just for being her* before? Her parents, maybe. But Roger loved her even when she acted like an idiot. He loved her *in spite* of her craziness. Her heart swelled with love for him. Biting her lip, she nodded. "Yes."

"Okay, because I have something important that I want to talk with you about. I was planning to save it for later, but I think we need to discuss it now."

Anxiety churned in her stomach. She didn't say a word.

"Remember how I said I've been thinking more domestic thoughts lately?"

Ashley was frozen, not sure where he was going with this.

"Darling, that's because I want to make you my wife."

Ashley wasn't sure what she'd heard was real. Was this really happening to her? A couple of hours ago, she'd thought Roger might leave her. Now he was proposing to her?

She watched as her beloved Roger knelt down on one knee, gazed into her eyes and asked, "My sweet Ashley, will you marry me?"

She flung herself onto his lap. "Yes, of course I will!" She smothered him with kisses.

"Wait, I have a ring," he said and pulled a box out of his pocket.

She laughed. She was so excited she'd forgotten about the ring.

It was a lovely, emerald cut diamond that fit her precisely. Exactly what she would have chosen. Leave it to Roger to choose the perfect ring for her.

Nestled in his embrace, they made out for what seemed like hours. All of a sudden, a funky smell drifted into the room.

"What's that?" Ashley asked. "Oh my God! The fudge!"

She ran into the kitchen and discovered the scorched concoction sitting on the stove.

Her first instinct was to cry.

Instead, she breathed deeply, glanced down at the ring on her finger, considered the unconditional love it represented then walked back into the other room.

"Hey, Sir, want to order a pizza?"

THE INTERVIEW

Caitlin Ricci

Dedication

This is for everyone out there who enjoys a little play mixed in with their work.

Chapter One

Mr Sims was much as she had expected — a chef from head to toe, coming into her building's lobby wearing a neatly pressed black jacket and chef trousers. He looked younger than she'd expected though, his twenty-five years looking more like twenty-one. Even in the grainy black and white security system feed, she knew he was going to be trouble. Jacob, as she fondly remembered calling him back when she'd first met him as a highly strung teenager fighting back against the pressures of living under his parents, had apparently grown up well.

Anne turned and checked her appearance in her bedroom mirror. Shaking her head, she knew the pretty, pale pink sweater and dark blue jeans wouldn't do for today. Maybe for meeting anyone else, but not now that she'd seen the all-grown-up version of Jacob Sims. He'd been cute as a teenager but that forbidden image had turned into something greater than simply attractive. She glanced at the security feed again and licked her lips. No, he was much more than what she had anticipated, and the thrill of having the handsome man so close made a shiver run along her spine.

She stripped quickly then put her jeans and sweater over the back of her cream reading chaise. It wouldn't take Jacob long to get upstairs, especially if he took the elevator. But she didn't need a lot of time to step into a short, flowing tan skirt and a button down lace shirt either. She'd been barefoot before, which was comfortable but not exactly sexy. Some strappy heels completed her outfit and she was sitting at her dining room table by the time a loud knock sounded on her front door.

"Come in," she called, adding a bit of a sultry edge to her voice. There was no guarantee the wide-shouldered, black-haired man would even be interested, she reminded herself, but it never hurt to try.

"Chef Mato?" he asked, entering her large apartment with quiet footsteps.

"Hello, Jacob," she greeted him, smiling. "Did you bring your knives?" Anne didn't get up to meet him, instead she crossed one leg over the other, letting her loose skirt slide up her thigh. She watched for any reaction, any telltale sign that he was interested in her. His father had said he'd been available, but parents rarely knew, and if he were seeing someone she'd stop this play. But if he wasn't, this afternoon was going to get very interesting indeed.

"Yes, Chef," he answered automatically. Anne nodded, pleased. He was disciplined and well trained. All of his professors at the culinary institute had said so. He'd probably called his parents 'Chef' more often than 'Mom' or 'Dad'.

He stood in her entryway, her beautiful kitchen between them. Though he said nothing, the way his eyes drifted to her double ovens, her gas, six-burner stove and the pristine white granite counter tops told her he was envious of her set up. Good, she'd worked very hard for many years and had given up a great deal personally to be able to have everything she did now.

"With your knives, you're all ready for the interview," she informed him. "Ale is my baby, the first restaurant I opened less than six months after graduating from the culinary institute. I was told that I was crazy for buying a restaurant when I was so young, that I needed more training." She curled her fingers around the spindled oak back of her chair. "But Ale has grown and blossomed for ten years now. It has been the restaurant to beat for the past four years in a row and I intend to keep that tradition going with the next executive chef to take it over."

"Yes, Chef." His response was strong and Anne believed he might be the one to take her restaurant over. His training certainly suggested it. And he had pride to spare.

"When your father suggested that I interview you for the position, I was hesitant," she continued. His face fell, but his smile didn't slip. She had to know that he could take criticism along with compliments. Maybe by the end of this interview, he'd figure out that everything was a test of his resolve to prove he could be her next executive chef. She would never allow someone weak to be under her, in bed or on the line. "But he assured me that you not only possess the necessary skills but also the heart for this profession. Do you think you do?"

His gaze didn't waver from hers. "Yes, Chef."

Smiling, Anne nodded. "Then don't prove him wrong. Make me your signature dish. My pantry and fridge are both well stocked. You've got an hour. Begin."

Unlike the last three idiots she'd interviewed, Jacob didn't hesitate at this stage. He simply acted. The first man she'd interviewed hadn't finished in the allotted hour, but at least he'd tried. The second had looked at her dumbly, not understanding what she was asking for. The third had made her a simple salad that had taken all of five minutes for him to toss together then over-dress. She'd thrown him out promptly.

Jacob glanced up at her from time to time as he gathered things from her orderly kitchen. She'd set up her home like she did her restaurant intentionally. The transition was effortless for her, as it should be for him. Though a chef didn't need to live his career outside of the restaurant, it should be in his everyday thoughts and actions. Quality, precision, timing. These foundations were everything, and mattered just as much as taste, presentation and creativity to her.

Anne watched him carefully, judging not only his knife work but his discipline as well. It took a rare person to thrive as an executive chef. The wrong choice in a new hire could kill an established restaurant. The right one would grow with it. Too often, owners settled for less than perfect because of a need to fill that spot in their line. Fortunately for Anne, she had no real need to move on. It was time and she had desires of opening a second restaurant. But there was no immediacy that came with that decision. She'd wait as long as she had to in order to find the perfect fit for her beloved Ale. Nothing less than that would do.

"Tell me what you're doing," she instructed.

He faltered for a moment, appearing unsure of himself, but he had to do this as well in her line. There were always times when an executive chef had to instruct a sous chef about a particular skill or style of doing something. In her restaurant she was the leader as well as a teacher. Her top candidate would have to be as well.

"I'm seasoning the potatoes with rosemary and a pinch of salt," Jacob answered her.

Anne nodded. "Why?"

His full lips quirked up into a smile. "Salt brings out the flavour of most foods, just like acidity does, and rosemary gives potatoes a sweet, earthy taste that will go perfectly with the steak I'm making."

He worked as he spoke, just as Anne had expected him to. Being a TV chef's son meant he'd probably spent many hours helping his mom prepare for an episode. Anne didn't know his mother well, not as well as she knew his father anyway, but she'd seen her shows a few times. She'd even watched her perform once a few years back, when Anne had been a guest chef on Taste, the network that aired his mom's programme. Sadly the name of it escaped her at that moment.

Jacob brought the steak out of the fridge, letting it warm to room temperature. Though she was proud of him for remembering to let the meat come to temperature before finishing it off, she showed no reaction. He had to know that he was doing the correct thing because it was what he'd been told to do, not because she encouraged him at each step.

She parted her lips and quickly licked them. He was beautiful to watch, his concentration on his task complete as he moved around her large kitchen. A warmth grew in her core and spread through her breasts and thighs at the sight of him. Her nipples strained against the silk of her bra and she took a sip of the cucumber water beside her, eager to sate her desire for him but needing to cool it for the moment. If he was as good in bed as he was in her kitchen, she'd be quite satisfied this afternoon. He would be too, she'd make sure of it of course...but she wasn't thinking about him for the moment.

Selfishness, ambition and drive were hardly unique to their field, but without them a good chef could never be great. And she needed great. Nothing less than that would do.

He pulled out her stove-top grill and waited for it to get hot. A bit uncertain of him and his methods, she watched him intently. He had to get this part right. Everything else had to be perfect as well, but potatoes could be saved, as could whatever else he served with her steak. But a steak, once ruined, was impossible to make right again. And so she watched, her breath catching, as he moved the potatoes around the pan with some butter and rosemary and waited for the pan to heat until that perfect moment when it was just right. He seasoned the meat with a bit of salt and pepper and put it down on the grill. The inviting sound of a loud sizzle went through her kitchen and she smiled, knowing he'd got that part right. He wasn't out of the clear yet but he was much closer, and he'd managed to impress her with his knowledge of simple food as well.

After washing his hands, he chopped fresh herbs, his wide shoulders moving under the stiff material of his chef jacket as he worked. His refusal to cross-contaminate her food was another bonus factor for him, as a firm grasp of the basics was the only foundation for growth. He tasted at each step, seasoning when needed. His skills were impressive but she wouldn't know just how much until she'd tasted his meal.

A few minutes later, he clicked off her stove and began plating her lunch. His hands were steady, his movements sure. The plate he presented her was less stylish than the ones his Las Vegas chef dad created every day, but they were simple enough for her Ale. The steak was the centrepiece, the red potatoes and asparagus creating a wreath around it.

"Describe it," she instructed him, her mouth watering as the sweet smells drifted up to her. And, she noticed with a further sniff, a hint of her signature Candied Pale Ale, a favourite at her restaurant. She hadn't seen him grab the bottle while he'd been cooking, but, as she watched, he quickly provided her with it and a glass.

"Chef, what I've prepared for you today is a simply seasoned rib-eye steak with rosemary red potatoes and garlic asparagus. I've finished it off with a glaze of your Candied Pale Ale, which has just the right notes of candied nuts and cinnamon to bring your meal together. Enjoy." He stepped back, looking proud of himself and satisfied with the dish he'd prepared.

As he should. The presentation of it was subtle and paired well with her restaurant's image. Also, the use of her ale was a bit of a genius move, and one none of the others had even considered. It showed that not only did he enjoy cooking and knew what went together, but that he was already familiar with her restaurant and the ingredients in the ales he would potentially be working with.

He waited off to the side while she cut into her steak. It was a beautiful medium rare. She hadn't given a preference and he hadn't asked, but he knew enough to know that the default when his customer hadn't given him a temperature was medium rare. It was the safest bet when dealing with all red meats and he was one smart cookie for remembering that.

After cutting off a piece of the steak, she took a bite and moaned with honest enthusiasm as the tender meat hit her tongue, the ale infused glaze aiding it in both sweetness and acidity to expertly balance the meat. She ate a little of the asparagus and the potatoes next. All nicely prepared, well-seasoned and correctly portioned for a dinner entrée.

Dotting her lips with a linen napkin, she hid her satisfied smile. "What did your father tell you when he sent you for this interview?" she asked, rising from the chair.

He looked surprised for a moment but quickly came to his senses and answered her. "He told me not to disappoint you. That a position at Ale could make my career, as it has for many of your sous chefs."

She set the plate aside, having had her fill of the light tasting. His skills were on par with what she'd expected and his knowledge was exactly what she was looking for. He was green but had the background to make up for any lacking in his training. And his skills weren't in question—his ability to follow orders and perform at the pass were, and she wouldn't know his abilities there for a while longer. However, those things could be trained into the right chef. She wasn't looking for an egotistical, highly experienced chef to run her Ale. What she wanted—and needed—was someone who could be worked with and moulded into being her next executive chef. An older, more experienced chef often came with his own ideas and lots of baggage. Anne had dealt with a few like that in her time and she wasn't eager to do it again.

"What would you do to Ale if you became the executive chef?" she asked him.

Jacob appeared to hesitate. "What would I do…? I'm sorry, Chef, but I don't quite understand what you mean. I wouldn't do anything. I'd run it the best that I could of course. But I wouldn't burn it down or anything like that." He chuckled, sounding nervous.

Anne smiled, hoping to ease his fears somewhat, though it probably wouldn't work. He was new to the world of being a professional chef—despite having watched it through his parents' eyes since he was a small child. But coming into a career of his own had to be a bit intimidating for someone so young. She remembered it being that way too. Thankfully, when she was even younger than he was now, she'd had a good mentor who had shown her more than simply how to julienne a jicama.

"Maybe you'd like to give the menu a bit of a facelift? My favourites are on there, what would you like to add to it?" she asked him.

The handsome man really was her last, and best, hope for a qualified executive chef. She didn't need him running because she'd scared him off this early. Still, if he couldn't take a bit of pressure there really was no hope for him in this field. Chefs were a bunch of competitive assholes sometimes, herself included, and there had been plenty of sous chefs who had called her a bitch either before or after she'd thrown them out of her restaurant. She refused to put up with morons or assholes for any reason.

He swallowed loudly. "I'd add some rarer game meets."

She twirled her hand. "Go on. This idea might have some merit."

"Well, there are plenty of steak houses around." He paused as she raised her eyebrows. "Though none nearly as good as Ale. Everyone knows it's the best."

Her ego placated, she smiled at him and he appeared encouraged by the gesture as he took a step closer and returned her smile.

"But maybe it could be even better if a few new choices were added. I'd keep them simply seasoned and present them in classical, easy to recognise ways.

Like the staple of steak and potatoes. Only with your dark oak ale and a bison steak."

Anne tapped her fingers against her chin. "The idea has potential. But bison, while a bit exotic, isn't impossible to find here. It requires a visit to a speciality shop instead of the big chains for a good cut, but it's still not extreme. Think bigger. What are your favourite meats that no one else has?" Anne could think of more than a few but hadn't considered bringing them into Ale because she didn't see the surrounding area as ready for a nice plate of anything more exotic than a roasted guinea hen stuffed with capers and a lemon cream sauce.

But maybe Jacob was right. Perhaps the market was growing up, their taste buds expanding in a new, more rewarding direction. A great steak was still a fantastic meal and she'd never allow the various cuts that she kept as staples on the menu to be taken off. But there was always room in a good restaurant to grow and change if it wanted to survive for another decade. And she planned on keeping Ale around for a lot longer than that.

"Rabbit," he began, looking as if he were thinking aloud as he leant back against the island and looked up at her old, rail station style lanterns. They were antiques transformed to work with modern technology—a blending of an old, stylish classic and modern convenience.

"That's a good start, but just offering a roasted rabbit dish won't cut it. Come on, Jacob, think a bit more. I know you've got something else under that shiny head of black hair. Give me something more," Anne demanded.

He blushed, whether from embarrassment or something else she couldn't tell, and she wasn't about to ask. He'd have to do better than that if he wanted this job, though if she were honest with herself, he was already miles ahead of anyone else she'd interviewed.

Jacob's green eyes met hers solidly. Anne challenged him, refusing to look away. He was young and needed discipline, training and more experience. She was willing to give it to him, in whatever capacity he wanted, but he had to know his place as well, and it would only be over her when she allowed it.

He looked away first and Anne smiled, knowing he'd start to learn his way soon enough. Especially if he stayed near her for any length of time. Which she secretly hoped he did.

"Ostrich," he blurted.

Anne raised a dark eyebrow. "What do you know of ostrich, Jacob? If I were to give you a loin, how would you prepare it?"

He fidgeted for a moment but quickly recovered, this time looking far more in control of himself and sure of his answer. "Ostrich is an exceptionally lean meat that takes well to a variety of flavours. A quick sear works for it, though roasting it allows for more flavour to get in there."

Though he sounded like he was reciting something out of a rare meats textbook, Anne had to give him credit for thinking on his feet. It was another skill all chefs needed to learn right away. She wouldn't allow him free rein with her brigade immediately, in fact she imagined that the transition would take a good six months before he'd truly be the executive chef she'd be comfortable leaving her Ale with. But he had a glimmer of the man she wanted in that position.

Among others.

Anne nodded and approached him, her heels clicking against the pale, travertine tile below her. She brushed her fingertips against the light stubble of his jaw and chin. He appeared uncertain, his arms frozen to his sides as she trailed her fingers down the side of his throat to rest against the exposed patch of his collar bone where the jacket split.

"Are you seeing anyone, Jacob?" she asked him. She had a code – if he said yes she would walk away. He'd get the job, he was perfect for it. But she would not explore this attraction to him outside of her own mind. But if he wasn't…well… That possibility was as tantalising as fresh strawberries with aged balsamic vinegar and rich chocolate custard. She licked her lips, the thoughts of her favourite indulgence reminding her of what else she enjoyed. Namely beautiful men like Jacob.

He shook his head. "I'm not. Are…" He swallowed thickly and Anne watched, fascinated as his Adam's apple bobbed against the pad of her thumb. "Are you?"

Smiling, she undid the first button on his jacket. "No. You've got a choice to make here, Jacob. And you've got the job, so don't think that your decision in this matter is at all dependent on your position at Ale. That one is sealed for you. This would be a private, extremely discrete matter between the two of us. Do you understand?"

"I think I do."

He sounded uncertain and his beautiful green eyes shifted to the side, further adding to her suspicion that what would come next would throw him off guard.

"I want you in my bed. For this afternoon at the very least." Anne undid the next of his buttons, a surge of heat spreading down her legs. She shifted, pressing her thighs together to relieve some of the pressure. "You'll do as I say and enjoy submitting to my desires above your own. Do well and this could be something more long-term. Share what happens between us with anyone else and you'll never be invited back."

His eyes went wide as he stared down at her and, for a fraction of a moment, Anne was afraid she'd misjudged him. But then he bent his head, opened up to her and offered himself for a kiss. She took his mouth eagerly, tasting the meal he'd made for her on his tongue and leaning into his touch as he brought his muscular arms around her back. He held her close, drifting his hands over her shoulders and back, trailing them down her spine.

She undid the remaining buttons on his jacket, the little black dots moving under her experienced hands. Someone else might have simply torn his jacket from him. But she knew how important a chef's jacket was in their profession and she wouldn't do that to him — or it — just for the sake of getting to him faster. She had plenty of time to enjoy him all she wanted. His jacket slid off his shoulders and she ran her hands over his arms and the sleeveless tank he wore underneath. It went as well, joining his jacket on the counter behind him as he reached his big hands down to cup her ass, pulling her tight against him. Anne lifted her leg and hooked it around his waist, giving him better access as he slid his hands to the slit between her thighs and hooked his fingers on the silk of her panties.

He tried to tug them down and she stepped away, not wanting to fuck him in her kitchen, because that was where this was leading. "Not yet, Jacob. In my bed," she panted, giving him an explanation as she moved farther away from him, putting some space between them. The separation was difficult for her and she glanced around, looking for a suitable surface for them. Finding none, she went back to her original idea of having him in her large and quite comfortable bed.

He nodded. "Show me the way."

Smiling, she took his hand and pulled him through her apartment to the last door at the end of the hall. She stepped into her beautiful pale blue bedroom. It was tidy and perfectly put together with a mix of Victorian touches and modern accessories. None of that mattered to her now though, as she moved Jacob to her bed.

"Undress me," she demanded, holding her arms out to him. She was worried he might become a placid man whom she could easily control. If he was, she'd be bored of him within the hour. But he surprised her by obeying her order in his own way. He lifted her onto the bed and covered her with his big body, resting her against the thick mattress. His hips dipped against the V in her thighs, pressing his hard cock against the silk of her panties as her skirt bunched up around her thighs.

His kisses were erratic—he worshipped first her lips then her cheek before he trailed his tongue down to her neck and he worked his fingers on the buttons of her blouse. The thin material fell away, exposing her breasts to him. Groaning, he rubbed the outside of her pussy through her panties, making her moist as he sucked at her hard nipples through the silk of her bra. He soaked the material then quickly moved on to the next, moaning into her breasts as he moved against her, grinding her into the bed beneath them.

"My clothes," Anne reminded him, gasping and eager to get to the next step, where she'd see a grown up Jacob naked and begging beneath her. But first he'd have to please her. Then, if he was good, she'd let him inside.

"Right. Sorry." He lifted himself up, balancing on one arm as he helped take off her shirt then reached behind her to undo her bra. She gasped as her bra came away, exposing her to the cool air. Her nipples tightened and she brought her fingers away from his thick shoulders in order to tease them into hard peaks.

Jacob kissed down her sternum, then her belly, circling her navel with his tongue then sliding her skirt and panties off in one quick motion.

"Fuck, you're beautiful," he gasped, bringing his hands up to her hips as he moved his tongue along her inner thighs.

Anne smiled. She kept in shape, fortunately keeping her curves in the process as well. Men loved her breasts and she enjoyed having them played with. "Now you," she said, nodding to his pants. She kicked off her heels then brought one of her hands to her swollen folds while keeping the other on her breast. She played roughly with her nipple, squeezing hard enough to feel pain as she watched him take off the rest of his clothes.

His muscular stomach ended in a thatch of dark curls and she followed them down with her eyes to his thick cock, standing proudly against his stomach. She licked her lips, imagining how good he'd feel inside her, how she'd stretch around him as he filled her. He got on the bed again, kneeling between her thighs, and stroked his cock from tip to base, spreading the clear pre-cum around. He leant forward, moving up her body but she stopped him with a firm hand on his chest.

"Not yet," she said, grinning as she slid her hand to his hair.

"No?"

Anne shook her head. "Lick me first."

It took a moment for him to figure out what she meant but when he did he gave her a little smile. She kept a firm hand on his head and spread her thighs, making more room for him on the bed. The first warm puff of his breath against her clit sent shivers through her, making her throb for him. Then his tongue pressed her stiff nub and all breath escaped her lungs. She tightened her hand in his hair and held him to her clit. He moved her thighs to his shoulders and she crossed her ankles over his spine, pulling him in even closer as he stroked her sensitive clit with his tongue.

Anne trembled against his mouth, moaning as he worked his way between her thighs and teased her clit. "Damn you're good at this," she panted. His deep chuckle sent breaths of hot air over her body and she shivered in his hold.

He slid a finger into her warmth, causing her to buck against him. A second finger quickly joined the first, stretching her and making her gasp. The heat in her core coiled into a tight ball, threatening to send her over the edge. She bit her bottom lip and shook her head. Just thinking about him being under her pushed her climax closer and she moaned loudly. *Not yet.* She'd come when he was in her.

"Jacob... Stop..." she gasped. "Fuck. I'm going to come."

He grinned up at her, his green eyes sparkling wickedly. "Then do it. Let me taste you."

Tempting as his offer was, she wouldn't give in that easily. "Soon. When you're buried inside me."

He gulped and nodded, slowly sitting back up. When he was kneeling, she crawled towards him then lay on her belly between his thighs. The length of his thick cock was in front of her and she pressed her cheek against it, feeling its weight against her cool skin. "Hands behind you, hang onto the footboard," she commanded as he reached for her. He hesitated. Though she was looking squarely at his cock, she saw his right hand clench then release. After a moment or two of indecision, he appeared to take her command for exactly what it was—an order—and did as she'd told him.

She breathed in his scent deeply and nuzzled the base of his cock with the tip of her nose. He was young, perfect and all male. Exactly what she needed at that moment. And, given a bit of direction, he appeared to take orders fairly well. She didn't doubt that if she kept him around there would be a few missteps here and there, but she could deal with them. She hadn't been around a well-trained sub in over a year and the peace of having a perfectly willing partner was so very tempting.

Anne licked her lips then ran them along the underside of Jacob's cock, making him jump erratically and suck in his breath on a wild hiss that sent shivers along her spine. He moved forward, pushing his cock against her mouth and though it may have been simply a reaction, it could not be allowed to continue. "Uh huh," she scolded him. "You move when I give you permission. Not before. This is my playtime. You had yours. Now be a good boy and hold still."

"Yes, Chef." His quiet acceptance sent a shiver of desire through her. As did his formal use of her title. Though she'd called him by his name, he hadn't broken formality and called her by her own. The difference he clearly placed between them thrilled and excited her, making her even wetter.

Grinning wickedly, she wrapped her fingers around the base of his cock and pulled upward towards his swollen head. She brought her lips to his sac, sucking him as she moved her hand over his thick length. She teased him, alternating between her hand and tongue as she stroked his shaft. The low noises coming from his throat told her he was becoming increasingly desperate for his own climax. Good, she wanted him on the edge—somewhere between desperation and madness was where she found her greatest pleasure. And today she'd be sharing that moment with him.

Smiling and very nearly throbbing with need, she slid back onto her knees, though she was sure to keep her hand on him, her pale fingers a brilliant contrast to the tanned muscles of his lower stomach.

"Lie down on your back, arms above your head," she instructed him.

"Are you going to fuck me now?" he asked softly, his warm green eyes following her movements as she rose from the bed.

Chuckling, Anne went to her dresser. It gleamed in the soft light of the room, its ebony surface recently restored to its original glory. It looked new, with barely a mark on it despite being from the early 1800's. She'd paid a hefty price to make sure of it. "Would you like that?" she asked, running her fingers along the gleaming surface of the dark wood. Aside from her knives, this piece was her most prized possession. And it held her greatest desires.

"Yes."

She pulled open the small top drawer and took out a soft, finely braided flogger that had cost her more than most chefs made in a month. But for the quality she desired, the price was no object. She brought it down with a loud smack against her outer thigh, testing the familiar weight of the piece in her hands and the bite of the strands against her heated skin before reaching in to pluck a small foil package from the box she always kept at the ready.

Anne turned towards Jacob, pleased to see that he had followed her instructions and stretched himself over the bed, his arms hanging loosely over her footboard. His heavy cock stood erect against his stomach, asking to be fucked, while the warmth of his gaze nearly begged for the same. Keeping the flogger close by her side, she walked around to the foot of the bed. Her thighs brushed against his fingertips but he made no move to grab for her. Bending low, she rewarded his control with a kiss.

"You grew up well, Jacob." She straightened up then pulled the silk ties from the bottom of the bed along with the thin pillow she kept for just such an occasion as this.

"Thank you, Chef." He watched her, tilting his head to see what she was doing as she placed a pillow under his wrists to keep them from becoming sore against the wooden footboard. She secured his arms above his head, checking each of his wrists to make sure the silk wasn't too tight.

"Has anyone ever tied you down before?" she asked, coming back to the side of the bed.

He shook his head and tested his wrists. "No, Chef."

Watching him carefully, she was pleased to see that the restraints didn't appear to upset him. There was no worry or fear in his face, only curiosity and the heady desire that flushed his tanned cheeks.

"You'll have a safe word," she informed him, her fingers stilling on the tight muscles of his forearms.

"I don't want one."

Smiling, she shook her head. "Too bad. I want you to say 'marmalade' if you need to be let go. Can you do that for me, Jacob?"

"Yes, Chef."

His breath caught as she joined him on the bed, placing a thigh on either side of his slender hips. Placing the flogger on the bed beside her knee, she carefully opened the condom wrapper and, after tossing the trash into the bin beside her headboard, slid the rubber over his engorged cock.

He made no protest to her safety concerns. Perhaps he was just that smart since he couldn't possibly have known that asking to go without a condom would have had him thrown out on his naked ass. She smiled down at him and positioned herself over his cock. Kissing him, she tasted herself on his lips and felt his cock jerk forward to hit her hand as she guided him towards her body. Anne gasped loudly as he entered her, her body easily adjusting to his unfamiliar shaft. She moved against him, breathing him in as his cock slowly pushed inside her.

"Fuck yeah," he groaned, breaking their kiss.

Anne moaned, agreeing with him fully as her heavy breasts rubbed against the thin hairs of his chest. She whimpered, lowering herself fully onto his cock then leaning back, trying him out. He was an amazing fit, large enough to fill her completely and thick enough to stretch her around his width. She rolled her hips, helping him hit all of the best parts within her, then reached for her flogger.

His eyes followed her hand as she lifted it then draped the fine strands over her sensitive breasts. "Know what this is?"

He shook his head.

"A flogger. The sensation of it hitting skin is delicious." She demonstrated for him on her belly, the wide patch of red lines and the heat that followed them making her shiver. His cock jumped and she smiled, knowing the unconscious reaction for what it was—an interest in knowing what the flogger felt like.

Anne brought the strands down gently against his chest, following the path of the flogger over his nipples with her eyes as she teased him. "Tell me now, Jacob, can you be marked?"

He sucked in a breath. "Yes, Chef."

Smiling, Anne nodded and brought the flogger a few inches above his left nipple. "Do you want to be?"

He squirmed and managed a small smile.

"Tell me."

His smile turned into a frown but he didn't exactly look upset. More confused. "I want to be marked," he tried, sounding hesitant.

Her smile quirked. "Do you really? That sounded more like a question. I think you can do better."

Jacob flushed and his green eyes grew brighter but he didn't back down. "Mark me please, Chef," he tried again.

Anne bent down and rewarded him with long kiss. "Very good. I'll give you anything you ask for, except freedom. You'll get that after you've come. But not until I tell you that you can. Unless you use your safe word, and then this will all be over," she said, leaning back. "Do you understand?"

"Yes, Chef."

"Good boy. Now, fuck me." Her voice ended on a hoarse groan as he immediately did what she'd asked, bringing his knees up and using his heels against her comforter for leverage. His thrusts were needy and erratic, showing just how turned on he was. Surprisingly she found herself enjoying the uncertain beat of his cock inside her pussy. Pressing one hand to his shoulder for balance, she kept up with him, moaning loudly as he moved inside her.

"Your tits look fucking amazing bouncing like that," he groaned.

"Such words coming from a beautiful mouth," she teased him. Anne tilted her head, moving her long hair all to the other side so that it could brush against her hard nipple and tease her further. Lifting the flogger, she brought it down experimentally against his shoulder, the faint red lines trailing onto his chest.

Though he stilled for a moment, he didn't stop and the cry that fell from his lips was one of passion, not pain.

"Like it?" she asked, her voice thick as she bent her head to soothe the lines with her tongue.

"Yes. Again."

She continued to lick his faint wounds. "Ask nicely."

"Whip me again, Chef," he said, his voice coming out as barely more than a panting sigh.

Smiling, she straightened up and brought it down across his other shoulder, shivering as the tendrils curled around her wrist before streaking over his tanned skin. His breath caught on a moan. She didn't ask him the next time, or the time after that as she brought the flogger down against his chest and stomach, each time making him jump.

"More. More please," he begged, moving his head from side to side against her comforter. His thick arms were bunched as he strained against the silk ties.

Anne leaned over him, the flogger falling against her hip as she tossed it to the side. Instead she grabbed his silky black hair between her fingers and gave him a sharp tug. He groaned and moved his face towards her arm.

"You're a serious kink," he gasped as she tugged again.

Grinning, Anne nodded and nipped at his chin. "You've got no idea. Now, stop struggling against the silk. We aren't done yet. Not nearly. Hope you didn't have anywhere to go this afternoon because you're not going to make it."

Jacob shook his head. "I'm yours for as long as you want me. All night even."

Anne released his hair and trailed her fingers down the side of his face, her short nails digging into his cheek. "We could get up to a lot of mischief if I kept you all night, Jacob." She leant back, his thick cock stilling as she moved. Anne considered his offer. A night of having this broad shouldered man under her, letting her play with him as much as she wanted was quite a tempting offer. She'd have to consider it fully. After she'd enjoyed him for now, of course.

Anne rolled her hips over him, sending shockwaves of pleasure through her core and up into her breasts. She ground against him, making her own rhythm as his fell away. He watched her, his mouth falling open as she reached up to cup her breasts and play with her nipples.

"Tell me what you'd do to me," she demanded. "If you had your hands free."

He swallowed thickly and licked his lips. "Slam your hips onto my cock and fuck you harder than anyone ever has before."

She grinned. "That's a pretty tall order. I usually like it rough."

"And I'd give it to you that way," he promised, his voice husky.

"Tell me more," she said, sighing as she brought her fingers to his mouth. Without her having to ask for it, he sucked her fingers until she pulled them away. Anne brought her moistened fingers to her clit, rubbing herself and his cock at the same time as she rose and fell against him in a steady motion.

Jacob nodded, appearing eager to tell her what she wanted to hear. "I'd take your hair and wrap it around my wrist and pull it back, forcing your head up as I fucked you from behind, so deep you'd feel it all the way down in your body and wouldn't soon forget what it felt like to have me fucking you. I'd make you beg, make you scream my name when you came around my cock."

Anne groaned between quiet laughter as she bent over him. She licked his nipples, causing him to squirm under her as he fought against the ties. "You think you can do all that?" she asked, not looking up at him as she sucked his hard nipple into her mouth.

"I know I can. Let me show you. Promise you won't regret it."

Anne trembled, the switch inside her loving to both be dominated and to dominate. And Jacob's words were exactly what she'd wanted to hear. A man who could talk like that was rare, but he'd be a real gem if he could back his words up with truth in his actions. She untied his hands in quick, sure movements.

"You have the control now, Chef," she said, making the transition deliberately obvious to him. "Don't make me regret it." Anne sat back, waiting for him to act as he rubbed his pink wrists. She didn't have to wait long—he brought his knees up quickly, forcing her to fall forward over his chest. He twisted his hand in her hair and yanked her head back as he brought her left breast to his mouth. He sucked hard on her nipple and squeezed her tender flesh hard enough to bruise her as he rapidly thrust into her wet pussy.

"Fuck yes, Chef," she moaned. "Fuck me harder. Harder, Chef, harder."

He did as she'd asked, eager to please her even when he'd been given control of her body, and she felt herself losing focus on top of him. She gasped as he released her nipple and went still under her. She pouted, wondering what the hell he was doing until he moved her off him, tossing her onto the bed beside him. He kept his promise and held onto her hair as he yanked her legs back against him.

"God, your ass is perfect," he said, running his free hand over her hip and butt cheek. Flushing deeply, she gasped loudly as his hand came down on first one cheek then the other. He squeezed, pulling at her soft flesh before he spanked her again.

Then, in one smooth motion that took her breath away, he entered her again and began pounding inside her pussy as if he hadn't missed a beat. She moaned, her breasts bouncing wildly with his thrusts as he tugged on her hair, forcing her neck back.

"Tell me you like it," he gasped.

Anne smiled. "I fucking love it, Chef. Your big cock feels so good in me."

He groaned. "Yes. Just like that. Tell me."

Feeling hotter than she had all day, Anne nodded as much as his hand in her hair allowed. "I knew I wanted you the moment I saw you come into my building through my security feed," she confessed. "You were cute years ago but now you're practically divine."

"Back then, when we met," he said between loud groans, "I knew I wanted you under me. You were my dad's friend, a professional colleague. And someone I didn't think would ever notice me."

Anne chuckled. "Oh, I noticed. But jail isn't exactly an ideal place for me. But now, now you're hardly off limits."

He released her hair to put both hands on her hips and Anne fell forward, her head resting against the mattress.

"I fantasised about you all through college and was so hard coming up here I was afraid I wouldn't be able to walk. Your breasts, your ass, the way you lick a spoon after you taste something on the shows you used to host. You made this chocolate torte once and moaned right after trying it. I fucking nearly came in my pants right there in the middle of class."

She smiled, his words thrilling her as his cock bounced inside her pussy. Anne reached between her legs with one hand and balanced on the other. She wasn't surprised to find her pussy soaking wet. Jacob was a fantastic fuck, one of the best she'd had in a long time. He smacked her ass again, sending shock waves of need through her body.

"I'm close," she moaned, the tight ball in her core coiling together and threatening to send her off to oblivion with the slightest provocation.

"All right," Jacob said, sounding out of breath as he sped up. "Tell me what you need."

Anne closed her eyes. Cutting off that one sense allowed her to focus on the others. The sound of his breath, the warmth of his hands on her hips, the thrusting of his cock into her pussy. His short nails dug into her skin and she knew there would be small crescent moon marks to go with the bruises tomorrow. Being marked by Jacob was nearly enough to throw her over the edge of her pleasure and send her cascading to the bottom. Almost. But she needed a bit more than that in this moment. "The flogger," she gasped. "Use it on me."

"You sure?" he asked, hesitating.

"Yes!" she hissed, nearly whining in her frustration with him. It was so simple, such a tiny task. And he had to question her on it and—

"Oh!" Anne moaned as the first swipe of the flogger came down across her back, surprising her. It wrapped around her arm, caressing the side of her breast before moving over her back and across to her other side. "Again, Chef, please mark me again. I need it. I want it so badly."

Without a word he brought the flogger down across her lower back. The tiny threads bit against the top of her ass, close to where they were connected. She threw her head back and moaned loudly. He whipped her again, this time without having to be told, as her pussy tightened around his cock.

"Oh yeah, Anne, come for me. Come around my cock. Scream my name," he groaned, tossing the flogger to the side and moved his hands back to her ass, digging his fingers into her sensitive flesh as he fucked her hard and fast.

He leaned over her back, taking her breast in his hand and roughly squeezing her nipple between his forefinger and thumb. She groaned and turned towards him, eager for a kiss.

"You like this huh? I saw you playing with your nipples. Damn tease you are. Tying me up so that I couldn't touch you too," he whispered. "Next time you're the one getting tied down while I fuck you till you're sore."

She grinned and kissed him again. "So sure you're getting a return invite?"

He chuckled and yanked on her hair. "Hell yes. You're enjoying this too much to make this a one-time thing."

Anne cried out, unable to say anything against his logic. Especially when the heat coiling in her belly exploded, sending a tidal wave of emotion and pleasure through her arms and chest, ending in her fingertips and toes. She slumped into the bed, unable to keep herself upright as the aftershocks of her pleasure worked through her body, leaving her breathless and boneless under him.

"Come for me," she whispered, watching him out of the corner of her eyes.

His green eyes bright, Jacob nodded and surged into her. A moment later he cried out her name as well, so loud that her neighbours probably heard him. But she couldn't bring herself to give a damn as he flopped onto the bed next to her, sweaty and breathless. Anne reached for him, taking his trembling fingers in her own as she closed her eyes and let a sex-sated exhaustion take its hold on her body and mind.

His phone interrupted the quiet moments that followed. Taking his first full breath in nearly ten minutes, Jacob slowly sat up. Anne lay asleep next to him, her steady breathing telling him all he needed to know about her state. He smiled down at her, loving that she'd enjoyed herself so much. He hadn't had a lot of experience with women, but none of the girls he'd slept with in college had done anything to him like Anne had. And it wasn't just the kink. He rose on trembling legs and reached for the nightstand, afraid of losing his balance otherwise.

Now to go find the source of what had disturbed his perfect after-sex moment with the hottest woman he'd ever been around, and the one he could easily see himself losing his heart to. He found his phone in the pocket of his pants and dug it out. The shiny silver face showed three new text messages. The first two, from his best friend, he ignored. Whether or not he was going to the party tonight was not on his top ten most pressing issues list for the moment.

The last one, from his father, also came with a voicemail—he must have got impatient. Chancing a look back at Anne to make sure she was still fast asleep, he silently left the bedroom, making sure to close the door behind himself. He wanted Anne awake, and very soon, but not until she'd rested for a bit. He wasn't nearly done with her yet.

"Jacob," his voicemail began, "Call me when you get this. I want to know how your interview with Chef Anne went. Remember, she can be hard on the chefs under her, but it's for your own good. If you let her teach and lead you she can take you places in your career. Just listen to her and do as she says. I know you'll do well."

Pressing the number to erase the message, Jacob snorted. His father had no idea how right he'd been. Chef Anne was bossy, demanding and sexy as hell. Even now, after having the best sex of his life, his cock protested being away from her as it started to get hard again. Shit, he had to get himself under control. He'd come in hard — leaving the same way almost seemed like bad form. But maybe Anne would help him out with that again. His gaze went to the closed door behind him and he imagined the sleeping woman he'd left on the bed. She was gorgeous, but there was so much more than that. He'd admired her for years, built his career around hers and had practically worshipped her since the first time he'd seen her cook.

He bit his lower lip, thinking better of pushing his luck with the older woman who had shown him just how she liked to control the men under her. And there it was. His cock got hard again at the image of Anne sitting on him, her big tits bouncing as she rode his cock. He'd been tied down and damn unfair that had been of her, but once she'd released him and he'd got to touch her, it had made the desire to do so much stronger. If every time was like that no wonder Anne liked it so much.

He'd done kink before with girls in his past. Sort of. It hadn't been anything like this. With them he'd been playing or simply trying out a fantasy or something he'd seen in porn. This was a full blown orgasm for his mind. Which sounded corny but actually made perfect sense to him, at least — Anne had not only turned on his body, but his brain had been engaged too. It was probably the most amazing sexual experience he'd ever had and he really hoped it wouldn't be his last chance with her. That would just be too miserable of a thing to consider. If he never got to touch her again, to feel her breasts in his hands or her full mouth sighing against his as he entered her... *No.* He shook his head. That wasn't going to happen. He wouldn't let it. Anne would just have to accept that he was in her life now, as someone to fuck silly whenever she wanted to if nothing else. He wanted more but he could settle for that. He knew enough to know that a woman like that just didn't come around all the time, and now that he'd found her, he wasn't about to just let her go that easily.

"Jacob?" she called from the bedroom.

He looked up, surprised to see her standing in the doorway, naked and seemingly proud of her body. When she turned he could see the red lines on her shoulders and back. She wore them proudly, even putting her hair up in a tie to show them off.

"I didn't give you permission to leave," she told him over her shoulder.

Jacob smiled, easily recognising that tone and once again knowing where he stood with her. "Yes, Chef. Sorry, Chef," he said, walking quickly to catch up with her. "Won't happen again."

Anne winked at him over her shoulder. "See that it doesn't. Now, I suppose we should talk about the executive chef position at Ale. Now that we've covered a few other positions of course."

Jacob laughed, catching her joke and sharing it with her. "I want it."

"I'd figured as much," she replied, nodding. "I'm going to take a shower. Join me and get cleaned off. Then we'll discuss duties, your potential salary and I'll take you to dinner there."

"At Ale?" he asked, surprised.

Her smile faltered for a moment. "Of course at Ale. That restaurant is my baby, stocked with all my favourite foods and preparing my best dishes to my specifications. Your restaurant should always be your first choice of where you'd like to eat. If it isn't then you need to change it so that it becomes so. Why? Is there something wrong with my beloved Ale?"

Jacob stared at her, the kinky kitten he'd had sex with turning into a full-blown defensive tiger at the drop of a word. And damn if he didn't find it sexy as hell. He smiled and went to her, pulling her into his arms and fitting her neatly against his chest. She looked up at him, not appearing hurt or upset, simply curious. As if she were waiting for his explanation before deciding whether to rip out his spleen or bake him her famous chocolate mousse cake.

"I just thought," he said, taking a breath. "That maybe you might not want to be seen as being improper with your new hire is all. People may start to talk." He shrugged, unsure of how his idea would be taken.

She laughed and ran her fingers through his hair, tugging gently on the strands. "People will talk regardless. They always do. And what woman wouldn't want to be seen with a handsome younger man on her arm? No, I think we'll be seen a lot over the course of our professional relationship."

He nodded, liking the sound of that. "And what of our personal one?" he asked before she could step out of his hold. "What about that relationship?"

She tilted her head to the side, appearing to consider his question. "What do you want to be? Sex toy, or something of a more permanent fixture in my bed?"

"Whatever you'll give me," he said, laying it out there for her. "You know we're good together. You can't deny that."

Anne smiled. "We do have a certain chemistry going. Don't we?"

"Yes," Jacob replied, eager to confirm her thoughts. "We do. And I want to see where that goes. Don't you?"

She stepped away and for a moment Jacob thought she might be rejecting him. Until she grabbed his hand and tugged him towards the bathroom. "I believe I do. But first, we wash. I don't discuss business when I'm naked. It's bad form."

Chuckling, he followed her into the bathroom and waited while she turned on the hot water in the shower. Like her bedroom and the rest of her apartment, this room was tidy, spotless and tastefully decorated. It seemed that most of the chefs he'd met had a need for order and control in common, though he'd certainly never asked if they were all into bondage like Anne was.

He checked the water temperature before she had a chance to, making sure it would be just right for them both.

"What are you thinking about?" She stepped into the water, the hot spray covering her shoulders and soaking her thick brown hair.

Jacob smiled as he followed her in. "How I want to be available for you whenever you've got a need." He moved his hands to her hips and pulled her close, fitting them together, his hardening cock resting on her navel.

She gave him a wink and turned in his arms. While he figured she'd just be getting the bar of soap behind her, she slowly bent, making sure not to break contact between them as she lowered herself in front of him. He groaned and rubbed against her ass, sliding himself between her cheeks until she straightened up. She was a tease but he was starting to figure out that she'd deliver on her promises, and he intended to have her every way he could.

"Oh, you'll be around," she said, handing the bar of soap over to him.

"I know." He smiled, quite happy about that.

Anne nodded. "As my new executive chef I'll have weekly meetings with you to make sure things are still going well. You'll give yourself over to me all morning, sometimes longer than that. These meetings might tend to run long some days. Think you can handle that?"

He laughed. "Hell yes. I'll be whatever you need, Chef."

Raising up on the tips of her toes, she gave his chin a little nip. "Good. I look forward to our next meeting. But for now I need you in a different regard."

Jacob nodded, eager to do anything for the woman in his arms. "Whatever you want."

She tilted her head back, letting the water fall over her face and chest. "Then wash me."

Smiling, Jacob reached for her full breasts, eager to please her again. His cock hardened all over again as he soaped up her full breasts and felt their weight in his hands. He'd never been with someone as strong as she, was but he was quickly beginning to realise that something different than what he'd had in the past was exactly what he needed now. He'd come to Chef Anne for a chance at being her executive chef, and he'd found so much more. His heart raced with all the possibilities that their new relationship would entail.

About the Authors

Wendi Zwaduk

I always dreamed of writing the stories in my head. Tall, dark, and handsome heroes are my favourites, as long as he has an independent woman keeping him in line.

I earned a BA in education at Kent State University and currently hold a Masters in Education with Nova Southeastern University.

I love NASCAR, romance, books in general, Ohio farmland, dirt racing, and my menagerie of animals. You can also find me at my blog

Elizabeth Coldwell

Elizabeth Coldwell is the author of numerous short stories and two full-length novels, 'Calendar Girl' and 'Playing The Field'. Her stories have appeared in the best-selling 'Best Women's Erotica' series and Black Lace's popular 'Wicked Words' collections. Formerly the editor of the UK edition of Forum magazine, she now contributes a spicy monthly column, 'The Cougar Chronicles', to its pages. When she is not busy writing, she is an avid supporter of Rotherham United Football Club and can be regularly found on the terraces at weekends, cheering her boys to victory (hopefully!).

Victoria Blisse

Victoria Blisse is a mother, wife, Christian, Manchester United fan and award winning erotica author. She is also the editor of several Bigger Briefs collections, and the co-editor of the fabulous Smut Alfresco and Smut in the City and Smut by the Sea Anthologies.

She is equally at home behind a laptop or a cooker and she loves to create stories, poems, cakes and biscuits that make people happy. She was born near Manchester, England and her northern English quirkiness shows through in all of her stories.

Passion, love and laughter fill her works, just as they fill her busy life.

Ayla Ruse

Handed a historical romance at the age of twelve, Ayla Ruse fell in love with love and with happy endings. Having grown up living life tasting a little of this and a little of that has not changed this attitude, but it's expanded her views. Love isn't always happy and it isn't always the way a person thinks it should be. Sometimes it's outside the box, and it's always a challenge.

The challenge of finding and holding onto this love is what drives Ayla in her fiction. She likes stories that strip love—among other things—down to the skin and tests the attachment and beliefs of the participants. Sometimes that test can come in the form of multiple partners, overcoming a desperate fear or even being sexually inventive.

Normandie Alleman

One day Normandie saw an interview with author Stephanie Meyer, in which Stephanie said that idea for her book, Twilight, came to her in a dream. Normandie determined that she needed to write down her next really good dream. Little did she know that vow would lead her to a career writing erotic fiction.

When she's not writing, Normandie has a busy life with a large family that relies on her. "There's always lots to do. I love to cook and bake, and I make a lot of big batches. My husband is an athlete and the boys are too. So they all eat a lot! There's never a dull moment at our house. Writing is my escape. I sit down with the dog and write while my kids are at school."

Normandie is married to her true love. She appreciates his ability to give her the male perspective on romance. "My husband is probably more romantic than I am, but he's also a real alpha male. That's a great combination that inspires me and keeps me on my toes!"

Caitlin Ricci

Caitlin was fortunate growing up to be surrounded by family and teachers that encouraged her love of reading. She has always been a voracious reader and that love of the written word easily morphed into a passion for writing. If she isn't writing, she can usually be found studying as she works toward her counseling degree. She comes from a military family and the men and women of the armed forces are close to her heart.

She also enjoys gardening and horseback riding in the Colorado Rockies where she calls home with her wonderful fiance, their dog and Blue Tongue Skink. Her belief that there is no one true path to happily ever after runs deeply through all of her stories.

All of the above authors love to hear from readers. You can find their contact information, website details and author profile pages at http://www.totallybound.com.

Totally Bound Publishing